Praise for *Messengers . . .*

"A fascinating story . . . through well written fiction, this book captures the essence of the ongoing reality."

"In *Messengers* Julie Gillentine has given us a magical tour through a world of fascinating ancient mysteries. We are invited to explore the unknown crevices of the past through the spiritual eye of a perceptive heroine, Alex, as she takes us around the globe on her heart's quest."

"This book dramatizes the inner search which thousands of people feel themselves to be embarked upon when they understand the mysteries of the Great Pyramid and Sphinx. This shamanic quest is personalized vividly in the characters Ms. Gillentine has created.

"To its authors credit, this book credibly conveys the challenge facing anyone who wishes to restore knowledge of our lost cultural heritage. *Messengers* creates a vision of ultimate success in attaining the knowledge we need to become our full selves."

"Julie Gillentine has written an exciting novel, rich in the mystical tradition of Dion Fortune, Joan Grant and Moyra Caldecott but with her own distinct and unique style.

"I found Messengers particulary engrossing, being personally involved in the same research concerning the Hall of Records in Egypt. I recommend it highly to all those interested in a timely and fascinating story."

Stephen S. Mehler, M.A.
Director, The Kinnaman Foundation

Messengers

Julie M. Gillentine

**Archive
Press
Boulder • Colorado**

Archive Press
POBox 11218
Boulder, CO 80301

This is a work of fiction. The characters portrayed are purely fictional and did
not receive the Edgar Cayce Readings that are attributed to them. Grateful
acknowledgement is made to the Edgar Cayce Foundation and the following
for permission to reprint previously published material:

Library of Congress Catalog Number: 97-93593

ISBN 0-9635211-7-9

Cover Painting:	S. David Mapes
Cover Design:	Julie Gillentine
Text Design Layout:	James Gillentine
Editor:	Janet Harris
Author Photo:	Emily Baldwin-Porizkova

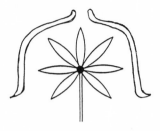

To Seshat

The great one, lady of letters and builders, mistress of the house of books.

"Her chief duties were connected with the writing of history. Happy was the king who was fortunate enough to have his name and deeds recorded by the reed pen and fingers of the goddess herself, and his abode in the next world built on the plan which she drew up in accordance with her attributes as the inventor of letters, lady of the builder's measure, and the founder of architecture."

E.A. Wallis Budge
The Gods of the Egyptians, Vol One

Tribute

For my husband Buz, who made it possible.

A great humility comes with the completion of a creative work. Creation is seldom a solitary act. I am deeply grateful to my family, friends and teachers for unending support, guidance, instruction and inspiration. Your love and acceptance of someone driven and often consumed by a vision has been my sustaining fire.

Julie Gillentine
Spring Equinox 1997

Contents

1
Resurrection

Spring had vanquished winter. Countless yellow daffodils danced in the spring wind beneath the ancestral oaks and maples in St. Joseph's cemetery. Pale-green leaves enveloped the gnarled limbs of the venerable trees like a delicate shawl of chartreuse lace. Wisps of cotton clouds dotted an azure sky.

Alexandria rode with her mother in the back of her grandmother's funeral limousine. The sleek interior of the indigo hearse was a chilling contrast to the glorious day. Funerals belonged in November when tears were disguised by icy rain, clinging like grief on tinted windows and dripping from ubiquitous, black umbrellas sheltering the mourners.

There was no warning, no illness, no goodbye. Only Emma's phone call in the early morning darkness: Gran had died peacefully in her sleep. Just like her to die at Easter, Alex thought. She always said the message was the resurrection, not the crucifixion. Now she can see for herself.

Alex rubbed her hand across the stiff and unresponsive leather upholstery. Her other elbow rested on the arm of the simulated walnut door. Grief and anger threatened to overcome a thin veneer of composure. Her stomach churned from the sickening sweet smell of floral air freshener and her mother's perfume. The atmosphere was stifling, but Alex felt as cold and trapped as if she were in a crypt.

Amelia Stuart's finely chiseled features were drawn and pale. She whimpered, twisting a delicate, white lace handkerchief in her hands.

"What will we do, Alex? I can't believe Rose is gone."

Alex looked at her mother dressed in black. A black veiled hat perched like a robin's nest on an elegant, blond French twist.

"Mother, if you don't stop whining, I might scream. I can't believe you wore black. It's May, not November. Look outside. Birds are singing, flowers are blooming. You look like a crow."

Amelia began weeping. Alex regretted her outburst. Her mother looked stunning in a tailored, black crepe dress. She'd turned sixty earlier in the year, but she looked much younger. Amelia Stuart's blond hair and regal bearing always drew admiring glances. It must be the ridiculous hat that put Alex over the edge.

"Alexandria, I don't know why you are so cruel. I'm not strong. You've always been your father's child." The porcelain features of Amelia's face were drawn with pain.

Alex wished it was November so the weather would match her mood. But she refused to wear black. She wore a suit of champagne-colored, raw silk which set off her curly mass of russet hair and her pale, ivory skin. The classic lines made her look taller than her statuesque five nine. An antique-looking brooch, the first piece of jewelry Alex ever created, held a pastel print scarf around her shoulders. The muted pastels, reminiscent of a Monet painting, did not dim an inner fire which glowed like fiery opals in aquamarine eyes.

The limousine stopped on the gravel road near the grave site. Alex breathed deeply to steel herself, then came around to help her mother out of the car. She opened the door and her mother gripped her arm. Amelia stared up at her daughter, through the veil of her hat, like a cornered black panther.

"I can't do it, Alexandria. I can't stand so close to your father's grave."

Alex pulled her from the automobile with as much gentleness as she could marshal. "Hold onto your hat. It's windy."

Alexandria supported her mother, who dabbed her eyes under the black veil with her white handkerchief. Alex steered her to a green canvas canopy, which covered a seating area for the immediate family. Amelia collapsed, weeping.

The metal casket glistened in the sunlight. Its cold, metallic surface was unsoftened by the floral blanket of tulips, jonquils, palm fronds and sweet-smelling white Easter lilies lying on top of it.

Father Michaels, long time friend of the Stuart family, read from his worn black prayer book. Alex noticed Father Michaels' black cleric's suit was as worn as his prayer book.

The priest's voice was a faint echo at the edge of Alexandria's consciousness. She recalled her father's funeral twenty-four years ago. Her mother had been inconsolable. She screamed and moaned, saying she wanted to die too. Gran kept her arm around the terrified twelve year old girl.

At least she's civilized today. The black veil is bad enough. God, please give me strength to deal with mother by myself.

Alex thought Gran would have hated the funeral but laughed at the hat. Gran wanted to be cremated. She thought burial was a terrible waste of land. Grandpa called her his perfect rose; he made her promise to lie next to him for eternity; she had not been able to deny him.

"Eternal rest grant unto her, O Lord," intoned Father Michaels.

"And let perpetual light shine upon her," replied the small congregation gathered at the grave.

Alex sighed. How many times in her life had she heard those prayers? They never gave her comfort. How could you have eternal rest if perpetual light shone on you?

A sudden breeze blew the sweet scent of funeral flowers to the mourners. Two white butterflies danced in a spiral flight over the casket and came to rest on an Easter lily. One of the butterflies slowly opened and closed its wings, as if to bow to its partner.

Alex was entranced by this bittersweet and delicate ballet. She imagined Grandpa, welcoming Gran to heaven. Gran would have adored the melodrama.

Alex recalled how her grandmother loved to decorate Easter eggs and hide them in the garden. She took immense pride in her clever hiding places. Alex never found all the eggs, and Gran never remembered where she hid them. God, she would miss her.

The priest was misty-eyed as he faced the family and read the closing prayer. "May her soul and the souls of the faithful departed, through the mercy of God, rest in peace. Amen."

Alex watched as the funeral director helped a sobbing Amelia to the limousine. She walked the short distance from the canopy and stood at the foot of her father's grave. The grounds of the cemetery were freshly mowed, and the smell of cut grass was strong.

Dappled sunlight filtered through the oak and maple trees. Daffodils swayed slightly in the breeze, and hungry baby birds chirped. They were all in a neat row, Grandpa, now Gran, Dad and the place reserved for Mom.

"By God, they won't put me in the ground. I'd rather have my ashes flushed down the toilet."

Alex turned to leave and noticed a man standing in the shadows near the canopy. Tall, thin and dressed in black, he reminded her of a character from Dickens. He looked like an undertaker. She realized she'd been vaguely aware of him before and wondered if he worked for the cemetery. He looks like a crow. No, she thought with a chill, he has a sinister quality, more like a raven.

*   *   *   *   *   *   *

Alex and her mother sat on hard, wooden chairs in Jeremy H. Trusdale's legal office, seats designed for interrogation. Exquisite oriental rugs and lush plants couldn't soften the ambience. This was a place of cold, hard facts. The atmosphere was not intended to provide warmth but to facilitate the revelation of guilt or innocence.

Gran called her old friend an archetypal Philadelphia lawyer. His mind was honed as sharp as a scalpel to dissect minute details. He was not daunted by complexity or ambiguity. His long career was marked by a succession of landmark legal victories. Alex wondered if the rumor was true that the building had been constructed around the Honorable J.H. Trusdale and his walnut mammoths.

J. H. loomed like a grizzly bear behind his solid walnut fortress of a desk. Counselor Trusdale was a hulking man whose hairy arms and hands looked unnatural protruding from the sleeves of a three piece suit. The immense wooden barrier was flanked by floor-to-ceiling walnut bookcases stuffed with weighty legal tomes. He knitted bushy, gray eyebrows and peered over the top of his spectacles at the assembled interested parties.

He was about to read the last will and testament of Rose Rodgers Stuart. He cleared his throat, signaling his intention to begin. Alex felt a wrenching anxiety in her abdomen.

"This is a complex document, thoughtfully crafted and revised over the long, full life of a remarkable woman. It was my honor to know her and my great pleasure to work with her," he cleared his throat again to mask his emotion.

"I, Rose Rodgers Stuart, do hereby make, publish, and declare this instrument to be my last will and testament, and hereby revoke all wills and codicils heretofore made by me."

There followed a lengthy list of gifts to organizations, charities, galleries and museums, scholarships to educational organizations, and special remembrances. A musical scholarship to the child of her gardener, a furnished condominium to her longtime housekeeper, her car to the mechanic who cared for it, a cruise to the owner of her favorite bookstore, and her piano to the nearby elementary school.

"Finally, I instruct that my home and all its remaining furnishings, artwork and artifacts be auctioned with the exception of my jewelry, the contents of my library, and my dog, Crystal. These I devise and bequeath to my beloved granddaughter, Alexandria MacKenzie Stuart.

"From the proceeds of the sale and auction, a trust fund is to be established and administered according to the attached codicil. The trust fund will provide income to my granddaughter and her mother, Amelia Stuart, my daughter-in-law."

No one spoke. J. H. scowled over his glasses again, assessing reactions with an attorney's trained eye.

Alexandria and her mother sat like stone statues. All eyes in the room were on them. Nothing would ever be the same. Her mother no longer needed her financial support. She was free to do as she chose. Alex realized she had no idea what that was.

*   *   *   *   *   *   *

Alex sat in the car in front of Gran's house, trying to work up courage to go inside. This had been her favorite place for as long as she had memories. She thought the vintage Victorian home looked like a castle with its turrets, spiral staircases and leaded glass windows with small diamond-shaped panes.

Memories flooded through her mind of make-believe dragons, wizards in blankets and dark queens robed in treasures from the attic. Alex and her friends wove magic spells, concocted powerful potions and saved the realm again and again from evil sorcerers. To think of strangers living here, and never seeing Gran again, felt like the bottom falling out of her world.

When she finally got out of the car, the noise of the closing car door could be heard inside the house. By the time Emma, Gran's housekeeper, opened the big leaded-glass door, Crystal had worked up momentum. She was so happy to see Alexandria that the enthusiasm of Gran's white Spitz nearly toppled her.

Alex laughed out loud, stooped to the floor dropping purse and bag, and threw her arms around the fifty pound mass of white fur. Devoted eyes looked out of a bright canine face. Crystal's body wagged her affection. Tears came.

"Crystal, I miss her so much already," Alex sobbed. The sensitive Spitz licked her face and whined.

Alexandria looked up to see tears streaming from Emma's pale blue eyes. Wisps of gray hair framed her kind, round face. She stood and embraced her grandmother's housekeeper and dear friend. They clung to each other a long moment. Emma had been part of the family for thirty years.

"Can I get you something to eat, dear? If I know you, it's been hours since you've stopped. You must be a bundle of raw nerves." Emma brushed the loose hairs from her face with the back of her hand. She removed a tissue from her apron pocket and wiped her nose.

"That would be wonderful. I'm feeling like a stretched rubber band."

"Come into the kitchen; the kettle's hot. You have tea while I see what I can come up with."

Alex sat in her regular chair at the big wooden table with Crystal beside her, chin on Alex's knee. Sensing her pain, the dog looked up into Alex's eyes, ears cocked. Her tail swept slowly back and forth on the floor. Alex stroked Crystal's head in a gesture that comforted both of them.

Emma poured steaming water into a porcelain tea pot and placed the tea things on the table in front of Alex. She turned on the gas burner, busying herself with familiar patterns.

Alex poured chamomile tea into a delicate china cup and added milk and honey. She closed her eyes and sipped the hot sweet liquid. "I thought I'd stay here this weekend and get started on the library," Alex said quietly.

Emma served her a bowl of steaming vegetable soup, with homemade bread, chunks of cheese, and hazelnut brownies for dessert. "Emma, this is fantastic." She ate in silence until she felt the soothing influence of the food calm her.

"I think I'll lie down for awhile."

"That's a good idea, dear. You haven't slept a wink these last few days."

Stomach full and bone weary, Alex collapsed in her clothes on the small single bed in her father's childhood room. This had been her room at Gran's since her father died, when she abandoned the frilly four poster bed upstairs. She felt closer to him here. Crystal positioned herself at the foot of the bed where she slept whenever Alex visited.

In spite of that warm presence, Alexandria felt alone. Hot tears traced rivulets down her cheeks and fell silently on the pillow. She closed her eyes and prayed for sleep.

Hours later Alex rolled over in bed. It was dark in the room. She thought she heard someone calling her name. She sat up and listened but there was no sound. She wondered what time it was. *I should probably get up and put on pajamas, but I'm just too damn tired*

She pulled back the bedspread and covers, slipped under them, curled up in a ball and lay her head back down on the pillow. A moment later she heard the voice again.

Her heart pounded. It sounded like Gran. "I must be dreaming."

"Alexandria, can you hear me? My dear, you must hear me."

"Gran? Is that you? I'm losing my mind. I must have fallen asleep."

"You were sleeping," the voice answered.

"I can't see you."

"Gran's voice giggled in the darkness like a teenager at a slumber party. "Of course you can't. Wait just a moment."

A door opened, and light poured into the room. Alex shielded her eyes from the brilliance. Gran took her hand, and they walked through the doorway. Outside, the air was warm and smelled of the sea. Gulls and pelicans screeched and dove toward the water in search of food.

Alexandria gaped at her grandmother. Years had vanished from her appearance. She looked radiant in a long, blue robe which accented the color of her sparkling eyes. Silvery hair was pulled back into a bun at the nape of her neck, accentuating her fine features.

"Holy Mother of God! Gran, you look beautiful."

"Why thank you, love," Rose Stuart replied, amused but beaming.

"Come along, Alexandria, we have much to accomplish."

They strolled along a broad avenue lined on both sides with towering palm and fir trees. Red and yellow hibiscus flowers spilled out of terra cotta pots placed along the walkways. Sand colored buildings lined one side of the avenue. The other side was bordered by a turquoise ocean. A warm breeze rustled the palm fronds and Alexandria's mane of red hair.

They turned into the entrance of a large white building constructed of a stucco-like material. The grounds were lush with brilliantly colored birds of paradise, orchids, lilies and plumeria. Heady fragrance permeated the air.

A large green parrot perched on a palm branch. "What's your name?" the parrot squawked.

"Alice in Wonderland," she laughed.

The two women entered an open doorway into a central courtyard where a sparkling fountain emptied musically into a meandering stream. Sunlight filtered through the lattice roof creating patters of light and dark green on potted plants.

"This looks like paradise," Alex exclaimed. "I'm glad I didn't put on my pajamas."

Gran's eyes twinkled with amusement and pleasure. "And so it should, Alexandria."

Alex turned and gasped, eyes suddenly wide, "Are we in heaven?"

"Oh my, Alexandria," Gran sighed. "Sometimes you do miss the obvious. Come on, there's someone waiting to see you."

In a room off the courtyard, two men faced a window, deep in conversation.

"Please forgive the intrusion, gentlemen, but our guest has arrived."

The men turned to face them.

"Daddy!" Alex screamed.

Philip Stuart grinned and held his arms wide. The huge form of the handsome Scot towered above the distinguished man at his right. Curly, red-blond hair framed blue green eyes the same color as his daughter. The joyous sound of his laughter boomed in the open room.

Alexandria ran to him, and he scooped her up in his arms. She felt twelve years old again. Warmth and love flooded through her like the rush of wine.

Alex stared at her father transfixed. "You look just the same. We're the same age. We look like twins."

"I still feel thirty-eight," he laughed. "And you, little Princess, have grown into a remarkably beautiful woman."

Alexandria blushed.

"Alex, I'd like you to meet a old friend, Miguel Piedra," Philip said, turning to the Indian man beside him.

Black eyes shone from a regal face. Jet black hair, laced with streaks of gray and white at the temples, surrounded a chiseled countenance. He was dressed in western clothes but Alex thought he looked like pictures she'd seen of Mayan chieftains. "It's a pleasure to meet you," she managed to say.

"The pleasure is certainly mine, Senorita," Miguel replied, bowing low. "So, this is the young lady who was named after the famous library huh, Felipe? Well, if she is as wise as she is beautiful, all will be well. Now, if you will please excuse me, I'm sure you have some catching up to do. We will meet again soon, I am sure."

Alexandria bobbed her head at him distractedly. "Yes, of course." She looked at her grandmother in disbelief.

Pointing to three stuffed chairs which surrounded a glass table Gran said, "Let's sit down, shall we?"

A handsome young man, dressed in white linen, brought a tray of fresh fruit and a pitcher of sparkling golden-colored liquid. He placed the tray on the glass table and poured the shimmering liquid into three silver goblets. He flashed a warm smile at Alexandria, who flushed crimson.

"A toast. To old times and new adventures," Philip said, raising his glass. He smiled, and the ruddy complexion of his Celtic features were illuminated. Gran mirrored the gesture. Alex lifted her glass with difficulty. She was so overcome by her father's presence she was paralyzed by joy.

"Alexandria, we don't have much time," her father said. "You won't remember all the specifics of this encounter so it's important that . . ."

"That's impossible!" she interrupted. "I've never forgotten the way you used to visit me in my dreams. Why did you stop?"

Philip and Rose exchanged glances, then smiled at her with love and compassion. "You closed your heart, Alex. It was your way of coping with the pain."

Her father reached over and took her hand. He lifted it to his lips and gently kissed it.

"I've missed you." Tears rolled down Alexandria's cheeks.

He smiled. "I have always been here." He squeezed her hand. "Things will happen quickly, but we'll help you. Events will unfold soon which were set in motion a long time ago. You have to get busy with the specific work you came to do. It's time for your mother to learn to take care of herself. I think you're ready."

"Alexandria, dear," Gran said, "you can visit us here anytime you choose. It's a simple matter of doorways. You'll meet our dear Miguel again soon. He will help you remember."

As her grandmother spoke, Alex saw images of temples, stone pyramids and white robed figures engaged in ceremonies.

"You must open your heart Princess, no matter how much it hurts," Philip almost whispered. "Listen to the voice of your heart; it's the gateway to your soul. Never forget how much you are loved."

Alex woke in darkness as the grandfather clock in the foyer struck three. Her heart beat as loud as the clock. She stared out the window at the stars a long while.

*   *   *   *   *   *   *

Still under the influence of last night's vivid dream, Alexandria made an uncharacteristic early start. She pulled on jeans and an over-sized shirt, twisting her hair on top of her head to keep the unruly curls out of her eyes.

Armed with a steaming mug of cinnamon coffee and a plate of Emma's warm, blueberry muffins, Alex followed Crystal into the library. She stood in the center of the large room and turned around slowly, absorbing the magnitude of the task. Three walls of the library were floor-to-ceiling bookcases which overflowed their capacity. Gran's antique roll-top desk bulged with papers, books, notes, post cards and letters from her wide and eclectic circle of friends. The matching secretary was crammed with knickknacks, newspaper clippings of Grandpa's discoveries and patents, vacation photographs and the innumerable spiral notebooks that were Gran's journals.

Alex placed her coffee and muffins on a stack of books and went to the window. The library overlooked the backyard and Gran's garden. She turned the handles of the big, leaded glass panes and opened them wide to the fresh air of a magnificent morning.

Dew drops sparkled like precious gems on green velvet as the first light of day shone upon them. Gran's pear, apple and cherry trees were in bloom, adding the delicate grace of their beauty, and the rich scent of their blossoms, to that of the hyacinths and lilacs. Purple irises, as large as a hand, framed a fountain with a statue of Saint Francis of Assisi. Several birds chirped and bathed in the little pool watched over by their patron saint. A robin sang which such intensity Alex thought its tiny breast might burst.

The garden has never looked more beautiful.

A cool breeze blew softly across her face. Alex closed her eyes and saw the place where she dreamed of her loved ones. She felt connected to both worlds at once; in the magic of that moment, she felt at peace. *Don't leave me again.*

Feeling some measure of resolve, she took a deep breath and plopped in the leather swivel chair in front of the massive old rolltop desk.

"There must be thousands of books in here, Crystal. I wonder why she wanted me to have this stuff?"

At the sound of her name, Crystal nuzzled under Alex's hand, sat on her hind legs and looked up at Alex in an unabashed request for affection. Crystal's ears flopped forward, pink tongue draping from the side of her mouth. Devoted eyes gazed up expectantly. Alex hugged the fluffy white dog.

"Let's get started."

She sorted by category: letters, books, cards, photographs, magazines, newspaper articles, bills, bank statements, reminders and lists Gran had written. Alexandria fought the temptation to look too closely at the items she sorted. She knew it would take forever if she succumbed. But some things were irresistible, especially the pictures.

Inside an old book, she found some black and white photographs of Gran and Grandpa with a group of people. A shiver crawled up her spine. A younger version of the strange, raven-like man she had seen at the cemetery stared at her from the photo.

Written on the back, in Grandpa's small precise print, was, "ALTERNATE ENERGY CONFERENCE, 1962." The title of the book was The Promise of Nuclear Energy. Alex placed them in a box for future reference.

Halfway down another big stack of papers, she discovered a manila envelope with her name written on the outside. Curious, she removed the contents. Inside were colorful Mexican travel brochures, a complete itinerary with airline tickets in her name. The destination was Palenque, in the Mexican state of Chiapas. According to the literature, Palenque was the site of famous Mayan ruins. The departure date was just three days away.

Alex sat back in the chair and stared at the articles in her lap. "This doesn't make sense."

The front door bell rang and startled her. Crystal barked and sped off to investigate. Crystal reappeared in the library accompanied by Emma, who was eclipsed by an exquisite arrangement of lilies, white roses and birds of paradise. The fragrance was intoxicating.

"Who sent those?"

"Here's the card, Alex. What does it say?"

"The Angels of heaven rejoice at her homecoming, sorrow not. It's not signed. Who on earth could they be from?"

"Who on earth indeed?" agreed Emma.

"Hand me the phone book."

Alex checked the number and phoned the florist. "This is Alexandria Stuart. I received flowers for my grandmother. Can you tell me who sent them?"

"No, Miss Stuart. We received a Western Union money order and message from Mexico City. It wasn't signed."

Alex hung up the phone and handed the plane tickets to Emma. "The flowers came from Mexico. I'll start packing. The angels of heaven have some explaining to do."

2
Revelation

Alex felt a mixture of guilt and excitement as she walked down the jet bridge to board the plane to Mexico City. The mystery of the tickets left a curious trail she felt compelled to follow. She still smarted from the conversation with her mother. Sheila and Emma would have their hands full the next ten days.

Alex had digested some of the reference material in Gran's library. The Mayan civilization captured her imagination. She knew her grandmother's interests were eclectic. She had not known the extent of her interest in archeology and ancient civilizations. Grandpa seemed like such a conservative physicist on the surface. She wondered what else those two explored.

Exhausted from hectic travel preparations, she fell asleep and didn't waken until the jet touched down in Mexico City. The airport teemed with a diverse populace. Mexican aristocrats and poor peasants jostled for luggage carts and and vied for position.

An undercurrent of tension pervaded the crowd. Rebel uprisings in San Cristobal de las Casas dominated

the news. Her mother was terrified that she traveled to
Palenque. The rebel base was thirty miles away.

Alex changed planes and boarded a smaller aircraft
to the city of Villahermosa in the northern part of the state
of Tabasco. The mood inside the smaller jet was a welcome
relief from the airport. She relaxed and read in the travel
guide how rich oil deposits brought a boom economy to the
city of Villahermosa. Sudden prosperity spawned satellite
antennas, luxury hotels, museums, art galleries, shiny new
shopping malls and traffic jams.

An hour and a half later, the pilot banked the plane
to descend. Alex stared at the swampy plains, dotted with
palm trees, which stretched from Tabasco to the jagged,
northern slope of the Chiapas sierra. Ducks and grebes
moved through the streams. Graceful snowy egrets flew
over small lakes and swamps, casting long, afternoon
shadows on the water.

Burgeoning vegetation covered the flat landscape like
a thick textured carpet. Rivers snaked across the terrain like
mammoth, brown Anacondas. Arching bridges spanned the
waterways at frequent intervals. Two lane, white roads took
their course from the geography rather than their
destination. She felt a shift, a slowing down, a movement
into another way of measuring importance.

Outside the airport, forty people stood in the sun
waiting to board a bus. Diesel fumes stung her nostrils, and
engine heat radiated from the bus.

Inside the air-conditioned bus to Santo Domingo de
Palenque, Alex felt another winding down in pace. The
driver spoke into a static-filled microphone. He spoke first
in Spanish, then English. "Welcome to Tabasco. We will be
in Palenque in two hours. Don't worry. It is perfectly safe
there. Revolutionaries are not terrorists."

A young German couple sat across the aisle. The
woman looked doubtfu, and frowned at Alex. "I hope he is
correct."

"I'm sure we'll be safe," Alex said and hoped she was
right. She stared at the landscape through the tinted glass

bus window. Indians worked crops of corn and tobacco in the fields along the two-lane road, setting small fires in their milpas in the ancient way of their forebears. Clouds of smoke hung in the air.

Tiny dwellings of gray cement blocks and wooden huts with thatched roofs peppered the fields. Carefully hung laundry, stretched on clothes lines, baked in the sun.

The bus pulled off the paved road onto a gravel drive. Dense jungle vegetation enveloped the narrow drive like a green tunnel. Wood and stone cabins with thatched roofs peeked from the tropical foliage.

A fragile truce existed between civilization and the jungle. A lapse in vigilance and the forest would eagerly wrap its green tentacles around the meager human structures. This seemed less true where huge, tree-eating machines cut wide gashes in the ancient forest to feed an increasing appetite for mahogany and ceiba wood in developed areas.

Alex checked into the hotel and exchanged credit card and keys with an attractive woman who spoke no English. She followed a boy, who struggled with her suitcase, to a casita.

Philodendron plants, with leaves as large as dinner plates, climbed up tall trees as parasites around the stone path. Banana plants hung within reach. Six inch butterflies, in brilliant hues of fluorescent yellow, blue, orange and black, floated as though suspended in hot, thick air. Insects hummed and buzzed. Parrots and macaws screeched in the tops of the tall trees.

The cottages had ceiling fans, but thee were no cooling units. A porch overlooked a stream that meandered through the hotel complex. Waterfalls cascaded musically throughout the grounds.

Alex decided to take a swim and cool off before dinner. The swimming area was cleverly fashioned from stones of different sizes to look like a tropical lagoon. Stone bridges crossed pools of various sizes. Small rock islands provided humans and lizards a place to bask in the sun. Tall date and coconut palms grew close together and created a small forest around the pool.

Alex dove into the water and swam under the surface to the other side. She emerged breathless, but refreshed and pushed herself up on the edge. She approached a counter with a large, thatched roof blanketed by yellow hibiscus flowers.

The handsome man behind the outdoor bar had high broad cheekbones, almond-shaped, ebony eyes and skin the color of burnt sienna. "Que desea, Senorita?" He smiled.

She returned his warm smile.

"Cerveza, por favor."

He pulled a Carta Blanca from a cooler. Ice crystals clung to the beer bottle.

"Muchas gracias." She smiled.

He nodded and grinned. Alex turned and collided with a fortyish blond man. He was tall and muscular. She looked up into the most beautiful gray eyes she had ever seen.

"I'm sorry," she said, trying not to stare.

"No harm done," he grinned. "Don't spill your beer; it's nectar of the gods in this climate."

"You're right," she laughed.

"Arrive today?"

Alex nodded.

"See you at the slide show tonight," he smiled.

Alex took a swallow of nectar and admired the tall form of the retreating Olympian.

* * * * * * *

The hotel provided an orientation lecture each evening. The meeting room was a larger version of the bungalows, built of mahogany, ceiba and stone with a thatched roof of palm leaves. Ceiling fans circulated the warm air.

An eclectic group of European tourists sat at round tables. Alex heard French, German, Italian and Spanish. The presenter was a local Indian. He arranged his slides in a carousel which he projected on the wall. He wore blue jeans and dirty, black boots with pointed toes. His short-sleeved, mint green shirt was held in place inside his jeans by a leather belt. It boasted a large oval buckle, which was barely visible underneath a protruding stomach. He rubbed his fingers through greasy black hair, as if it were in his eyes. Alex thought he'd lost his soul to progress.

A Styrofoam cooler, filled with Coca Cola, Orange Crush and beer beckoned from back of the room. As she leaned over the cooler to pull an Orange Crush from the ice, the speaker glanced at the sterling silver necklace she wore.

One of her favorite designs, the necklace was a stylized cross, resembling Philodendron vines climbing a tree. The two arms of the cross curved upward and inward, extending out from the center of the cross, branching into a stylized U. Tiny crystals and pieces of jade, carnelian and turquoise lined the edges.

His eyes widened. His probing stare made her skin crawl. She sat at one of the tables and met his gaze.

"Buenas noches, Senores y Senoras. My name is Pepe Paniagua. Welcome to Palenque."

Alex thought his presentation seemed forced, a caricature created for the foolish tourists. She found his tone ingratiating, almost obsequious.

The handsome blond man she encountered at the pool came in and sat next to her. Not a single blond hair was out of place. His shirt and shorts looked starched and ironed. He smelled of Aspen aftershave, her favorite. Alex heart beat faster, and her palms were sticky. She felt like an idiot. This guy's probably an anal-retentive bore. What's the matter with me for crying out loud?

"As you can see from this aerial view, even today Palenque sits in grandeur," Senor Paniagua continued.

The slide projector hummed. Small insects circled in the light, and the fan blew dust particles in the hot air.

"She is the jewel, the emerald, most beautiful of all Mayan centers. Palenque rests at the foot of a chain of hills, which are covered with the tall trees of the rain forest, just above the flood plain of the Usumacinta river. A small stream runs through the site and flows underneath the Palace complex through a vaulted aqueduct.

"The mission of Santo Domingo was founded in 1564, on the savanna of Tumbala, by a Dominican padre. It received the addition of de Palenque, or palisade, when the Spaniards ordered high walls built to protect themselves from the unfriendly natives resistant to conversion."

Pepe smiled, but his expressions was without humor. The projector clicked as he advanced the slides and pointed to pictures of stone temples, describing the buildings nestled within the green forest.

"The last slide is the Temple of the Cross of Palenque," he said and looked directly at Alex.

"When it was uncovered, three beautiful carved panels were discovered. In the center was the image of the World Tree of the Mayas. Two human figures are on each side, and many glyphs tell a great story."

He paused, then advanced the slide. The projector clicked. Alex was shocked to see the same cross she wore around her neck. In spite of the heat, she shivered. She created the design herself. She had never seen anything else like it. Pepe called it the World Tree.

Echoing her thoughts, Pepe said in a flat tone, "This is the only cross of its kind in the world."

He paused, turned off the slide projector, and switched on the lights.

"Tomorrow you may see brilliant parrots and macaws flying above the trees. If you are lucky, the gods may give you a feather. It is a special sign. If it rains, you can hear the roar of the howler monkeys.

"Wear insect repellent; otherwise you will be lunch for the bugs! And you, lovely Senorita," he said, looking at

Alex and pushing his greasy hair off his forehead, "wear much sun lotion to protect your fair skin."

Alex did not like Pepe Paniagua. He barely concealed the resentment he felt for the touristas, but he was happy to take their money.

"You are fortunate; tomorrow you have a special guide. His name is Francisco Trujillo. He grew up here but is studying archeology at the University in Mexico City. Ask him anything about Palenque.

"Rise early, and eat breakfast before the heat. After site-seeing, you can siesta. Sleep well, amigos."

The group filed outside. A cacophony of insect sounds filled the humid darkness. The acrid smell of smoke from peasant cottages and the sweet fragrance of flowers permeated the night air.

"We haven't been properly introduced," the blond man said to Alex. He was a full head taller than her. "I'm Erik Anderson. I couldn't help noticing the exchange that took place inside." His brow was furrowed, and the remark was phrased as a question.

Alex stopped and looked at him. "I'm Alexandria Stuart. Most people call me Alex. What exactly did you see?"

"You have something he thinks has value. He's curious how you got it. Frankly, so am I. Your necklace looks just like the cross on that slide."

Alex frowned and resumed walking. "Not that it's really any of your business, Mr. Anderson."

"Erik."

"I design jewelry. I was stunned to see my cross on the temple wall."

"No offense, but it appears it was someone else's cross before it was yours. I didn't like that guy. Are you traveling alone?"

Alex laughed. "You're going to protect me right? Why should I trust you any more than him?"

They reached her bungalow.

"I plan to keep an eye on you."

Before she could object further, he strode off toward his own cabin. She went inside and slammed the door. Alex found the man annoying, but had the irrational thought that he didn't even try to kiss her.

3
Reunion

The travel alarm beeped at six. Alex groaned and punched the snooze button. She considered abandoning the early breakfast idea.

Ten minutes later, the alarm beeped again. She swung her legs over the side of the bed and stared at the bathroom, willing herself there. She struggled to the shower, turned on the water and stepped inside onto cool white tile. Alex closed her eyes while lukewarm water poured over her. She dreamed of a siesta.

Alex dried off her body but left her copper ringlets wet. Turning to throw the towel over the curtain rod, she almost stepped on the largest spider she had ever seen. The dark brown arachnid was larger than her hand.

She screamed, dropped the towel and ran out of the bathroom. This was the stuff of nightmares. Summoning all her courage, she covered the spider with a plastic glass.

Alex smeared sunscreen on her face and arms and threw on a cotton shirt and long pants. She pulled on socks and hiking boots purchased for the trip. Grabbing camera, sun hat and insect repellent, she hurried to breakfast.

Alex joined the other guests at a large round table. She was ready to consider the next bus back to the airport. Shy young girls in westernized clothes brought pitchers of milk and coffee to the tables. Frijoles, rice, eggs and tortillas were served family style in big bowls and platters. Smaller bowls of tomatoes, peppers, onions, salt, lemon and butter provided spice and seasoning. There was honey and cinnamon for the coffee.

Alex asked for a Coca Cola. "I can't imagine drinking coffee in this heat." She noticed everyone else at the table had mugs of coffee, and she blushed at her thoughtlessness.

Erik Anderson walked in a few minutes later and sat next to her. Alex thought he looked like an Eagle Scout in a khaki shirt and shorts with numerous pockets and pouches. He probably had a Swiss Army knife stashed in one of them along with a flash-light, compass and magnifying glass. Maybe even a cellular phone.

Her heart raced, and her face reddened. This was lunacy. She had nothing in common with this man. She was glad she could blame it on the heat and the bloody spider.

"Morning," Erik said, with a broad smile. "Feeling all right? You look flushed."

Alex, mouth full of beans and tortillas, glared at him. *Christ! I might have known he'd be a morning person. He looks like a toothpaste commercial.*

Erik ate with enthusiasm and commented on each item, speculating on preparation and ingredients. Alex ate in silence, wishing golden boy would take the hint.

"Mind if I join you on the van?"

"Suit yourself," she shrugged.

"Excellent," Erik said, undaunted.

After breakfast Alex walked outside to wait for the van. Already the air was steamy. Cicadas buzzed and hummed. Butterflies and dragonflies seemed to float in slow motion in the heavy air. A breeze blew through the open porch and felt like silk against her moist skin.

Eight people piled into the van. The driver exited the hotel complex and headed toward the archeological site. Tall trees and thick vegetation grew to edge of the narrow paved road which curved steadily upward around steep turns. The heaviest rains in Mexico created a rich tropical forest between the ruins and the mountains.

The van driver entered the archeological area and parked the vehicle. He led them down a dirt path to the entrance to the ceremonial complex. Countless earthen mounds covered with dense green vegetation showed how much of the ruins' story lay uncovered.

The eclectic group of mostly European tourists walked a short distance and stopped in an open area at the entrance to the archeological site. A group of Mayan Indians, dressed in traditional long white robes with shoulder-length, raven black hair stood to one side. They were called Lacandones, one of two indigenous tribes who resisted immersion into the modern world.

Hand-made arrows, ceramic pots, colorful dolls, bead necklaces and bright woven belts lay on blankets on the ground. Dark eyes radiated power and strength that came from living close to magic of the earth. Alex sensed an intrinsic dignity and poise, and was drawn to them.

A light early morning rain blew in over the mountains, creating a green mist, which enhanced the otherworldly feel of the place. Gray stone buildings looked stark against the background of soft green foliage.

Alexandria was moved to tears by the timeless beauty of Palenque. Even in its ruined state it was awesome. She tried to envision the original grandeur. She also felt a mounting curiosity.

"It is my pleasure to introduce your guide, don Francisco Trujillo," the driver said with drama.

"Good morning," Francisco said with a trace of an accent. He was slight of build with nut brown skin. Kind black eyes were creased at the corners promising frequent laughter. He wore blue jeans, running shoes, a plaid cotton shirt and a red baseball cap. Alex liked him at once and thought Francisco was a delightful contrast to Pepe Paniagua.

"The ceremonial center of Palenque is not the largest Mayan center," Francisco said, "but it is beautiful even now. At this time of day in the mist," he smiled, and circumscribed the surroundings with his arm, "it looks magical.

"Palenque was a western Maya center. One of its ancient names was City of the Sun's Daily Death. Implied in the daily death of the Sun is a daily resurrection. The sun was reborn each day at the eastern city of Tulum.

"We are standing roughly in the center of the site, which covers twenty-four square kilometers," Francisco said. "More than four hundred temples and buildings are buried within that area. Only a few have been excavated.

"The architecture was well suited to the humid climate. Tall roofs, with double vaulted ceilings, porticoes and doorways helped to keep the rooms cool. The ingenious use of small windows, shaped like an inverted letter T, symbol of the Wind God, brought in the god's cooling breath."

They followed Francisco across a mowed area and stood in the shade of a temple.

"The stucco decoration at Palenque is the most delicate and sophisticated of any Mayan area. The violence and sacrifice seen at other centers is not reflected in the frescoes here. Whatever its true Mayan name, Palenque seems to have been a place where tranquility prevailed.

"Directly ahead is a complex of buildings, which covers about an acre, known as The Palace. It is a network of vaulted galleries, courtyards, porticoes and underground chambers which went through many changes during its long history.

"To the right is the famous Temple of the Inscriptions, where a fabulous tomb was discovered. Please follow me."

The group trudged to the base of the pyramid.

"This temple is the highest structure at Palenque," Francisco said. "Until recently, it was thought to be unique in the Americas. Archeologists discovered a new tomb in 1994, one hundred years older, and just as fabulous as the ruler-priest Pakal's. We believe his grandfather is buried there. What other fantastic surprises might be asleep in the jungle?"

Alex felt a mixture of excitement and vertigo as she contemplated the single narrow stairway. Francisco led the ascent of the Temple of the Inscriptions. Eight stepped terraces formed the base of the pyramid; the actual temple was on the ninth level.

She perspired as she climbed the steep stone steps. The rest of the group was silent and intense. When they reached the top, they were breathless. Bottled water came out of day packs like champagne corks at a wedding. Alex gulped half a bottle and leaned against a stone wall. Her chest heaved from the exertion in the forbidding climate.

Francisco, who looked untaxed, gave them time to rest before the climb deep into the tomb inside the pyramid. "This structure is similar to an Egyptian pyramid, even the Great Pyramid, in terms of difficulty of access to the inside. Unlike the Great Pyramid, it contained a tomb and rich treasures."

The mountains and the surrounding countryside were visible from the top. The elevated position provided a commanding view of the great plains which stretched like an unbroken sea of green between the ruins and the mountains.

Francisco's tone was reverent when he spoke again.

"The Mayas believed the universe was created when First Father raised the sky from the earth to form a cross. This is the World Tree. The center is called the heart of the world. The arms of the cross are the four directions. A god resides at each corner.

"Ready to enter the tomb?" Francisco smiled. "You must be very careful."

Erik positioned himself next to Alexandria. The steps inside the pyramid were hewn from large pieces of stone, some rounded, others jagged. Most were covered with moss and lichen and were slippery. The ceiling above the stairs was vaulted in a typical Mayan arch.

Steep, damp steps inclined straight down for fifty feet. The stone stairway made a sharp right turn on a small landing, another right turn for twenty steps, and ended in a stone anteroom outside the burial chamber. The crypt was small with an arched doorway.

Stalactites, grown from centuries of darkness and moisture, sparkled like jewels over the massive sarcophagus. Pakal's body, his jade funerary mask and rich treasures had long since been moved to the safety of the museum in Mexico City.

The nine lords of the underworld encircled the walls surrounded by the hieroglyphic inscriptions which gave the temple its name.

"When they discovered Pakal's tomb," Francisco said, "the floor outside the burial chamber was covered with cinnabar. Red is the color of the rising sun and symbolized resurrection. The ancient Chinese had a similar custom to help the spirit gain access to eternal life. The Spanish named their mission Santo Domingo. Domingo means Sunday, but also Easter, and Resurrection."

"Red represents east. South is yellow. The setting sun in the west is black, and north is white. The center of the wheel of directions is green, for the great World Tree and the earth. We know the directions were important to our ancestors, as they are to Indians today," he continued.

"Much of the true meaning of these symbols is hidden, but there are Mayan shamans today who still know the old counsels."

Francisco and most of the group started back up. Alex and Erik remained, gazing at the remarkable tomb.

"Nowhere else but Egypt did people build massive pyramids like this," Erik said.

I think there's a relationship. I came to get a first hand look." He removed his hat and wiped perspiration from his forehead with his sleeve.

"I read somewhere there are pyramids in China, but the government is hiding them," Alex said. "They looked as large as the ones in Giza."

"Are you sure it was China?"

"Yes, positive. Francisco just said the Chinese also used cinnabar. That sounds lke a link."

"I'll check it out. I was supposed to come next month, but my team leader had a family emergency, so they gave us time off now. I wouldn't have met you."

"What kind of team?"

"I'm working in Egypt with a group of scientists from multiple disciplines. I'm the computer guy. John Anthony West, the group's leader, believes the Sphinx was weathered around its lower half by water, not wind and sand."

"In a desert?"

"He covered up the head of the Sphinx and showed a photograph of the body to some geologists. He asked them to identify the pattern of weathering. The geologists agreed; it was classic water weathering. Turns out there was that much water in Egypt thirteen thousand years ago."

Alex's eyes widened as the implication registered.

Erik smiled. "Exactly."

She looked at him. "My grandmother believed in ancient civilizations."

"I'm intrigued by the science; I'll leave the history books to someone else."

They climbed the slippery, stone stairs from the tomb in silence. When they reached the top of the pyramid, Alex's breathing was labored. Her head ached, and her clothes were soaked with perspiration. They rested and shared a bottle of water.

Alex's heart thundered as she stared down the narrow stone steps on the outside of the pyramid. The descent was treacherous; a misstep could prove fatal. Alex and Erik descended the pyramid with care and joined the group. When she reached the ground, Alex was suffocating from the heat and humidity.

They followed Francisco to the next temple. He stopped in a grassy area where three temples formed three arms of a cross. A massive hill, covered with foliage, filled the fourth point. Alex was overheated and exhausted. She sat on a stone bench which circled banana trees.

"Archeologists believe these temples were used for ceremonial purposes," Francisco said. "Some of the most exquisite murals were found which tell the story of creation on a cosmic scale and also relate the personal story of the accession of the throne of Chan Balam, son of Pakal. The information on these murals is a rare treasure because it survived destruction by the Spanish friars.

"The temples were named for their sculptured panels. Human skin was red, but the skin of the gods was blue, similar to Egypt. The temple facing west is called the Temple of the Foliated Cross."

"The Temple of the Sun faces east. Inside are the head and body of a great serpent and a large war shield. The Mayas perceived the path of the sun as a serpent. The double headed serpent was a symbol of kingship, similar to the Egyptian uraeus, the cobra which appears on the brow of the Pharaoh.

"The one in the north, looking south at the forest, is known as the Temple of the Cross of Palenque. It contained the beautiful carving of the World Tree. The originals are in museums.

"Climb the pyramid you choose," Francisco said. "From the top of the Foliated Cross Temple you can see all of Palenque and for miles in any direction. I will wait here in the center to answer questions."

Alexandria marshaled her flagging strength and climbed the temple of the Cross of Palenque. Erik followed her. She ascended the terraced stone steps. The temple had been reconstructed, and a replica of the three part mural depicted the Mayan World Tree. Alex entered the temple at the top of the pyramid. Inside it was cooler, and she felt the lingering sacred energy of the place. She gazed at the marvelous sculpted reliefs and tried to probe their meaning. She placed her hand over her necklace and thought of Gran. What a strange and humbling synchronism.

She turned to look at the ceremonial center and the horizon, lost in contemplation of the green landscape. She stared at the temple of the sun and felt a quiver of recognition. Palenque had a haunting familiarity.

"It's so beautiful," she whispered.

"And so compelling," Erik said softly.

Erik's voice startled Alex from her reverie. She looked at him. His sensitive, intelligent eyes drank in the surroundings.

He knitted his brow. "This center was abandoned six hundred years before the Spanish arrived. What happened?"

"Their origin is curious too," she agreed. "It's as if their civilization sprang to life fully developed, like Egypt and Sumeria. The beginning and ending aren't connected to anything. It's like what you said about these pyramids and those in Egypt. What if the two cultures were related?"

"That's why I'm here. The similarity of the pyramids seems too much of a coincidence." Erik sighed. "Ready to climb down?"

"I guess," Alex said. She didn't want the moment to end. She felt an affinity with these temples and was also feeling intoxicated by Erik's proximity.

As they descended the stone steps, Alex mourned their faded majesty. When they reached the ground, they noticed a distinguished Indian man talking to Francisco. He wore dark slacks, a white shirt, and a straw hat, like a Panama. Except for Mayan features, he looked like a European tourist.

Francisco waved and walked toward them. Erik tensed. Francisco smiled, "I'd like to introduce my grandfather, don Miguel Piedra. He's visiting from Mexico City."

The man smiled and riveted powerful dark eyes, like sparkling obsidian, on Alexandria's blue-green ones. He bowed. "My pleasure. Alexandria, a beautiful name, like the city of learning in ancient Egypt."

Alex froze. This was the man she met in her dream of Dad and Gran. She tried to speak and found she couldn't breathe. She grabbed Erik's arm to anchor herself but, with the combination of unfamiliar heat and shock, she collapsed.

Alex wakened to see two concerned Mayan faces with hawk-like noses, looking down at her. Their brown muscular bodies were framed by bright sunlight and the background of the forest. They wore multi-colored ties around their waists. Bracelets of woven leaves circled their brown wrists and ankles, and ornate necklaces covered their chests. Brilliantly colored feathered headpieces crowned their heads.

She looked into the fierce, almond shaped eyes of the young man who supported her. Alex felt incredible longing and a sense of recognition. She breathed deeply, closed her eyes a moment, and the vision passed.

"Are you okay?" Erik asked.

She was unable to respond.

"Alexandria! Are you all right?" he demanded.

"I've never fainted. I'm embarrassed."

"Allow me to assist," don Miguel said. Before Alex could object, he moved behind her. He placed his right arm under hers and his left arm held her left elbow. With a strength that startled her, he lifted her to her feet. Erik's astonishment over Miguel's uprighting of Alex showed in his open-mouthed stare.

Alex brushed herself off and looked from one to the other. She was confused and a little frightened. She wanted to be angry, but Erik's startled face made her laugh. His expression changed from an open-mouthed stare to a scowl.

"Why don't we have something cool to drink and talk about ancient history?" Miguel asked.

"Very well, professor," she said a bit sarcastically, "I'm extremely interested in an ancient history lesson."

"Alex," Erik blurted, "You need to rest. You're shaking. We need to get you out of the sun."

Alex's struggle with her conflicting emotions about Erik manifested as annoyance. "We'll talk in the shade," she said and marched off in the direction of the trees.

Don Miguel followed, and a fuming Erik brought up the rear. Miguel could barely conceal his amusement at the drama between the overheated shrew and her unsuccessful tamer.

Alex stopped in an inviting rest area behind the Palace complex, beside the stream. Water cascaded over rocks, creating a musical sound. Stone benches circled the trunks of huge Ceiba trees. A breeze moved the thick air.

Don Miguel handed Alex a bottle of water. She tilted her head and drank it without a breath. It tasted like liquid gold. He gave her another and she drank half, then splashed water on her hands and face.

Alex glanced around to see if anyone else was in the area, then looked directly into Miguel Piedra's eyes. "I've seen you before."

Erik leaped to his feet. "Just a damn minute. I don't know who you think this senor is, but he's got a lot of nerve."

Miguel gave him a piercing stare, then his face softened and he smiled.

Alex spun around and glared at Erik, "What is it with you? This isn't the boy scouts."

Erik's eyes looked hurt, then the scowl returned. He opened his mouth to speak, but don Miguel raised his hand in the Indian gesture of silence before speaking.

"You are right, young man. My apology, you do not have the benefit of Alexandria's previous knowledge. Shall I tell him why you reacted as you did?"

"By all means," Alex said, "I'd like to hear this."

Alex was surprised and looked at him expectantly. Erik looked wary; his scowl deepened.

"A week ago I had a remarkable dream," don Miguel began, looking first at Alex, then Erik.

Alex was surprised and looked at him expectantly.

"The dream took place at Palenque. I saw the great center at its zenith. It was called ChaKanPuTun, City of the Rains. The buildings were magnificent. The temples were covered in white stucco, and the friezes and murals were painted in brilliant shades of turquoise blue offset by red like cinnabar.

"The citizens looked as if they stepped off the sculptures. Proud Mayan faces and colorful clothing looked at home in these surroundings. Avenues and paths were lined with beautiful trees and flowers. The City of the Rains was a majestic and sacred place."

He paused and looked around at the ruined Palenque of the present. He was silent, deeply thoughtful.

"Memories are bittersweet, are they not?"

"Oh brother," Erik said, rolling his eyes.

"Be still," Alex said.

"In my dream, I was a priest, on my way to what is now the Temple of the Cross, to perform a ritual to dedicate a new temple rebuilt over one destroyed in an earthquake."

Alex tensed and moved to the edge of the stone bench.

"I walked across the plaza, past the Temple of the Inscriptions, and stood at the bottom of the steps. I was joined by attendants, dressed in white robes woven from fibers of trees in the forest, and embroidered in beautiful designs with threads that matched the temple frescoes.

Alex closed her eyes and was transported back in time. The pungent aroma of sacred copal incense wafted in the air. White smoke curled from the bowls of incense. A drum beat a steady, deep reverberation. She watched the priest and his attendants climb the steps of the pyramid from her perspective at the top, inside the temple. The muscular body of the priest was adorned with woven cords and wraps in red, green and blue. He wore a head dress of feathers and leaves which symbolized power. A necklace of jade beads hung around his neck.

"We climbed the steps of the Temple," Miguel said, "stopping at each group of steps to recite a portion of the ritual. Seven groups of steps symbolized different aspects of reality. When we reached the top, a young priestess waited in the alcove. She assisted me with the ceremony.

"Inside the temple, the great World Tree was painted bright blue, red, green, black, yellow and white. Its name meant 'raised-up sky.' The World Tree wasn't an abstract symbol; it represented the union of earth and sky at that moment. The images on the tree were the constellations in the night sky at the time the temple was dedicated."

Don Miguel stood, placing his white Panama hat on a log. His figure was framed by gray stone pyramids and green jungle. His modern clothes seemed out of place.

"From the top of the temple, every word could be heard throughout the plaza. The ornate roof combs acted as acoustic devices. I remember some of the words."

Miguel raised his arms toward the sky in the timeless gesture of invocation. The voice that thundered from his mouth no longer seemed his. The spirits of all the shamans who ever lived seemed to speak through him.

> "Mighty Hunab K'u, Great Lord of Creation,
> who dwells at the center of the fourfold universe,
> the heart of the world where all is one.
>
> Bless us Wakah-Chan, Great World Tree.
> Protect us First Father, Shield of the Sun.
> Nourish us First Mother, with Divine Maize.
>
> Come forth through the opened portal
> into our Holy Place.
> Receive the offerings we have prepared for you.

Grant us sustenance from the Spirit Realm.
We are humbled, we are grateful.
We honor your presence in our world."

"I looked at the young woman who had been my assistant. The face was that of a beautiful young woman with red hair. She was accompanied by a blond man and a large white dog." Alex was startled back to ordinary awareness.

"I knew I had to come to Palenque to pursue the meaning of such a powerful dream. When I met you today, I recognized you at once." Miguel smiled. "I assumed from your melodramatic reaction that you recognized me also."

Erik scowled at Alexandria. "A pretty story."

Alex exhaled and realized she'd been holding her breath. She stood and turned to look at the Temple of the Cross. Only the back of the hill and the top of the temple were visible from their vantage point.

She stared at the green mound and the stone steps that curved up and around the back. When she turned to face them,her face was pale, and her eyes were moist.

"My grandmother died a week ago."

"I'm sorry," Miguel said gently.

"The night of her funeral I saw her in a dream. My father, who died when I was a child, was with her."

Alex was composed as she spoke, but tears spilled out of her eyes. She absently wiped them from her face with the backs of her hands.

"There were beautiful temples in that dream too. They seemed to be made from sand and stucco and overlooked an ocean. In that dream I was introduced to you, don Miguel. You looked exactly as you do now. My father told me it was time to do the work I had specifically come to do, and that you would help me.

"The next morning I found an envelope with the tickets for this trip. My grandmother arranged it before she died.

"There's also this."   Alex pulled the silver chain and cross from her shirt.

"I made it myself. I thought it was an original design."

"Intriguing," he replied. His black eyes sparkled with intelligence and curiosity.

The cheerful stream cascaded over rocks. A macaw called overhead. "It's strange," Alex said, "but in some ways this place feels more familiar to me than my own home. I'm confused. Can you help me, don Miguel?"

He put his arm around her shoulders. "I will do all within my power to help you, Alexandria. Please, sit down. I must ask you a question."

Alex sat on the stone bench under the tall trees. She placed her sun hat on a rock and twisted her damp hair in a pony tail. Her blue-green eyes searched the sharp features of his countenance.

"I'm not sure where to begin." Miguel smiled at Alex, his expression was kind.

"Make it up as you go," snapped Erik.

"Is your grandmother's name Rose Stuart?"

"This is getting rich," Erik said and wiped his forehead with his shirt sleeve.

Don Miguel's face changed like a storm moving across a landscape. He leveled an icy stare at Erik. When he spoke, his voice was like a dagger. "Because I believe your role may prove to be central to this drama, Senor Anderson, I will be patient with you. But heed me, young man, I may not always be.

"What is unfolding here fits into a larger scheme than you can yet imagine. If you can keep your ego and hormones at bay, you stand to learn a great deal. If you demonstrate strength of character, you may realize the deepest desires of your heart.

"Protectiveness is noble, but you can help Alexandria most by assisting her with this puzzle she's inherited. Have I made myself clear?"

"Perfectly," Erik nodded, "How about this for clear? Go to hell!" He bolted like a stallion escaping the corral.

Alexandria had watched astonished, as don Miguel, looming larger than life and terrifying, delivered this blistering manifesto. She was appalled by Erik's response.

Miguel shook his head as they watched him disappear over the rise.

"I met your grandparents in Boston at an archeological symposium. I believe it was the early sixties. Your father was still alive. He and I were close to the same age and became friends. They visited me twice in Mexico."

"I wonder why I never met you," Alex said.

"After your father's death, we kept in touch through correspondence. Someone notified me when Rose passed. I sent flowers."

"What kind of flowers?" Alex's heart raced.

"Roses, of course, lilies, and birds of paradise."

"Those flowers arrived the day I found the envelope. In fact, at the same time. There was a beautiful card, but it wasn't signed."

"Curious," Miguel smiled, "I wonder what the next surprise will be."

"I'm tired of questions and sick of surprises. I need answers."

4
Raven

Alex sat on a large rock and stared at the gray stones of the Temple of Inscriptions enveloped by emerald jungle. Sticky clothes clung to her moist skin, and her face ached from sunburn. The air itself seemed damp.

"You look like you need a siesta," don Miguel said. Except for his modern clothes, Alex saw him as a Mayan lord on a temple frieze. High cheekbones and a sharp nose endowed his face with haunting dignity.

"I'll take you back to your hotel so you can rest before dinner. This climate is taxing."

She sighed audibly and looked up at him. "I'm miserable, but you look unaffected." She wiped her forehead on her sleeve.

"I was born here. Your body is more attuned to the cold." Miguel offered her water. Accepting the bottle, she consumed the remaining contents.

Alex had difficulty breathing. The heat made her nauseous. "I feel like I'm surrendering to weakness."

"You've been under a strain, and today's events have added to it."

They walked back through the Palenque complex to the parking area. Sparse clouds looked like smoke in a sky as hot as blue flame. The sun had reached its zenith, and the jungle baked in a tropical oven. Birds and monkeys were silent.

Alex noticed the Lacondon Mayas at the entrance. They were small people; barely five feet tall. Their black eyes were bright with intelligence. Their gentle demeanor radiated an openness of heart which touched her.

Men and women kept their black hair long. Lacondon men dressed in ancestral white cotton robes and wore simple sandals, or went barefoot. Even in this two thousand year old archeological site they seemed anachronistic.

Handmade items lay on brightly colored, woven blankets spread on the ground against a backdrop of jungle foliage. One of the men beckoned to don Miguel.

"Excuse me," he said. Don Miguel looked tall next to the Lacandon. His modern clothes, walking shoes and straw hat contrasted with the plain white robe. A broad smile illumined his face as the man gave Miguel a necklace made of textured brown seeds from the rain forest. The beads resembled carved coffee beans.

Miguel held the necklace up. "A gift for you, Alexandria."

Alex blushed. Miguel gestured for her to join them. "This is Chan Ka. He wants to place the beads over your head."

Chan Ka smiled and looked at her out of wise eyes that were childlike in their innocence. She leaned forward to accept the necklace. Everyone smiled and clapped.

"Tell him they're beautiful, don Miguel."

Miguel spoke in Mayan. Chan Ka grinned and nodded. Then his expression became serious. He looked directly into Alexandria's eyes and said a few words in his Mayan dialect. Miguel translated.

"He says he would like to have your necklace."

Her eyes widened. She grasped her necklace in a protective gesture. Alex looked at don Miguel for help. His face was impassive. She could make another necklace. Why did his request offend her?

Everyone was still; the moment seemed eternal. Alex wanted to take the bead necklace off and throw it at him. She fought the urge to run.

As if in response, she heard her father's words. "Listen to the voice of your heart, Alex. Remember how much you are loved."

She sensed his presence and felt a stabbing pang of guilt. She was ashamed, and her reluctance evaporated. Alex removed her necklace. Her hands shook as she lifted the ornate silver cross over Chan Ka's head. Stepping back, she saw her treasure against the white fabric of his simple garment. A deep sense of rightness stirred in her.

A chorus of "Ah's" emanated from the small group.

She recalled the Cross of Palenque she had seen on the temple wall earlier. It belongs with Chan Ka. Alex looked into the eyes of this outwardly simple man and connected to his inner power. He returned her look with a commanding presence and spoke again in Mayan.

"He will wear it with honor," Miguel translated. Then he moved to Alex's side and touched her elbow. "Ready for that siesta?" She nodded.

Miguel guided Alex toward an ageless blue pickup truck. The vehicle was covered in mud and dust but seemed structurally sound. He opened the passenger door and helped her inside. Alex felt dazed. She had no awareness of don Miguel starting the engine, or riding in the truck, other than a vague sense of bouncing on the road.

She was jolted to alertness when a car swerved on the other side of the road and headed directly toward them. Alex screamed and pitched forward. She braced herself against the dash.

Don Miguel wrenched the steering wheel to the right and drove into a ditch. The other car did not stop. As it passed, Alex thought the passenger looked familiar. She didn't see the driver but felt a sense of malice.

"Don't worry; we're not harmed. Help will arrive soon."

She wanted to believe him, but that did not prevent tears from filling her eyes. She was frightened, and her heart throbbed in her chest.

Two men materialized from the brush.

"Where did they come from?" Alex was amazed.

"They live in the area," Miguel said.

The men climbed into the ditch and helped them out of the truck. Alex clamored out of the ditch and collapsed on the ground beside the road.

Two cars arrived, and four men emerged from each vehicle. They laughed and joked in Spanish and Mayan, expressing the good natured banter of close friends. Alex understood enough to know they were teasing don Miguel about his big city driving. The mood was almost festive.

They easily extracted the truck from the ditch. Miguel climbed in and started the engine. One of the men helped Alex into the truck. They resumed their journey in silence.

Alex felt an undercurrent. She thought Miguel's quick response had prevented serious injury, but she didn't believe the mishap was accidental.

When they reached her hotel, don Miguel came around to open her door. Alex thought he seemed comfortable in any circumstance.

"Try to rest, Alexandria. Do not think too much; you are safe here," Miguel smiled.

Alex returned his smile. "I'm too tired to do anything else." She walked to her cottage in a trance and checked on the spider. She was relieved to discover the plastic cup and its eight-legged inhabitant were gone.

*   *   *   *   *   *   *

Alex rolled over, and looked at her watch. It was six o'clock. She'd slept three hours, and the afternoon sun cast long shadows in the room. Stretching, she realized she was famished.

She dressed in a long, goldenrod dress. She wore large brass earrings and added a gold chain with a simulated topaz bangle. Her loose mass of red hair softly framed her sunburned face. Alex looked in the mirror and was pleased with her reflection.

She shook her head. *I hate to admit how much I want to see Erik.* She left the cottage and walked through the jungle grounds to the restaurant.

"You look better, Senorita," Miguel said as she approached.

"Don Miguel, I didn't expect to find you here."

Miguel laughed. "It's a shame to waste such loveliness on an old man."

Alex was embarrassed. She thought don Miguel was handsome. Silver hair, laced with streaks of black, contrasted with his dark, flashing eyes. His angular Indian features seemed chiseled into his striking countenance. He looked comfortable in beige slacks and a blue, short sleeved shirt.

"I feel like a fool. Today was like a dream, almost surreal. I'm stunned by my response to this place. It seems so familiar somehow. Meeting you, after dreaming about you, was a shock. Everything to do with my necklace has been unnerving. Too many accidents and coincidences. Mr. Anderson is making me act like a mindless teenager. Whatbothers me most is Gran buying the tickets. What's happening, don Miguel?"

Don Miguel smiled and gestured dramatically with a wave of his arm and a deep bow. His movements were as agile and graceful as a ballet dancer.

"Your destiny, Senorita," he said. Then he stood up straight and clicked his heels.

Alex laughed but felt helpless.

A waitress approached and showed them to a table on the wooden veranda overlooking the swimming pool and grounds. Sparkling light filtered through the palm trees. The angle of the sun's descent gilded the trees and water with luminescence.

"What would you like to drink?" the waitress asked.

"Beer, please," Alex said.

"Mineral water," Miguel said.

Alex gazed at the philodendrons, hibiscus and tall coconut palms which were filled with the sounds of parrots and macaws. Noisy cicadas competed for mates. Classical flamenco guitar music drifted from a radio in the background.

"It's so beautiful, Miguel, so vital. The temperature and latitude heat up the life force until it explodes in intensity and diversity. Everything teems and boils to express itself. Quite unlike a Philadelphia winter."

Miguel smiled, and his wise eyes twinkled. "Your thoughts have taken a philosophical turn. There's a danger in taking life for granted in a tropical climate. If winter never comes, you can become careless.

"Speaking of philosophy, did you know your grandmother believed in reincarnation?"

Alex laughed. "It always comes down to philosophy. Yes. Gran's world view influenced mine. I spent so much time with her, I absorbed a lot. Reincarnation makes sense to me. It helped place my father's death in perspective. Gran called it a 'karmic necessity.'"

"What did she mean?"

Don Miguel watched Alex intently. His elbows rested on the arms of the chair, and his thumbs and fingers formed a triangle at his chest. His chin perched on the tip of the pyramid.

"It was part of the agenda for his life, and dealing with that loss was part of the life plans for those closest to him," Alex said.

"I see."

Alex looked into Miguel's eyes which seemed to emit sparks of light. She laughed and pounded her fist on the table. The silverware jumped. "That's it! Meeting you is a karmic necessity."

Miguel laughed, a hearty sound, which came from the center of his being. "Each life has a purpose, Alexandria. Yours is being thrust upon you. In reality, you have called it forth. Fate is not an external process.

"I agree we have a purpose for meeting, a karmic necessity, if you will. We don't have much to go on at the moment. We still have some time."

Alex knitted her forehead. "What's your life purpose, Miguel?"

He smiled, and his face brightened.

"A fair question. My studies have been somewhat unconventional and have carried me to unexpected vistas and different realms of consciousness. I have devoted my life to studying the way of the Mayas. The living shamans continue the ancient traditions. I see my purpose as helping them integrate that knowledge and reclaim their heritage. Although I am half Spanish, it is my heritage too. There are prophecies that say the time is at hand."

"You sound like Gran. No wonder you two were friends."

Don Miguel smiled. His profile was outlined by the half-light of the setting sun. Alex thought he looked strong and wise. She felt safe and was comforted by his friendship with her grandparents.

"Don Miguel, I don't think the incident with the truck was an accident."

He looked at her. "No, I don't believe it was."

Alex thought she detected concern in his kind eyes. The waitress served large plates filled with beans, rice, tortillas, sliced avocados and tomatoes. Alex took a bite of beans and rice. She closed her eyes to savor the flavor and texture.

"This is wonderful."

Miguel laughed.

Erik approached their table. Freshly showered, he wore long khaki pants and an olive green tee shirt. He ignored don Miguel and stared at Alexandria.

"Won't you join us, Erik?" Miguel asked, pointing to an empty chair.

Erik didn't answer. He continued to stare at Alex.

Alex smiled and felt like an infatuated teenager. "Sit down and have a beer. We just started."

Don Miguel ate his dinner and appeared to ignore them. The waitress reappeared.

"I'll have what she's having," Erik said, as he sat next to Alex. "How do you feel?"

"Physically, much improved. Psychologically, I'm not sure."

"You look wonderful."

Alex blushed. She was aware of her face producing a vacuous smile of its own accord. Feeling awkward, she groped for something to redirect the course of conversation and turned to don Miguel in desperation.

"Miguel and I were discussing a troubling experience we had today."

Startled from his trance, Erik wheeled around to look at Miguel. Alex and Erik both focused on don Miguel, who had a mouthful of food and a glass of water in his hand. They waited for him to recover. He put his glass down, swallowed and cleared his throat.

"After you left us, I offered to drive Alexandria back here. We had a mishap. Alex and I believe we may have been intentionally forced off the road."

"What?" Erik directed his eyes toward Alex.

"I didn't have a chance to tell you, Alexandria, but my family checked on the car," Miguel said. " Jose Sanchez rented his automobile to a European. The man asked several curious questions, paid in advance and insisted on giving him extra money. It was Jose's car we encountered today. The man never returned it, and they found the vehicle abandoned.

"Did you notify the police?" The volume of Erik's voice increased. Alex was surprised by his strong reaction.

"You're making a scene," she pleaded.

"You're damn right I'm making a scene. It doesn't smell right. Something's rotten in Denmark, and it started when this guy showed up," Erik pointed his thumb sideways and cocked his head at don Miguel.

"That's ridiculous. It started years ago with my grandparents. But I don't know what 'it' is. Stop making don Miguel the enemy and help me figure this out. You're wasting testosterone."

The waitress delivered Erik's dinner. Alex resumed eating beans and tortillas. They glared at each other over their plates.

"How about a safer topic?" Don Miguel ventured. "I'm interested in your work in Egypt. Years ago, I encountered the daunting master work of Schwaller de Lubicz. It is wonderful someone is pursuing it."

Erik sat back in his chair, anger and dinner momentarily forgotten. "You actually read *Le Temple de l'Homme*?" I've never met anyone outside of our project group who even heard of it."

Alex was amused by Erik's reaction to this news and struggled to suppress a smile. "What are you two talking about?"

Miguel's expression was unreadable, but Alex thought she detected a brief sparkle in his eyes.

"He was brilliant, if controversial," Erik said. "*The Temple In Man* is a three volume behemoth. He's the one I mentioned who believed the Sphinx was weathered by water. That makes the big lion thousands of years older than mainstream Egyptologists insist.

"John Anthony West, the force behind the project, had the idea to prove the thesis geologically. I think we've done that. It's pretty clear-cut actually. Oops, forgive the pun," Erik grinned, warming to his topic.

"Until we have twelve thousand year old pot shards, it constitutes academic heresy to the Egyptologists."

"Who does West think built the Sphinx?" Miguel asked.

"He postulates an earlier mother civilization. The A word; Atlantis. He hasn't endeared himself to the Egyptological establishment."

"Gran was interested in this topic. She talked about a psychic who had lots to say on Atlantis. I think it was the same time frame," Alex said.

"Edgar Cayce," Miguel said.

"You know about Edgar Cayce?" Erik asked, wrinkling his forehead.

Miguel laughed. "Ancient civilizations are my passion, too."

Alex watched the interaction between the two men. A thought struck her. "Ancient civilizations were Gran's fascination too. In my dream, there were temples and pyramids. My father said I had work to do, and that you would help me, Miguel. I don't see what I have to do with ancient civilizations."

"Our path will be revealed. We must watch for the signs," Miguel said.

"I believe you," Alex smiled.

"It has been a long day for me. I will take my leave and see you in the morning. Buenas noches," Miguel said.

"Good night, don Miguel." She kissed him on the cheek. Erik merely nodded.

Alex yawned. "It's been a long day."

"I'll walk you back to your cabin," Erik said.

They walked to her bungalow in silence. The tropical night air was balmy. A full moon rose in the east. When they reached the door, Alex looked up at Erik.

"I appreciated the company."

"I've been a jerk. I don't know what's wrong with me. I have this strange need to protect you." His boyish face looked contrite.

He reached for her hand. His touch was electrifying. She felt a current of energy throughout her body. She stared into his eyes. Erik kissed her, a brief velvet touch on her lips. The smell of his breath aroused her, and she felt a sudden rush in her solar plexus.

"Buenas noches, senorita bonita."

She opened the door and went inside. She leaned against door to steady herself. I am totally out of control; this is ridiculous.

Alex put on a cotton nightgown, sat on the bed and tried to write postcards. She couldn't concentrate on anything but Erik's kiss. She attempted a few entries in her journal but threw it on the floor.

She stretched out on the bed and was mesmerized by the slowly circling ceiling fan. Alexandria turned out the light and lay on her back in the darkness. Outside insects hummed, and a dog barked in the distance. The pungent juxtaposition of tropical flowers and decaying vegetation permeated the night air. Alex's mind was full of nagging questions as she drifted off to sleep.

*   *   *   *   *   *   *

Storm clouds gathered in a sickly yellow sky and painted menacing black streaks across the horizon. Thunder rumbled. The air was laden with the pernicious stench of sulfur, and a harsh wind blew dry leaves and dust into whirlpools. Giant sycamores thrashed as strong currents of wind battered them.

Alexandria ran across a forbidding landscape, clothed in a long robe, searching for something. She felt an ominous foreboding.

A huge raven swooped from the sky, cawed in a threatening voice and dove toward her. She ducked, and the bird missed her. A light appeared ahead of her like a beacon. A woman ,clothed in purple raiment like a goddess, held a lantern; shebeckoned in the darkening gloom.

Alex ran faster. She had to reach the goddess before the raven attacked again. She climbed up the side of a mountain. Rocks broke loose and tumbled down the slope. She stumbled as she stretched in a supreme effort to reach the lady.

At last, Alex stood in front of the awesome figure. The goddess handed her a silver sword. She felt the weapon's power enter her body like an electric shock.

She whirled to face the evil raven, who had grown larger than human size. Her heart pounded, and her lungs ached.

Alexandria swung the heavy sword in a wide arc and severed the raven's head. The monstrous head fell to the ground, beady black eyes staring open. Foul, green slime oozed from the headless neck. Alex stared at the disgusting sight, her hands still clenched around the hilt of the sword. She turned to the goddess whose hair and robes blew nearly horizontal in the wind.

The porporate goddess fixed a severe gaze on Alexandria. "Do not fail in your appointed task."

A volcano rumbled deep inside the mountain and erupted in a massive convulsion. A paroxysm of steam and lava hurtled rocks and sparks skyward. Fires raged, and molten lava streamed down the sides of the mountain like the end of the world.

Alex woke screaming. She couldn't comprehend where she was. She heard pounding and someone shouting her name. Erik kicked the door open, and it banged against the wall like a cannon blast.

He rushed inside and cradled her in his arms like a child. "It's all right. It was only a dream," he repeated several times.

Erik held her while her emotion slowly changed from hysterical sobs to quiet tears. She recovered enough to ask for tissues. She blew her nose and looked at him out of red, swollen eyes.

"I haven't had that dream since childhood," she said. "Parts of it change, but I'm always attacked by a black raven.

I dreamed a lot about that hideous bird when I was little. Tonight I chpped its head off. "

He put his arm around her. They sat that way for some time. "My father used to wake me, just like you did." She smiled. Erik reddened.

"The nightmares stopped after he died. I always thought it had to do with his death.

"I think I can sleep now. I wouldn't mind if you stayed in the other bed."

"We'll both worry less," he said. "Lie down. I'll be over here."

"Thanks," she whispered.

"Go on, under the sheet."

Alex was asleep before her head touched the pillow.

5
Respite

Alex woke as the first rays of morning light shone through the window creating white streaks on the green bedspread. Her face ached from sunburn, and her head throbbed. Erik slept in the other bed. The raven's face flashed across her mind, and Alex remembered the stranger at Gran's funeral. She'd called him raven.

She sat up too fast and felt as if she had a hangover. She hobbled to the bathroom to take some headache medicine and dressed in cotton shorts and camp shirt. She hated to wake Erik, so she left a note.

Alexandria walked through the hotel grounds, relieved that the morning air was cool. Noisy parrots called overhead. In spite of the bright morning, Alex couldn't shake the dark emotion of her dream.

Don Miguel sat on the restaurant veranda, sipping coffee. "Buenos dias, Senorita," he said, lifting his mug in salute. He stood as she came to the table and helped her into a chair.

"Difficult night?"

"I had a nightmare that I had many times as a child."

"Do you want to talk about it?"

"Over breakfast?" Alex laughed and tried to calm herself. She was nauseous.

The morning sun burnished her hair like polished copper. Her delicate features were drawn, and her fingernails dug into the palms of her clenched fists. Unnamed anxiety gnawed at her abdomen.

"The basic elements of the dream are usually the same," she said. "I run across a frightening landscape, chased by an evil raven. I meet a goddess-like being who gives me a sword.

"In the past, I woke screaming when the raven attacked. Last night I killed it."

Miguel listened with single-minded attention. Alex shuddered when she described the raven's death.

"I screamed. Erik was outside and pounded on the door. I kept screaming, so he kicked the door in. He held me like a little girl just like my father did when I had that awful nightmare. When I was ready to sleep again, I asked him to stay in the other bed. He's still asleep."

A young waiter brought coffee, and Alex was startled back to the present and awareness of Miguel. She looked into the depths of his warm, dark eyes. Miguel smiled, and the gesture soothed her raw nerves and aching vulnerability. She wished she could go back to the time before Gran's death. Alex sipped coffee and picked at her eggs and tortillas.

"Shamans believe dreams are of central importance," Miguel said. "Their work includes interpreting dream symbols. Your dream is a powerful message."

Alex exhaled, and realized she'd been holding her breath. She sat back in the chair and pushed her hair away from her face.

"I mean no disrespect, but I felt powerless."

"You sensed danger and imminent crisis. You found a mighty Spirit Being who gave you a wondrous weapon, and you defeated your enemy. That is powerful.

"The sword is an ancient symbol of truth, Alexandria, representing the ability of the intellect to cut away the non-essential. The language of dreams is symbolic. The end of the world signifies transformation within you.

"Fulfilling your appointed task, once you know it, requires courage and strength of will. You will be provided with what you need."

"I want to believe you," Alex said.

"Faith in yourself is more important."

"I remembered something else this morning," she said. "I saw a strange, sinister man at Gran's funeral. He was tall, wiry and dressed in black. He reminded me of Poe's Raven. The man gave me the creeps. When I went through her things, I saw him in a group picture with Gran and Grandpa that was taken during a conference."

Erik approached the table and scowled. His gray eyes brooded like storm clouds, but wrinkled clothes and unruly blond hair diminished the impact of his annoyance. He looked like a small boy rousted prematurely from his nap.

"Why didn't you wake me?"

"I thought you needed the rest."

"I heard some of that mumbo jumbo, professor," Erik sat down and glared at them.

Don Miguel took a deep, audible breath. He clasped his hands and placed his arms on the table.

"Alexandria, a respected shaman lives a day's walk from Palenque. I would like to offer help from the Mayan way through a technique called the shaman's journey. Its purpose is healing and the restoration of power. The practice is part of a congruent body of knowledge which has worked for thousands of years."

"A fool's journey you mean. Eight hours through the jungle to see a witch doctor?"

Erik looked toward Alex for confirmation, but she ignored him.

Alexandria evaluated don Miguel. He radiated quiet power. He was secure, fearless, master of any circumstance. Erik exuded fear.

"I want to try," she said.

"Has he cast a spell on you? You'd be at the mercy of a voodoo merchant."

"We'll leave this morning. I'd like you to accompany us, Erik. I share your concern about Alex's well being."

"It means a lot," Alex said.

"It's a cinch I won't let you go into the jungle alone."

"Good" Miguel said. "Pack two changes of clothing. Bring plenty of water, sunscreen and insect repellent, and don't forget a hat. Meet me here in an hour."

Alex was suddenly ravenous and consumed the untouched eggs, beans and tortillas.

*   *   *   *   *   *   *

Alex and Erik joined don Miguel at eight-thirty at the entrance of the hotel. Miguel wore a wide-brimmed straw hat, khaki pants and a long sleeved shirt. He grasped a carved walking staff in his left hand. A small pack hung from his shoulders.

Francisco Trujillo, don Miguel's grandson, and their guide from Palenque, stood with him. Francisco wore jeans, long sleeve shirt and a New York Yankee baseball cap. He held a curved wooden stick that resembled a serpent.

"Francisco will be our guide," Miguel said.

"Wonderful," Alex said.

Erik bordered on sullen.

"It is a pleasure to see you again," Francisco said, with a smile that wrinkled the corners of his brown eyes.

"The jungle is magical," he continued, "but can be treacherous to those who do not know her ways. You dressed well."

Francisco handed Alex and Erik a stick, five feet in length, and a half-inch in diameter. "A walking stick is a good idea for balance." Alex was surprised by the staff's strength and flexibility.

"We will pass through parts of Palenque which are not excavated. It is a lesson in humility to see how the earth has consumed the structures of man.

"Let's begin," Francisco said and turned toward the malachite wilderness.

They hiked for two hours in silence through the steamy forest. The path Francisco followed was invisible to Alex, but he proceeded as if it was a paved road. Vines, branches and thorn bushes caught her clothes.

Alex felt faint when Francisco signaled a halt. Two massive balsa wood trees grew close together and created a clearing in the small space between them.

"This is a chico zapote tree," he said. "These zig zag machete cuts were made by chicleros. The resin is used to make chewing gum. During the rainy season, it runs like milk. The modern world's appetite for gum led the chicle hunters deep into the forests where they discovered many of the ruins."

Francisco looked up. The forest canopy towered high above. Birds and monkeys volleyed for their share of the jungle's bounty in the treetops. "These giant trees are ceibas, the Mayan World Tree, through which souls rise to the heart of heaven.

"Drink as much water as you can," Francisco said. "Rest a few minutes, and eat some nuts and raisins."

Alex felt better when they got underway. Light filtered through the leviathan ceiba trees, some of which grew to five hundred feet. The width of their trunks and vines made them look like mutants.

Nature provided each living thing with an ingenious means of protecting itself. Harmless looking vines grew deadly thorns; others oozed poisonous sap. Insects were cleverly disguised to become invisible in their surroundings. Everywhere the hungry trees and vines consumed the stones of ancient dwellings.

Two hours later, Francisco halted for lunch next to a fresh water stream. The jungle scintillated with heat. Several large pieces of stone from earlier temples had tumbled into a usable formation. Each of the travelers chose a stone and retrieved food and water from their packs.

The hotel prepared lunches of thick, salted tortillas, boiled eggs, tomatoes and limes. Alex mashed a boiled egg inside a tortilla and blended tomato and salt. She rolled the tortilla around the mixture and bit into her creation. It tasted delicious. She squeezed fresh lime into her water and drank half a bottle.

"This is a place of great antiquity," Miguel said. "Mayan legends say the first builders came across the ocean from the east. It may be older than archeologists believe."

"Gran talked about colonists from Atlantis starting over in Egypt, Mexico and Peru," Alex said.

"Flood myths exist in many cultures," Erik said, forgetting to be angry.

"Ancient Mayas were fascinated with time," Miguel continued. "They looked backward and forward to distant epochs."

Miguel placed a large rock on the ground with a smaller one next to it.

"They developed an amazing calendar which works like interlocking wheels. One wheel had twenty day signs; the other wheel had thirteen numbers. As they turned, the cogs connected. The priests interpreted these conjunctions. Certain combinations were fortunate, and others were dangerous.

"Time was depicted as a walker, a god bearing his load, traveling around a great circle. The hours, days, months and years were all seen as gods bearing the burdens of their place on the great wheel.

"The Mayas used a three hundred and sixty-five day solar calendar, and a two hundred and sixty day sacred calendar based on the helical rising of Venus as morning star. Special calendars watched Venus and the Moon."

"The ancient Egyptians also used multiple calendars," Erik said. "Solar and lunar calendars were used for admistering the goverment and other cycles. Their sacred calendar was based on the star Sirius, brightest star in the sky. The helical rising of Sirius signaled the annual flooding of the Nile and the start of the new year.

"I believe these calendars were related in antiquity," Miguel said.

"I read that the Mayan calendar ends on the winter solstice in 2012," Erik said.

"That is a misconception," Miguel said. "What ends on that date is the fifth sun of the Mayan calendar. Five suns of fifty-two hundred years are a world period of twenty-six thousand years.

"The Mayas were great astronomers and understood the phenomenon of precession of the equinoxes. One complete cycle of precession is an enormous time to us, but it was a short cycle to the Mayas. A truly grand cycle, a new creation, began August 13, 3114 BC. It represents a measure so vast it can only be conceived of as multiple big bangs," Miguel laughed.

"Why was time so important?" Alex asked.

"The Mayas, like the Hindus, saw the universe existing in alternating cycles of creation and destruction. They created a cosmic clock to predict and prepare for the periodic cataclysms."

Miguel wiped his palms on his knees. "Forgive me, I've talked too much. We should be on our way."

"Fill your containers with pure water from the stream," Francisco suggested. "Wash your hands and face; it is refreshing."

They walked for hours, stopping periodically for short rests. When Alex thought she must stop, or die in the jungle, a tiny settlement materialized. Excited children ran from thatched huts. Shy women peeked around doorways. Dogs barked, and chickens clucked at the unfamiliar visitors.

Francisco halted the group at the edge of the living quarters. Children danced around him as he distributed candy and stones he collected on their walk. He tossed his baseball cap upward, and three boys raced to snatch it from the sky. The children laughed and pointed at Alex and Erik. When don Miguel addressed them, the children eagerly ran toward him.

A Lacondon Maya emerged from one of one of the huts. Dark hair brushed his shoulders. He wore a white robe, and the cross of Palenque hung from his neck.

Erik gaped when he spotted Alex's cross around the man's neck, and he shot her a baffled look.

"Chan Ka," Alex gasped.

Francisco bowed his head and spoke to Chan Ka in Mayan. He pointed at don Miguel; Chan Ka nodded. Francisco pointed to Alexandria and spoke again.

Chan Ka looked at Alex. She remembered those powerful eyes and realized he knew she would come. Surrendering the necklace was a test.

"What's happening?" Erik demanded. "How did he get your necklace?"

"I gave it to him."

Chan Ka embraced Miguel and Francisco. He turned and went inside the thatched hut.

"We must follow," Francisco said.

Alex walked behind them. She was nervous, but she trusted Miguel.

"What is this, 'Mother may I'?" Erik asked.

They followed Francisco into the simple structure built of mahogany branches which had been tied together in the same manner for millennia. Guano palm leaves formed the thatched roof.

Simple furnishings included a hammock and a seat made from a felled tree trunk. A wooden table leaned against the wall. Hooks held empty tin cans, rope, and a bow and arrows. An oil lantern rested on a piece of wood. Three round stones formed the hearth in the center of the earth floor. Chan Ka sat on a blanket on the earthen floor. Francisco and Miguel sat on the tree trunk, and Alex followed their example.

Erik joined her, scowling.

Don Miguel spoke in Mayan, then opened his pack. He pulled out a beautiful woven blanket and gave it to Chan Ka. Alex wondered if the blanket was offered on her behalf, in exchange for the shaman's assistance. She guessed she was being tested again.

She remembered her good luck crystal. She dug it up on a girl scout camping trip and had carried it for twenty-five years in a little leather pouch. Alex didn't know what Chan Ka would think, but it was one of her treasures. She decided to offer it as a gift.

Alex reached inside her pack, remembering the little girl scout who carefully threaded plastic strips through the once-stiff leather. She stood up and handed her gift to Chan Ka. His sparkling obsidian eyes penetrated her soul.

Chan Ka closed his eyes as he held the pouch. He slowly opened the flap. Reverently, he removed the clear quartz crystal ,holding the shard between his thumb and forefinger so everyone could see. The crystal was the size of his index finger.

The shaman turned the crystal in the light that shone through the mahogany slats. Alex saw a tiny rainbow flash. Chan Ka looked at Miguel and spoke in a strong voice. The only thing she understood was her name. Alex feared she had offended him.

"Chan Ka says you have offered a gift of rare worth. It is a powerful zastun, a stone of light. Before you leave, he will talk to the stone to see your path. Chan Ka will do what he can to help," Miguel said.

Alex looked at don Miguel. "What are the Mayan words for 'thank you'?"

"Hunab Ku, boh ti ketch," Miguel said.

Alexandria crossed her hands over her heart, closed her eyes, and bowed her head. "Hunab Ku, boh ti ketch," she said. She raised her head and smiled at Chan Ka. When their eyes met, energy exploded in her heart and solar plexus. A flash of light blinded her momentarily. When her vision cleared, Chan Ka nodded.

"I will tell Chan Ka of your dream," Miguel said. When he finished, Chan Ka was silent. Then he stood and spoke a few words.

"We will perform the ritual tomorrow night," Miguel translated.

Francisco and Miguel rose on cue from some from some invisible signal. Alex stood and felt dizzy. Erik got up in time to steady her. The small group left the hut and walked a short distance to a cleared area in a grove of orange and lemon trees. Banana, papaya, avocado, cotton, chili, tomato and wild tobacco plants grew among the trees. Hives of stingless Mayan honey bees buzzed in hives in log openings.

Don Miguel and Francisco removed woven cotton hammocks from their packs and expertly attached them to the trees. A Mayan woman, who never spoke or made eye contact, strung hammocks for Alex and Erik.

Another woman brought beans, tortillas, peppers, tomatoes, bananas, mangoes and a large container of water. She served hot chocolate, a royal treat, in special bowls. Francisco built a fire at the center of their camping circle. Hungry after the long hike, they ate without speaking.

"Are there always three stones in the fire circle?" Alex asked, looking at the fire.

Miguel smiled. "Yes. Through the hearth we invoke and honor the powers of creation. The three stones represent the stars in the belt of Orion, the place of creation. Souls are born in the hearth and ascend to the heart of heaven through the ceiba tree which is the milky way."

"Woman's domain is the hearth at the center," Francisco said. "Man's domain is the field. He is hunter and farmer. Together they create harmony and self-sufficency. When children are born, the female afterbirth is burned in the hearth; the male's is placed in the top of a tree to be eaten by birds."

"Speaking of Orion," Erik said, "Robert Bauval, another Egypt worker, realized the three pyramids of Giza are laid out as a precise mirror of the three stars in Orion's belt. The constellation is placed in the heavens in the same relationship to the Milky Way as the Giza monuments are to the Nile."

"Bauval's most stunning discovery, through astronomical computer models which move the stars back and forward in time, was the perfect alignment of the belt stars of Orion and the pyramids occured at sunrise on the spring equinox in 10,500 BC." Erik said.

"Isn't that how old John West claims the Sphinx is?" Alex asked.

"Bingo," Erik said. "That's also when Edgar Cayce said the great pyramid was built."

"The path of the soul is written in the stars," Alex said and was surprised by her own words. The three men stared at her, and she blushed.

Don Miguel smiled. "That is true. My study of mythology indicates that stories are coded in all world cultures as if they originated from one source, and they all use the constellations as their stage.

"Star pictures and their stories have always carried a message of history , prophecy and the soul's journey. "

"Why is Orion so important?" Alex asked.

"Perhaps because he is so large and easy to recognize," Francisco said.

"In Egyptian mythology, Orion is connected with the myth of Osiris, god of resurrection," Erik said.

"All the civilizations are telling the same story. I believe there is a great mystery here that relates to birth, death and rebirth," Miguel said.

They stared at the fire in silence and watched as the crackling flames faded to glowing embers.

"What happens tomorrow, don Miguel?" Alex
asked.

"You and I should eat little during the day. We will
meet in the morning, and I will tell you what to expect and
the significance of what will happen tomorrow night."

"I'd like to listen," Erik said.

"Fine," Miguel said.

Francisco banked the fire for the night.

Alex curled up in her hammock, staring at the
twinkling stars visible in the circular space created by the
clearing of trees. She identified the Great Bear, the Little
Dipper and the North Star, Polaris at the tip of its handle.
Draco wrapped its dragon's tail around the celestial north
pole. She wished she could see Orion.

Insects hummed in the darkness. Alex was grateful
for the smoke and embers of the fire which kept the
creatures of the night at bay.

I hope I'm doing the right thing.

*   *   *   *   *   *   *

After a breakfast of coffee, tortillas with honey and
sliced mango, don Miguel led Alex and Erik to a clearing
close to the nearby stream. The three sat on tree trunks.
Morning light filtered through the trees.

Alex felt apprehensive and took several deep breaths
to relax. Pride precluded a change of mind.

Miguel's black and gray hair was wet and brushed
back from his face, accentuating his high cheekbones and
hawk-like nose.

"The shaman's journey is a practice which is at least
fifty thousand years old," Miguel began.

"It is essentially the same wherever shamans are in
the world. Where people do not have sophisticated
technology to aid in diagnosis, they use other means.
Individuals who can sense, or see, the illnesses of others
are prized. These ways of healing have flourished in

indigenous cultures for thousands of years because they work."

"Why is it called a journey?" Alex asked, her brow furrowed into a question. Her red hair was pulled back from her face.

Miguel made a cross in the dirt with a rock and drew a circle around the cross.

"Shamans see the world in three levels: upper world, lower world and this one of ordinary reality. A shaman must learn to travel between the three worlds, to climb the Mayan world tree, the Wacha Chan."

Miguel paused and looked at them, his Indian features highlighted by sunlight. His words conveyed a way of knowing unfamiliar to the western mind.

"Ancient Mayan kings performed this act through ritual sacrifice in the temples and pyramids. The king represented the people. He made the sacrificial ascent for the sake of the people and was aided by the priests. Mayan shamans still carry on the great idea."

"Why was it so bloody?" Erik asked.

"It was not always so," Miguel said. "I believe the height of what archeologists call classic Mayan civilization is but a shadow of what went before. Those memories are still buried."

"That's what we believe in Egypt also," Erik said.

"In your case, Alexandria, I will journey on your behalf to the lower world of the spirit realm to obtain a nagual, or guardian spirit. The acquisition of a power animal will strengthen your will. Once you have such a guardian, you may journey in the other worlds to seek answers to questions, for teaching and healing."

Time seemed suspended as they sat in silence. The air was warm and heavy. A welcome breeze moved through the trees, shifting the pattern of sunlight on the ground. Alex became aware of the calls of the birds. Miguel you.

"I will spend the day in preparation. Spend time alone. Reflect on the questions that trouble your mind.

Search your heart for the meaning of these esperiences. I will see you after sundown."

Alex and Erik were quiet after Miguel left. She walked to the water's edge and stared into the stream. Clear water cascaded over rocks that were sculpted by the waters constant movement.

Erik joined her and took her hand in his. She turned to face him. His gray eyes darkened, and his expression was serious.

"Why are you doing this? I have no right to tell you what to do, but it could be dangerous."

She looked into his troubled, gray eyes.

"Next to my father, I loved and respected my grandmother more than anyone on earth. She sent me here for a purpose, and it involves don Miguel. It must involve you too, Erik. I need to know what that purpose is."

He relaxed and tried to smile. "I can't fathom what's happening, but in the words of my personal hero, 'The game's afoot, Watson!'"

Alex laughed. "You would be a Sherlock Holmes fan. You're anal-retentive enough."

Erik jerked his hands to his chest as if he'd been shot. "You wound me to the quick, Lass, yet I cannot deny it."

Alex kissed him on the cheek. "I'm glad you're on the case, Sherlock. Would you mind if I spent some time alone?"

Erik left, and Alex sat on a blanket near the water. She extracted her spiral notebook from her pack. She dated the top of the page and reflected on Miguel's words. She listed the clues: dreams, the Cross of Palenque, raven and the mystery of ancient civilizations. Where was the meaning?

Why did you send me here Gran?

6
Rainbow

Miguel came for Alex at dusk, and she followed him into the darkening jungle. They arrived at a cleared place in the forest where Chan Ka's helpers built a fire and burned copal incense. Holding the crystal to his forehead, the shaman danced and sang. He placed the new blanket on the ground.

Don Miguel lay on half of the blanket and instructed Alexandria to lie beside him. Her head ached, her throat was tight, and her stomach growled audibly.

Drum beats reverberated in the dark accompanied by shaking gourd rattles and chanting. Alex breathed rhythmically as don Miguel had instructed and started to gain control of her nerves.

The tempo of the drums and rattles increased. Alex drifted in the darkness on the hypnotic sounds, losing ordinary awareness. She didn't know much time elapsed when the rhythm of the drums changed. She felt Miguel move next to her. He knelt beside her and placed cupped hands on her stomach. Don Miguel blew air into her navel with great force. Then supporting her back, he helped her sit up. He placed his cupped hands on the crown of her head and blew again. She imaged whales spouting water.

"Open your eyes," Miguel said. "I have brought your guardian from the Lower World."

Chan Ka spoke in Mayan. His voice crackled with energy.

"I have brought a small whale, a dolphin," Miguel began. "It appeared four times in different forms. First, I saw the dolphin as a white marble sculpture, larger than life size, in a Grecian garden. Then I came upon a rock garden where a large, green hedge was pruned in the shape of a dolphin. Next, my attention was drawn upward, where a single dolphin-shaped cloud swam across the sky. Finally, a real dolphin emerged from the waters of the ocean. I grabbed it to my chest and ran back to this place.

"You must honor your power animal by dancing its energy. Help Dolphin experience this world, and she will aid you miraculously when you travel in her domain," Miguel said. He turned and spoke to Chan Ka in Mayan.

Chan Ka answered. Alex longed to understand his words.

"He says your nagual is a good omen. Your nature is fiery, and your guardian is a water creature which will balance your spirit. Dolphins and humanity have an ancient kinship. We both came from the sea but they returned to their source.

"These magical creatures sense the energy fields of other beings and always approach those who are ill or pregnant. Dolphins have power to heal through the sounds and energy they emit. It is not just one dolphin but Dolphin, the power of the whole species, who comes to aid you.

"Chan Ka's final words were, 'beware the danger of weakness.' Sleep now. Tomorrow morning we will leave."

Miguel rose and helped Alex stand. She was lightheaded as Miguel guided her through the forest to their camp. Erik and Francisco were not there. Alex collapsed into her hammock. She had crossed a threshold into a new reality and been blessed. She closed her eyes and let the warm darkness enfold her like a black velvet blanket. Inhaling the smoky scent of the fire, she recalled the dolphins at the national aquarium who performed with grace and joy, in spite of their captivity. Alexandria called forth an image of the ocean.

"Dad and Gran, I swear to you, I'll see this through."

She fell asleep and dreamed of pink marble temples where she worked and studied high on a cliff overlooking the sea.

*   *   *   *   *   *   *

Alex woke before daybreak to the morning sounds of parrots and macaws searching for breakfast. Her companions were asleep. She walked the short distance to the nearby stream and knelt by the water's edge. After drinking three delicious handfuls, she splashed the pure water on her face and neck and ran wet fingers through her tangled hair. Alex considered submerging her head.

Something caught her eye that resembled a bright green garter snake. A brilliant, neon green feather dangled from a bush. Ten inches long, the green plume looked like decoration from an Art Deco hat. She picked up the feather and twisted it in the light; perhaps Miguel or Francisco could identity the bird it came from.

Refreshed and ravenous she returned to camp. Miguel and Francisco folded their hammocks and placed them in their packs.

"Look what I found," Alex said, holding the feather in front of her.

"A Quetzal feather," Francisco said with a look of awe. "A great treasure. They are secret creatures. We hear their song but rarely does anyone see one."

"A good sign," Miguel agreed.

Erik sat up in his hammock, rubbing his tousled blond head.

"What does the bird look like? It must be huge."

"The Quetzal bird is brilliant green with a red chest, but it is quite small. The body is only five inches. This feather is from the tail which can be three or four times as long as the body," Francisco said.

"Nice going, Watson," Erik said.

Alex grinned. "It's beautiful."

"We will walk to a nearby village today. My brother, Pablo, will meet us and drive us back to Palenque," Francisco said.

Erik frowned, "Why did we have to walk here in the first place?"

"It was a necessary part of the journey," Miguel said.

"Can we eat first?" Alex asked, looking worried. The men laughed.

After breakfast they went to Chan Ka's hut to say goodbye. Alex showed him the Quetzal feather. He held it in his hand, turning it slowly to admire its beauty. He smiled, and his black eyes dancing with childlike wonder. He returned the feather to Alex and spoke to Miguel.

"Chan Ka looked into the stone of light. He says you are called to this work, Alexandria. You must become h-menob; a shaman. The crystal showed him a vision. He saw the three of us searching for something, digging in the ground. A tiny Quetzal bird battled a large raven overhead. The little bird was valiant. Although challenged severely, the tiny warrior triumphed. Chan Ka said to guard this feather well; it holds a promise."

Tears of joy welled up in Alex's eyes. "I will."

Chan Ka gestured for her to come forward.

Alex approached the shaman and stood in front of him. He started to remove the cross necklace. She looked alarmed and raised her palm.

"No. The cross belongs here," she said.

Chan Ka understood without translation. Impulsively, she hugged him then wheeled around and left the hut.

They followed Francisco to his brother's car. Alex and Erik were quiet during the return trip. Francisco, Pablo, and Miguel talked and laughed. Alex understood some of the words, but her attention drifted in and out of their conversation.

When they reached the hotel, Miguel said, "Tomorrow I will teach you to journey to the lower world."

"I'm ready, and I have a magic feather to prove it."

* * * * * * *

After an early breakfast, the three returned to Alex's hacienda to begin her exploration. "You must journey first to the lower world," Miguel said, "where you will meet your power animal and experience the shamanic state.

"The lower world represents the emotions and must be entered through a real place which has power of you. It could be a spring, a cave, or a hollow tree trunk. When I beat the drum, see yourself standing there. Examine the place thoroughly, see its details. This is important.

"Enter the opening in your imagination. You will be inside a tunnel which will take you deep inside the earth. If you see other passage ways, do not take them. Move only straight ahead. When you emerge onto a landscape, you will meet your power animal there.

"This is your first journey, Alexandria. Don't expect too much. Look at everything closely, and try to remember as much as you can."

Miguel closed the blinds to darken the room. He brought a drum and copal incense.

"When you are ready, tie this kerchief around your eyes. You need to be in darkness."

She squeezed Erik's hand before she covered her eyes. Breathing deeply to calm herself, she visualized her entry point. She chose a secret cove along a stream at the Matthews farm. A wizened elm sheltered the inlet and a trickling waterfall tumbled into stream.

She imagined herself in that spot, then pictured herself diving into the center of the waterfall and entering the earth as don Miguel had instructed. She signaled him to start drumming.

Don Miguel struck the drum in the quick, staccato beats of the preparatory rhythm, then altered the tempo to a rapid, steady pounding. Alexandria entered the opening and found herself in a large, tube-like tunnel about eight feet in diameter. The aroma of brown, loamy soil filled her nostrils. The earthen sides of the tunnel was ribbed and stretched out in a gentle downward slope ahead of her.

She looked at her clothes and feet, realizing she was barefoot and dressed in a short skirt and halter top. Her body was tanned and muscular. Alex felt a primal urge to run. The vibration of the drum gave her speed and momentum, and the deep reverberation drove her onward into the fertile womb of the earth.

Alex ran tirelessly into the tunnel, past openings which branched off the main artery. She did not detour as Miguel had warned. A small circle of light formed ahead in the tunnel, and she ran toward the luminous disk.

Alex emerged from the darkness of the interior passage onto a bright, sunlit seascape. She shielded her eyes from the sudden brilliance. Humid, salt air stung her nostrils.

As Alexandria's eyes adjusted, she examined her surroundings. She stood on a golden sand beach which surrounded a lush, turquoise lagoon. To her left tall, rocky cliffs overlooked the ocean. A waterfall cascaded over the rocks into the lagoon. To her right, a pine forest grew to the water's edge.

The blue-green water of the lagoon trembled, and the silvery face of a large, bottle nose dolphin appeared. Alex thought the creature smiled. Certain the dolphin was female, Alex ran into the water to meet her.

Alex spread her arms, and Dolphin came up out of the water on her tail fins. They greeted in a gesture resembling an embrace. Alex had never known such spontaneous joy. Dolphin's eyes sparkled with light. She slid back into the water and made a series of clicking sounds. Alex heard a voice inside her head.

"Climb on my back, Child."

Alex didn't hesitate. She clambered on Dolphin's silky, gray back and heard the voice in her thoughts again.

"Do not fear. You will not fall. My desire to carry you will hold you fast. We will journey far, you and I."

Dolphin arched her body and leaped into the air like a gymnast - then dove under the surface of the waves. The sea water was warm. Alex could see clearly and was able to breathe.

Hundreds of shiny, translucent glassfish swam in precision, turning and twisting in unison like an underwater drill team. A yellow and white spotted flatworm posed by a flame colored sea fan. Bright yellow anemonefish, with cobalt blue bands around their faces, swam among the anemones. The spines of a brilliant orange sea urchin exploded from the rocks like a fireworks display.

Alex saw crabs, jellyfish, starfish, a sea turtle and a stingray. A shy moray eel poked its head from a crevice on the ocean bottom.

Dolphin swam into a Kelp forest. Sunlight from the water's surface shimmered through the long fronds of dark green vegetation, creating a haunting, primeval sanctuary. Stones and columns of rock rooted in the ocean bottom looked like ruins of an ancient temple.

White fire coral, yellow feather stars, brain coral, and red rope sponges protruded from rocky beds in the sand. Gray moonfish with bright yellow fins and tails surrounded them. Alex laughed at a spiny pufferfish that looked like an aquatic porcupine. Dolphin clicked, and the sound was amplified by the water.

Dolphin swam out to the open sea. Once away from shore, a group of dolphins greeted them with a chorus of effervescent clicks and whistles and swam around them in circles. Further out, great Orcas surfaced, sprayed and crashed into the waves.

Dolphin turned back toward land, racing through the waves at astonishing velocity. Alex had not known such euphoria since childhood. This beautiful being radiated unfathomable happiness. Dolphin turned her lithe body straight up and soared through the air. Circling in the sky, Alex saw the beautiful lagoon from above. Sunlight shimmered on the aquamarine surface, creating dancing prisms of light. Gulls and pelicans flew with them.

Impossibly, a glorious rainbow shone in a cloudless sky. Dolphin flew across the fluorescent colored arch, then banked like a big bird, circled downward in broad spirals and came to rest on the golden beach.

Alex slid off Dolphin's back and knelt on the sand in front of her. She looked into the sea creature's magnificent eyes and felt unconditional love. Alex kissed Dolphin's silvery snout.

"Thank you, Dolphin. My heart is full."

Dolphin's eyes twinkled with merriment.

"You have a great heart, traveler, but it is not yet full. You have scarcely touched its capacity. Your journeys here will help fill the chalice. I'll be with you as long as our work together requires. Do not forget me while you sojourn in the world of form. Farewell, little mermaid."

Alex heard four loud drum beats which called her back to ordinary reality.

As quickly as she appeared, Dolphin vanished into the sea. Alex turned and scanned the gray cliff face for the opening she came through. She entered the cave and ran through the tunnel, back the way she had come, matching her pace to the rapid, staccato drumming. When she reached the opening at the other end, she came up through the waterfall into her secret place.

Alex felt the drum beats, which assisted her return. Miguel struck the drum hard four more times, signaling the end of the journey.

Alexandria became aware of the room, the bed, the kerchief over her eyes and the fragrance of copal. Inhaling, she removed the blindfold and looked around in a state of rapture.

"How was your first journey, little mermaid?"

Alex looked at don Miguel. "Why did you call me that?"

Miguel smiled, and his black eyes danced.

"I don't know if I can find the words," she said. "I was really there. I could feel, touch and smell."

"Try to tell us what happened," Miguel encouraged.

"I ran through a tunnel inside the earth until I saw an opening. I came out onto a beautiful seascape. I met Dolphin and went for a thrilling underwater roller coaster ride on her back. I saw incredible sea life. We swan with a pod of dolphins in the open ocean. Dolphin flew through the air over a rainbow," Alex said in awe.

"A profound first journey. Multiple senses are unusual in the beginning. As Chan Ka said, you have potential as a shaman."

"What happens now? I don't have the answers I came for, just more questions," Alex said.

"We have been reunited," Miguel smiled. "Now we must go our separate ways and return to our ordinary lives until the next step is revealed."

Alex looked at Miguel and Erik. She'd known these two men only a week, but she didn't want to part from them. It seemed she had known them all her life.

"Waiting is not my forte," she said.

7
Return

Alexandria stared out the oval airplane window as rain streaked across its plastic surface and intermittent lightning briefly illumined the black clouds. She wished she'd taken the aisle seat.

The flight from Mexico was delayed and rerouted to avoid the violent spring storm. Alex barely touched her meal, just managing to gobble up the chocolate frozen yogurt before turbulence made eating impossible. She needed to go to the bathroom, but the captain had directed the passengers to remain seated.

The gray-haired woman in the seat next to her tensed her muscles and gripped both arms of her seat. Her eyes were closed, and her lips mouthed a silent prayer. Alex felt sorry for her. She was visiting her son's family, and she said this flight was her worst nightmare.

Alex was relieved when they approached the airport. The plane bounced and pitched as the pilot descended through dark clouds onto a rain swept runway. Local time was three P. M., but the sky was black.

She breathed a prayer of gratitude as the jet taxied to the gate. Alex looked at her seat mate and saw tears run down her cheek.

"You were brave," Alex said, touching her arm. "I love to fly, and I thought this flight was awful. Now you can relax and enjoy your grandchildren." The older woman smiled.

Alex glimpsed Sheila waiting at the gate as she emerged from the jet bridge. Her friend waved a hand decorated with bright red fingernails and bangle bracelets.

"You look a little green, Kiddo," Sheila teased, after they hugged. "I told you not to drink the water."

Alex managed a smile. Everything about Sheila was round: mouth, eyes, hair and figure. She fondly referred to her friend as the Queen of Hyperbole. Sheila's favorite color was black because she thought it was slimming. She adored Alex's designs because they were fluid. Sheila wanted to do a funeral motif for her upcoming fortieth birthday.

"Mumsie's been a handful," Sheila said. "She's called Emma, or me, twice a day. Thank the Goddess, she connected with Arthur Livingston at the bank. He's been a prince, Allie. They've actually done lunch a time or two." Sheila flashed a wicked smile and glanced at Alex out of the corner of her eye. "Don't ya' love it?" she said in her best Mae West voice.

Alex laughed out loud.

While Sheila helped Alex with her bags, Alex spotted her seat mate across the luggage carousel, surrounded by adoring grandchildren. She was radiant; memory of the terrifying flight was erased.

Alex envied her. She was reeling from the stressful flight and shock of reentry into her own culture. The Philadelphia airport seemed unnaturally quiet after the manic chaos of Mexico.

The two friends climbed into Sheila's black Lexus and headed out of the airport. Alex stared at rainy streets and tried to process her surroundings while Sheila checked messages on her car phone. The city seemed manicured and antiseptic.

Alex smiled at her friend while she drove and talked. Sheila made a comb of her fingers. Red talons poked through shiny black strands, sweeping her chin length hair across the top of her head. Terminating her last call, she zeroed in on Alex.

"Well?"

"It's been an incredible week," Alex said. "I thought Mexico was another planet; now home seems alien. I feel like I've been wandering in a dream world.

"Speaking of dreams, do you recall the one I had the night of the funeral?" Alex asked.

"Where you saw your Dad and Rose?"

"They introduced me to a man named don Miguel Piedra and said he was an old friend. I met him in Mexico. He's a shaman, and he knew Gran."

Sheila's eyes widened. "You're kidding."

Alex grimaced. "I fainted when I met him. I blamed it on the heat. He had a dream about me too; that's why he was in Palenque.

"That's just the beginning. I had a nightmare I used to have as a child. It stopped after Dad died." Alex paused.

"Something else?" Sheila asked.

"I met another man, a computer scientist who works in Egypt. His name is Erik Anderson, and I've got a ridiculous crush."

"Sounds like a full trip; I want the juicy details."

Alex sighed. "I have a million questions and not many answers."

Sheila turned the corner of Gran's street. Alex braced herself, but the sight of the real estate sign in Gran's yard felt like a kick in the stomach.

"It's only a house, why does it hurt so much?"

"So much love was breathed into this one it's alive," Sheila said. "You have to grieve the loss of the house too."

When they reached the door, Crystal's barks were strident. Alex felt her heart stop, then adrenaline kicked in and pounded started inside her chest. She clutched the wet railing on the porch to steady herself.

"Crystal!" she shouted through the door.

Emma opened the door; her normally cheery face was contorted by tears. Her starched white apron was wrinkled from twisting, and she pushed loose wisps of gray hair from her face.

"What's wrong?" Alex asked, fighting a rising panic.

Crystal continued to bark, a high-pitched noise which grated on Alex's nerves. The dog turned her head toward the hall and yipped louder.

Alex realized Crystal wanted her to follow and moved in that direction. Crystal padded toward the back of the big house and stopped in front of the library door.

Alex was momentarily paralyzed. Crystal did not relent. She barked again, an urgent sound. Sheila peered inside the doorway and turned a stricken face toward Alex, whose heart beat so hard she could feel the arteries pulsing in her head.

Alex forced herself to look into the room. The priceless antique desk and secretary were overturned, their contents dumped on the floor. Books were strewn across the carpet, or piled in crumpled stacks as if awaiting the torch of a mad zealot. Alex was so angry she was shaking. Fingernails dug into her palms.

"Call the police, Sheila," Alex said.

Alex left the library and returned to the front of the house. Emma was rooted in the foyer.

"When did this happen?"

Emma struggled to regain her composure. She blew her nose and stuffed the tissue in her apron pocket.

"We just discovered it. Crystal and I went to the market. The minute she came in the house she went right for the library, barking like a fiend," Emma said, crying again.

"It's not your fault. Have you looked through the rest of the house?"

"Nothing else was touched," Emma said.

"Sheila's calling the police. They'll want to ask you some questions," Alex said, hugging her.

Alex walked back to the library in time to overhear Sheila talking to the police dispatcher. She hung up as Alex walked in.

"Philly's finest are on their way. I think sherrys are in order," Sheila said.

"Capital idea," Alex said. "A triple for Emma. This is damn odd and damn upsetting."

They adjourned to the kitchen to wait for the police. Sheila poured three glasses of sherry. "Here's to Sherlock Holmes," she said.

"I wish he were here," Alex said, thinking of Erik.

The sherry burned her throat, but the warmth quickly spread into her blood stream. The alcohol deadened her nerves and slowed things down. The telephone rang, jarring her short-lived reverie.

"Hello?" Alex said. Silence was followed by a click, then a dial tone.

"Who was that?" Sheila inquired, directing a scrutinizing look in Alex's direction.

"Wrong number," she said.

"Maybe not," Sheila frowned.

The doorbell rang and jangled her nerves again. Crystal rushed to answer it. Alex followed the dog to the front door and held her collar as a precaution. When Alex opened the door Crystal wagged her tail.

A large uniformed police officer stood beneath a golf-size, black umbrella. "I'm Sergeant O'Reilly. Hello, Crystal."

"Come in. I'm Alexandria Stuart," she said, opening the door wide, gesturing for him to enter.

Tall and broad, O'Reilly's frame strained the upper limits of police height and weight requirements and the seams of his uniform. His round Irish face was brightened by red cheeks and nose. Streaks of gray dignified his curly red blond hair.

The sergeant closed his umbrella and wrapped it on the porch to dislodge rain water. That gained points with Emma who watched from the hall. He stepped inside and removed his hat. Alex deposited the umbrella in the large container by the door.

"I was sorry to hear about your grandmother's death, Miss Stuart. She was a fine lady."

Sheila approached the foyer smiling. "How do you do, Captain? I'm Sheila Goldman, friend of the family."

O'Reilly nodded. "It's Sergeant, but thanks for the vote of confidence."

"Names and titles are funny things. I'm thinking of changing mine to Goldwoman."

O'Reilly stared at Sheila. He started to speak, then changed his mind. Alex stifled a laugh, which resulted in a strangled coughing noise.

"Let's look at the library," she suggested.

O'Reilly examined locks and windows and took Polaroid photos of the room.

"When did this happen?"

"This morning," Alex said. "Emma Martin, my grandmother's housekeeper, discovered the damage when she returned from the market."

"Anything taken?"

"We aren't sure," Alex said.

"Any ideas about who might be responsible?"

"My grandparents' collections seem intact, as do his geodes and minerals. He was an eminent scientist who did leading edge research," Alex said, shaking her head. "Sometimes it was controversial."

"Get the housekeeper," O'Reilly directed.

"Aye, aye, Captain," Sheila saluted and went to find Emma.

Alex bristled. "She's frightened, Sergeant."

Emma was visibly shaking when they returned.

"I just need to ask you a few questions, Mrs. Martin," O'Reilly said.

Alex was annoyed with O'Reilly's tone. Did he suspect Emma, for Christ's sake? She sat next to Emma while he questioned her. O'Reilly took careful notes and nodded frequently as she spoke. After what seemed an eternity, he closed his notebook and rubbed his eyes.

"This was a professional job in terms of entry, but the library looks like vandalism. Put the room to rights. Pay attention to any pattern you see."

"Can I call Henry and the maintenance fellow to upright the furniture?" Emma asked.

"Have them bring boxes for the papers. I'll stay here until this mess is straightened out," Alex said.

When Alex showed O'Reilly out, she spotted her mother heading up the walk and cursed the rotten timing. Amelia Stuart looked glamorous in a white linen suit, carrying a colorful jungle print umbrella. She tiptoed through small puddles on the sidewalk. O'Reilly nodded to her from under his black umbrella.

Alex embraced her mother and kissed her cheek. "Mother, what a nice surprise. I didn't expect you. Your hair looks lovely."

"I can see that you didn't. You hadn't even phoned. What was that policeman doing here?" Amelia spoke the word with distaste.

"Someone broke into the library," Alex sighed.

"I told you not to go to Mexico. I knew something dreadful would happen. It was very selfish, Alexandria. "

Crystal padded into the hall and honed in on Amelia.

"Keep that dog off me. This is a new suit."

"Dammit, Mother," she said, collaring Crystal, "This would have happened whether I was in Mexico or not." Alex wished she were sure.

Amelia stepped inside and stuffed her umbrella in the caddy.

"Hello, Sheila dear. It was sweet of you to get Alex at the airport; she never asks me."

"You hate the airport, Mother."

"Isn't is dreadful about the library?" Amelia said, ignoring her. "I can't bear to think of criminals being in this house."

Sheila hugged Amelia and winked at Alex behind her back.

"Mother," Alex asked, deciding that the best defense was a good offense, "Sheila told me about that nice man at the bank, Arthur Livingston isn't it?"

Sheila's eyes became huge, and she shot Alex a conspiratorial look from behind Amelia's back.

"Arthur's a dream. I don't know how I would have managed without him since you abandoned me. We're having dinner this evening," Amelia said.

Alex was prepared to capitalize on that comment when the doorbell rang again.

"What the hell is going on?" Alex shouted.

Sheila helped Crystal answer the door. The realtor stepped into the foyer.

"Mrs. Bartholomew, this is a bad time," Alex said.

"Pay no attention to me, Dear. You won't know I'm here. I need to get a few tiny points clarified before the open house," the realtor said.

Inwardly, Alex groaned as Mrs. Bartholomew marched off with her mother in tow.

Alex and Sheila headed toward the kitchen for coffee and chocolate chip cookies. They sat at the big wooden table and kicked off their shoes.

"Okay, I've waited long enough. Let's hear about the stud," Sheila said through a mouthful of cookie. "Vital statistics first."

Alex grinned. "Tall, blond and handsome with brooding, gray eyes that belong in a gothic novel. Being around him made me feel sixteen. The bad news is he's anal-retentive and pushy," she frowned.

"Sounds promising," Sheila said, raising and lowering her eyebrows and pushing her hair out of her face.

The phone rang again.

"I can't believe this day.

"Hello, Erik." Alex batted her eyes at Sheila, who mimed Greta Garbo, holding a long cigarette holder.

"There's been an interesting turn of events," Erik said. "The Egyptian government won't renew West's license; he's stirred up too much controversy. We got a bonus check, and yours truly is out of a job. What's up with you?"

"Someone broke into my grandparents library."

"Are you all right?"

"We're fine; no one was home. The police have been here. The odd thing is, nothing seems to have been taken."

"You need the strong, silent scholar's touch. I can be there tomorrow to help you get things organized."

"You have to look for a job," Alex said, as she paced around the kitchen with the portable phone, gesturing as she spoke. Sheila laughed, watching her antics.

"A few days won't hurt. I can't resist a library."

"I could use the help."

"It's settled. See you tomorrow."

"Bye," she said, pushing the off button and slamming the antenna into the top of the phone.

"This is better than cable," Sheila howled, grabbing two cookies. "I'm outta here for now, but I'll be by this weekend to meet blondie."

"Damn he's arrogant. I can't wait to see him."

8
Romeo

Erik's phone call the previous night had rattled her, and Alex was on the verge of chewing her fingernails. She couldn't sit still, and when she stood she paced. Crystal matched her movements, and they collided at every turn.

She felt like a dizzy teenager spending an impossible hour deciding what to wear. She wanted to look fabulous, but she didn't want Erik to suspect she'd taken half the morning to accomplish it.

Since she designed a signature line of clothing and jewelry, Alex had more options in her closet than some retail stores. After evaluating skirts, jeans, slacks and shorts, she settled on khaki pants and an aquamarine print shirt.

Grappling with a jewelry selection, she tried green turquoise set in gold, malachite and silver, and the African trade bead necklace. She chose jade with gold wire trim. An inch long, the piece of jade was shaped like a tear drop. Matching earrings dangled from gold wires twisted to look filigreed.

Alex stood at the upstairs bathroom mirror and fussed with her makeup to get the colors right. She rubbed and blotted until it looked like no make up at all, just the effect she wanted.

Satisfied, she galloped down the big spiral staircase with Crystal in pursuit. She went to the kitchen to brew a pot of coffee and considered a shot of whiskey.

Long after Alex thought she would detonate from a critical mass of anticipation, Crystal barked. In a flurry of scraping paws trying to get traction on wood floor, Crystal arrived at the front door before the bell rang.

Alex was so startled, she was momentarily pinned to the chair by centripetal force, as if she was descending the first hill on a roller coaster. Instead of the warm, noncommittal aura she'd planned to display, she suffered from stage fright. She wiped moist palms on her slacks and took a deep breath.

Crystal sat in front of the door, tail wagging eagerly.

"Some guard dog you turned out to be. You haven't even smelled this guy, and you're ready to let him in."

Alex opened the huge door, summoning her warmest, noncommittal smile. Crystal nearly knocked Alexandria down in her attempt to tackle and lick Erik.

Holding aloft a large bouquet of apricot colored roses and baby's breath, Erik rubbed Crystal's head with his free hand. He wore blue jeans, loafers and a white polo shit.

"How are you, girl?"

"Not bad, how about you?"

Erik laughed, and Crystal barked.

"Ordinarily, she's a good judge of character," Alex said, feigning concern.

Crystal licked his hand and wagged her tail double-time. "In my experience, dogs of Crystal's caliber are impeccable judges of character. I'd stake my reputation on it," Erik smiled.

Alex leaned against the door jamb, arms crossed at the elbows. "I bet you would."

Erik offered the roses to Alex. A recalcitrant lock of blond hair lay across his forehead. His gray eyes were enhanced by his white shirt. The smell of his Aspen cologne was more compelling than the roses.

Alex thought he looked like a boy who had just picked a handful of wildflowers for his mother's birthday. All semblance of detachment evaporated. She couldn't believe how glad she was to see him.

"They're beautiful."

"You're beautiful; the flowers are merely pleasant. I also have a bottle of respectable champagne in the car."

Crystal pronounced her approval with a short bark.

"There's one other thing," Erik said.

"What's that?" Alex asked absently, visualizing candlelight and romance.

He disappeared down the front walk and returned with an animal carrier. Crystal growled.

"My cat sitter had an emergency appendectomy, and I couldn't find anyone to take care of Sheba. I hope you don't mind."

Alex was speechless. Crystal barred the door.

It took her a moment to recover. "As in the Queen of Sheba?"

Alex stared into the cat carrier. Wide ice-blue eyes peered out of a furry, white orb. Alex noticed Sheba's blue, rhinestone collar with a heart-shaped identification tag.

"How precious. The collar matches her eyes."

Sheba hissed. "She's frightened," Erik said. "She's really quite affectionate."

"No doubt," Alex said in a tone as icy as Sheba's eyes, "like a Black Widow spider on her wedding night."

Alex exhaled in frustration and headed for the spiral staircase. "You and her highness will sleep upstairs," she called over her shoulder. Erik followed, and Crystal brought up the rear.

Alex had prepared her favorite guest room. The rose and dark green room was decorated with Victorian antiques. Print curtains matched the wall paper, and a small French writing desk overlooked the garden.

She stopped at the door. Erik walked past her without speaking and headed for the window. Placing the cat carrier on the floor, he leaned on the window ledge and looked at Gran's handiwork.

"I'll find a place to board Sheba tomorrow," he said.

Alex felt guilty tears well up in her eyes.

"We'll sort it out later. Come downstairs when you're unpacked and survey the bomb site."

She turned quickly so he wouldn't see her cry and took the spiral stairs two at a time, leaving Crystal as sentinel at the guest room door.

*   *   *   *   *   *   *

Alex sorted pictures and letters in a small space she cleared on the library floor. She placed them in the temporary storage boxes Emma procured so she could focus on the books.

She glanced up as Erik appeared in the doorway. He changed into gray slacks and a black and white print shirt. She thought he looked gorgeous. As he surveyed the room, a pained look washed across his face.

"This is heinous," he said.

Alex thought it was an odd word to use, but guessed her father and grandfather would agree. "Nothing seems missing; not even the geode and mineral collection. This thief was very particular, or stupid."

"Or he didn't get what he wanted; which means he'll be back," Erik observed.

"That's what Sergeant O'Reilly implied," Alex said, frowning. "Gran only left me her jewelry and the contents of the library."

Erik scowled, "And the tickets to Mexico."

Alex looked at him. "Are you suggesting there's a connection between what happened here and the incident in Mexico?"

Erik moved a stack of papers on the love seat and sat down.

"I'm not ready to make that leap, but your grandmother left you a message."

Crystal approached and put her head across Erik's knees. He rubbed her ears with both hands; her tail swept the carpet in appreciation. She looked at him out of the sides of her big brown eyes.

"Tell me about Duncan Stuart," Erik said.

Alex sat back from the papers she sorted. Her hair formed a fiery halo around her pale face. She stroked the coolness of the jade pendant as she spoke.

"A tall order. Grandpa's degrees were in physics and chemistry. He was an idealist and visionary first, and a scientist second. He was a member of the Manhattan project during the second world war, the folks who gave us the atomic bomb. Somewhere around here there's an eight millimeter film of the atom bomb test. It's eerie to watch the mushroom cloud form. He grew ashamed of that episode; he didn't think the end justified the means."

"It seldom does," Erik said, pushing his hair back.

"Most of his research involved energy. It was his passion to find alternatives to fossil fuels. He was a fan of Nikola Tesla and believed in free energy."

"That an unpopular view in some quarters."

Alex nodded. "Grandpa did original research for Ultrasound, which directs an electrical current through a crystal to create sound waves. That's how Crystal got her name. Gran said he spent so much time with crystals she needed one of her own."

Erik smiled. "Were all those papers really in those two pieces of furniture?"

Alex looked at the mess in the library and laughed.

"Gran was a world class pack rat."

She stood, and pushed her hair back. "I'm starving. Let's check Emma's progress with dinner."

They walked into the kitchen where preparations were underway.

"Smells magnificent," Erik said.

"Erik Anderson, this is Emma Manchester, kitchen magician," Alex said fondly. "Her culinary prowess is legendary."

Emma blushed, and smiled. Erik grinned and extended his hand. "An impressive introduction."

Emma flushed scarlet. She wiped her hands on one of her perennial white aprons careful not to dampen the blue cotton dress underneath. She pushed loose strands of silky gray hair away from her pleasant round face. Rosy cheeks framed a mouth that often curved upward in a smile. Kind blue eyes looked up at the young man who was a foot taller. Extending her hand, she practically curtsied.

"Pay no attention to Alexandria. She always exaggerates; it will be her undoing," Emma said, nodding her head sharply.

Alex and Erik laughed. Erik approached the stove, peering into the cooking pots with keen interest and an air of authority.

"What's the menu?" he inquired.

"Cucumber bisque with fresh dill, spinach crepes, asparagus with ginger sauce and wild rice. Creme brulee with fresh raspberries for dessert," Emma answered.

"I don't think Alex exaggerated."

Emma reddened. "Alexandria's a vegetarian, so it's always a challenge."

"Me too," Erik said.

"I didn't realize that," Alex said, surprised.

"Perhaps Mr. Anderson would select the wine?" Emma blurted, gaping at him.

"Please call me Erik," he smiled.

Alex had never witnessed such a reaction from Emma. She felt amused and faintly annoyed.

"Follow me, steward. I'll conduct you to Duncan Stuart's secret cellar. Few venture there and live to tell the tale."

Alex opened the door at the back of the kitchen, revealing a small hall and another door. A flashlight and a rusty coffee can rested on a small wall shelf. Handing the flashlight to Erik, she lifted the coffee can which revealed a large set of brass keys.

"Do those belong to the warden?" he asked

She opened the other door onto a steep staircase.

"Hold onto the railing and watch your head."

Erik bent over to avoid hitting his forehead on the door frame. Alex flipped a switch, and a dim light came on overhead. They descended twenty steps into a musty cellar. Dampness muffled the sound of their steps. Alex pulled a chain which hung from the ceiling, and a bare bulb blinked on.

A dozen wooden wine racks stood against a stone wall behind a wrought iron gate. A large, brass pad lock secured the opening. Alex inserted the brass key, and the old lock reluctantly succumbed. The gate creaked like a cheap sound effect in a horror movie.

Alex chuckled. "Grandpa used to let me come with him when I was small. I was frightened, but I thought it was a great adventure. I always held his hand tight and imagined creatures living in the shadows. He didn't let on he knew how scared I was."

Erik smiled.

"He never oiled the gate; it was part of the game. Grandpa blew the dust off the bottles with great panache and told me why the wine was special. I miss him."

Erik was right beside her, and she could smell his cologne. She felt her color rise and her pulse quicken. For once, she blessed the dim light. His gray eyes reminded her of an unpredictable winter sky. His blond hair had fallen across his forehead again.

"Emma usually guards this place with her life. She's formed a high opinion of you."

"It's mutual; she's a jewel."

Alex nodded. He continued to look at her.

"White or red?" Alex asked with equanimity she didn't feel.

Instead of answering, he lifted her hand to his mouth and kissed her palm. His breath was warm on her hand. Alex closed her eyes and felt the warm tide of desire rise in her body. She hadn't felt this way in years. She opened her eyes and saw a matching need mirrored in cloudy gray eyes.

Erik took a deep breath and squeezed her hand. "White, definitely. Let's see what we have here." His eyes darted over the wine racks, pulling out bottles. He whistled, gasped, moaned and made other sounds of admiration as he analyzed the labels. After careful scrutiny, Erik chose a white Bordeaux and a rare vintage Chardonnay.

"This is a connoisseur's collection. Your grandfather had exquisite taste," Erik said.

Alex laughed. "Grandpa used to say, 'Life's too short to drink bad wine.'"

"Admirable motto; we'll toast his wisdom this very eve."

Alex rolled her eyes but couldn't help smiling.

They replaced the padlock on the old gate and climbed the stairs. Alex walked in front. She could feel his eyes on her; it made her dizzy. Her face was flushed. When they returned to the kitchen she felt Emma's penetrating gaze and thought she detected approval.

"The first order of the evening is a toast," Erik said. "Although my champagne pales next to the treasures of your vintner's cellar, it is nevertheless a gesture symbolic of the occasion."

Alex thought Grandpa's Scottish heart would be pleased by this borderline pompous Scandinavian with such unlikely charm. Gran would have adored him and rejoiced at the fire he'd ignited in her granddaughter.

Erik popped the cork on the champagne bottle with two moves of his thumbs. It made a joyous sound and not a drop was spilled. He poured the pinkish, effervescent liquid into crystal flutes. The bubbles sparkled in the light.

He faced them and raised his glass.

"To beauty," he said to Alex who reddened. "To grace," he said to Emma who beamed. "And to Duncan and Rose, 'Life's too short to drink bad wine.'"

Alex and Emma exchanged glances and giggled like school girls. They lifted their glasses to touch Erik's. "Here, here," they said, downing healthy portions.

The telephone rang. Irritated by the interruption, Alex answered the phone in the kitchen.

"Hello?" She heard a click, then the dial tone. Alex frowned and replaced the receiver. "Wrong number," she said, a little too quickly.

Erik stared at her, then seemed to decide not to pursue an interrogation.

Emma placed her glass on the counter and smoothed her apron. "You go on into the dining room. Dinner will be ready in two shakes."

The octagonal shape of the dining room formed the base of the largest turret of the Victorian house. Six large windows admitted the last rays of the sun. A red and blue octagonal oriental rug lay under the table.

Emma placed Erik's roses in a cobalt blue vase and spread a crocheted white cloth on the antique table. Silver candelabras held glowing blue tapers.

"Emma has a gift for making things special," Alex said.

"It helps that she loves you so much."

"How about a little 'Nachtmusik?'" She felt the affect of the champagne as she inserted the tape in the player.

"Mozart, perfect," Erik said.

Dinner was a blur of music, delicious food, vintage wine and pleasant conversation. After dessert and coffee they returned to the library.

"This place sobers me up in a hurry. When I dreamed of my father and grandmother, he told me it was time to do the work I came to do. I don't have a clue what that means, but I believe you're part of it," Alex looked at her lap when she spoke.

"I intend to be," Erik said.

Alexandria felt a longing for union awaken in her heart.

"I can't face any more tonight," she said. "How about an early start tomorrow?"

"Eight-thirty?"

"That's early all right," Alex laughed.

They walked to the foot of the staircase. He kissed her softly. "Sleep well."

"You too," she smiled, trying to be light.

She plopped on the bed in her little room on the first floor. *He didn't even try to make a pass at me.*

Alex lay awake, imagining herself lying naked next to Erik Anderson in the rose and green room, a deliciously scandalous thought. She remembered his kiss on her palm in the wine cellar, shivered at the thought and imagined kisses in other places.

Recalling his gorgeous muscular body in his swim suit in Mexico, Alex allowed her mind to drift where it would, vowing that tomorrow she'd get more than a good night kiss.

9

Recourse

Alex woke to an overcast sky, heavy with moisture and the tension that precedes a storm. Her head ached from too much wine, and her back hurt from sleeping in the small bed. Crystal was gone.

She showered and dressed in comfortable jeans and a Native American tee shirt from Santa Fe. The aroma of coffee drew her to the kitchen like a magnet. Alex strolled into the room, ignoring Erik who glanced up from his newspaper. Woven straw place mats and bright plaid napkins decorated the table. A plate of hot pecan rolls, a pitcher of orange juice and a carafe of coffee promised salvation.

Alex poured a mug of coffee and walked to the kitchen window. Gulping her first dose of caffeine, she watched Crystal in the garden.

Swallowing the last of the coffee, she turned to look at Erik, who peered tentatively over the top of the newspaper and Ben Franklin spectacles. Sheba, tail arched high in the air, ate from a dish on the floor next to Erik's chair.

"Morning is not my best time," she said.

He held up the carafe. Joining him at the table, she positioned her empty mug under the pitcher. Erik smiled and put the newspaper down, revealing the same Santa Fe tee shirt.

Alex grimaced. "I'll laugh later; right now my head hurts." She bit into the soft dough and crunchy nuts of a warm pecan roll and moaned. "I may live."

"Emma left sandwiches."

Alex nodded. "She has weekends off."

Fortified with coffee and pecan rolls, Alex took a deep breath and looked at Erik. "Shall we?"

Erik had already moved the boxes filled with papers and documents into the hallway. Stacked four deep, they almost reached the ceiling.

"I still can't believe those two pieces of furniture held that stuff," he said, pointing at the boxes.

Alex walked into the library and discovered that Erik had organized the books in stacks.

"How long have you been awake?" she asked, a blush rising on her cheeks.

"Four hours. I've arranged these by topic."

She sat on the love seat. "You should have wakened me."

"I owed you one from Mexico," he said.

"Thanks. Did you notice any pattern?"

"In some cases, individual books were pulled off the shelf and tossed in piles. In others, they dumped the whole shelf, or left a row untouched. The stacks of books on the floor are mainly science.

"This library is amazing. Titles ranging from physics to metaphysics: eastern philosoph, mythology, atomic energy, chemistry and alchemy," Erik shook his head. "Three shelves on Atlantis, pre-Columbian Mexico, Egyptian and Peruvian History. Contrast that with solar energy, laser and quantum theory. I found twenty books about Edgar Cayce and this collection of tarot cards.

Alex laughed. "My grandparents shared a passion for knowledge. There used to be a card catalog, but I haven't been able to find it. Grandpa was as organized as Gran was random."

"I grew up around this stuff," Alex said. I thought everyone believed in reincarnation and had tarot readings."

Sheba joined them and perched on the back of the love seat like a gargoyle.

"Why look inside books?" Alex asked.

"Your grandmother obviously thought the books were important."

"Grandpa's notes," Alex said, not hearing him. "Where are Grandpa's notes?"

The front doorbell rang. Crystal jetted off to perform her customary security check. Alex followed her and was surprised to hear growling. She left the chain attached and opened the door just enough to peer through the opening.

A tall, thin man with a beak-like nose stood on the porch. Crystal growled again. Alex smothered a gasp and stared into the small black eyes of the man she called raven.

He appeared to be in his sixties and wore an expensive black silk suit and bowler hat. He grasped a walking stick and a leather valise in his left hand. A mere line of a mouth was etched between a pencil-thin moustache and a sharp pointed chin. He smiled, and Alex thought the gesture looked unnatural on his face.

She summoned poise. "Can I help you?" .

"Good morning," he said through his forced smile. "I am Rudolph Selig. I was a colleague of Duncan Stuart's, your grandfather, I presume." His deep baritone voice was a startling contrast to his avian demeanor.

"That's right," Alex replied. Her body shook but Crystal, who growled and pulled forward, served as a diversion. She held onto the dog's collar to prevent her from going through the door. Ever since the nightmare in Mexico, she associated this man with that dream.

"Your dog seems high strung," Selig said.

Alex had no intention of making this easy. "She doesn't like strangers."

"I'll be brief," he said, not bothering to hide his annoyance. "Your grandfather and I had an arrangement whereby I would receive his research papers when his wife died. I have come to examine his files and make arrangements to collect them."

"I'm not aware of any such agreement. It's not mentioned in my grandmother's will."

"I have a document which clarifies everything."

"You'll have to provide our attorney with the documentation. I'm not authorized to negotiate or release anything." Alexandria's heart pounded as she wondered why Gran left her the books.

Selig stiffened. "It would be helpful if I could evaluate the quantity of files and records I will be transferring."

"This is not a good time. I'll be happy to put you in touch with our lawyer," Alex said.

"I won't take a moment of your time." He tried to smile, and the gesture gave Alex chills. "I'm sure it would be easier on you in the long term, Miss Stuart."

Alex met his stare. There was enmity behind his patronizing smile. "That sounds like a threat."

Selig tried to soften his features and form them into another smile. "Not at all. I merely meant it might facilitate the eventual exchange of records."

"You're assuming there will be an exchange of records," she said, fighting to keep revulsion from her voice. He did not reply but held her gaze.

They stood that way a moment, then prompted by some inner urging, Alex changed her mind. "Perhaps you're right; it might be good for you to see the library today."

He looked briefly surprised. "You are most astute, Miss Stuart," Selig said, in a charming voice laced with an undercurrent of sarcasm.

Alex held on to Crystal, whose ears were back, and wanted to have her way with the intruder. Alex opened the door just wide enough for Selig to enter. He stepped into the entry hall and removed his hat, revealing sparse graying hair brushed straight back in an attempt to cover his bald head.

Alex shut the big door and spotted Erik, emerging from a concealed spot in the hallway. She surmised he'd been listening. "I'll take Crystal to the kitchen."

He extended his hand to Selig. "I'm Erik Anderson, friend of the family."

Alex smiled and was relieved her back was to them.

"How do you do," Selig said.

"Mr. Selig worked with Grandpa," Alex said, returning from the kitchen. "He claims they had an agreement about his research papers. He expects to receive Grandpa's material now that Gran has died," Alex said evenly.

"Really?" Erik asked, as if intrigued by the idea.

The three walked silently to the library. When they reached the library door, Selig stared at the boxes.

Alex entered the library first and turned around just inside the door. Selig followed, and Alex detected a genuine look of concern on his face.

"Why are those boxes in the hall?" Selig inquired.

"Apparently, you aren't the only one interested in my grandparents' library," Alex said.

"Someone broke into the house. Erik's helping me restore order; books and papers were everywhere yesterday."

"Do you know what's missing?" Selig asked, eyes darting rapidly over the room.

"No," Erik replied. "Perhaps you could speculate, Mr. Selig, since you were so familiar with Duncan's work. What might someone be looking for?"

"The police thought Grandpa might have hidden money or valuables," Alex added.

"Interesting theories," Selig replied in a flat tone. "I'm afraid my comments would be just that, speculation. My interests are purely scientific."

Selig perched on the edge of a wing back chair in front of the fire place and positioned hat, briefcase and walking stick across his knees. His arms stretched across them, clutching his belongings.

Alex noticed his hands, slender fingers with uncommonly long nails for a man, meticulously manicured and filed to sharp points.

Selig placed his hat and walking stick on the table and opened his valise, removing a large manila envelope. Carefully unfastening the clasp, he extracted the contents and placed the documents on the table. His movements were precise and mechanistic.

"These are copies of correspondence, photographs and research reports which span the years of my association with your grandfather."

He bent the fingers of one hand inward toward the palm and regarded his nails as he spoke. "A copy of our agreement is included. I have waited a long while for this data, Miss Stuart."

Sheba jumped on the coffee table and sat on the stack of papers facing Selig, swishing her tail. He winced and sneezed. He glared at the cat and Alex, who was beginning to like Sheba.

Selig closed his briefcase, placed his hat on his head, and rose from the chair.

"I regret troubling you today under these upsetting circumstances. I'll be in touch with your solicitor as you suggested. I'll provide him with additional copies as your feline seems to have appropriated these." He pursued his lips in apparent distaste.

Erik moved to see Selig out.

"Good day, Miss Stuart," he said, tipping his hat. I hope you find the villain who desecrated this library."

"So do I, Mr. Selig."

Alex walked to the library window and looked outside. The air had been heavy all day as a storm approached from the southwest. When Erik returned, she looked toward him.

"The weather's a great backdrop for a melodrama."

"Meaning the plot thickens?"

"Do you think there's a connection between Selig's visit and the break-in?"

"I don't believe in coincidences, and I don't think we've seen the last of Rudolph." Erik removed Sheba from the table and flipped through Selig's papers.

She kept her back to him as she spoke. "Do you remember the stranger I described at the cemetery the day of Gran's funeral?"

"Yes?" Erik said. She could feel him stiffen.

"You just met him."

"Damn. Why didn't you give me a signal? I would have handled things differently."

"Which he would have sensed. I acted like I'd never met him, which is true enough. I knew most of my grandparent's friends and associates. I never saw that man before the cemetery."

"You're probably right," Erik said, "although I loathe admitting it. There's a land mine in here somewhere, and we might step on it."

Alex recalled the raven from her nightmare. She didn't want to remind Erik of that coincidence right now; better not toss a grenade in the mine field.

Erik joined her at the window and put his arm around her shoulders. She rested her head against him; her skin tingled every placed they touched. He lifted her chin and kissed her. Alex closed her eyes as his lips touched hers. Her body responded with desire.

Nearly losing her balance, Alex placed a hand on the bookcase to steady herself. She heard a noise like a metal lever shifting. Before she had time to react, the bookcase pulled away behind her, and she fell backward.

Erik tried to catch her, but they tumbled into the opening created by the receding bookcase and landed on the floor in a dark room.

"Are you okay?" Erik asked, chuckling.

"Fine," she said, standing and brushing off her seat.

"I'll be damned," Alex laughed. "A secret room. I can't believe Gran never told me."

Erik felt his way in the dark, looking for a light, while their eyes adjusted to the dimness. "I think I found a flashlight," he said, clicking it on.

He shined the flashlight around the room and spotted a lamp on an old wooden desk. Alex turned it on, and the solitary fluorescent desk lamp cast a dim light in the study.

"Merciful heavens," she said. "Look at this stuff. There's the card catalog."

The hidden room was twelve feet square without windows or overhead lights, accessed by a door that masqueraded as a bookcase. Erik procured another lamp from the study, turned it on.

He whistled through his teeth. "This was a working laborator.,"

Apothecary jars, beakers, tubes and bottles lined shelves which hung over a work table. Dozens of dusty three-ring binders marked with dates and experiment names lined the shelves of another bookcase. Books were crammed and stacked into spaces in between. Three large file cabinets flanked the other wall.

"No wonder nothing's missing from the library; here are Grandpa's notes," Alex mused.

"I thought the wine cellar was amazing," Erik said, shaking his head. "Books on magic and more on alchemy. Whatever Selig's after, he'd have a heyday in here."

Alex pulled open drawers in one of the file cabinets and flipped through manila file folders. "The top drawer has stuff on crystals. The next two seem to be energy related."

Alex spied a folder labeled ALTERNATE ENERGY CONFERENCE.

"I just remembered something," she said. "The day after Gran's funeral, I found a photo in an old book taken at a conference in 1962. Selig was in the picture with my grandparents."

They looked at each other. "Energy," they said at the same time.

"Maybe if we get this mess cleaned and organized, we'll discover something," Alex said.

By eight o'clock rain seemed imminent. Exhausted, they stopped to admire their work. A cold front blew in ahead of the storm, and the temperature dropped from a humid seventy-eight to sixty-two. Selig's visit had cast a pall, and the old house felt damp. Erik built a fire in the stone fireplace in the kitchen.

"Let's order pizza and sample your designer beer," Alex said.

"Chief Oshkosh red lager micro brew to you."

"Whatever," she laughed.

She phoned for pizza and procured pewter mugs from the pantry. Erik poured red lager while Alex lit beeswax candles in brass sconces on the mantel. She spread a red table cloth and placed candles on the table. The wet logs hissed and popped in the grate as the smell of burning cedar filled the room.

"This was my favorite room as a child; especially with a fire. So much has happened in such a short time, but I sense that behind seemingly random events I'm supposed to glean a course of action. Right now it looks like a needle in a haystack."

"I never thought I'd hear myself say this," Erik sighed. "Maybe you should call don Miguel. I don't know why I have such a strong reaction to him. Maybe he represents things I don't understand and can't control."

"Maybe he can come while you're here. Three blockheads are better than one."

Erik smiled.

"Speaking of blockheads, my friend Sheila's dying to meet you. How about I ask her to bring breakfast?"

"Perfect. I don't think my brain can handle any more input tonight," Erik laughed.

They cleaned up the dishes and walked to her room. When they reached the doorway, Erik scooped her into his arms and carried her across the threshold. Alex giggled uncontrollably.

Erik gently placed her on the tiny bed and lay down beside her. His cologne was intoxicating. Emma would not be back tonight, she realized.

Light from the big street lamp on the far corner shone through the window. Rain streamed down the leaded glass panes creating kaleidoscopes of twinkling patterns in the reflected light.

They kissed and wrapped their arms and legs around each other. Erik kissed her neck and ears; her body came alive with desire.

Sheba jumped on the bed and bumped her head into theirs. Alex was startled, then laughed. Crystal padded into the room and barked.

"Intruder alert," Erik said. "This will require some orchestration," he said, furrowing his brow.

The phone rang. "I'll probably regret this," Alex said.

"Hello? You have rotten timing Goldwoman. Come by about ten tomorrow and bring breakfast."

"Where were we?" he said, nibbling an ear.

The phone rang again. "Ye Gods," Alex said.

"Hello? Don Miguel, I was planing to call you in the morning. Wonderful. We'll see you tomorrow."

Alex hung up the phone and sat up. She kissed Erik on the cheek. "He already has his tickets."

He squeezed her hand. "It isn't time yet."

Alex nodded. "I want my mind to be on one thing."

They walked to the door. His lips parted and covered hers. They shared a long kiss.

"I'll climb to the tower and leave the beautiful princess in the dungeon," he said.

"Good night, sweet prince. Thanks for everything."

Alex opened the window to hear the raindrops on the roof and smell moist air laden with the fragrance of flowers and grass. She hugged her pillow and watched the water trace patterns on the glass.

10
Reprisal

Priestess Una rose from her sleeping place and walked onto the terrace overlooking the ocean. She shaded her eyes with her hand and squinted into the morning sun; the dawn mist had nearly evaporated. The sea was peaceful, the salty breeze a caress on her face and skin. Behind her the gauze curtains of her room rustled gently.

To the west, sea and sky met in a hazy fusion of blue and green. Far below the cliff where she stood, gulls and pelicans called as they searched for morning food in the sheltered bay.

Una looked fondly at her mother's garden. Lavender clusters of wisteria hung from a trellis, bending their branches like plump bunches of grapes.

Fragrance from hanging baskets of plumeria, honeysuckle and jasmine filled the air. Round marble pots brimmed with colorful petunias, impatiens and lilies. Honey bees gathered nectar from the floral bounty. No one believed her mother would get anything to grow so high up on this rock, but she proved them wrong.

Breathing the beauty of her home, the young priestess walked back inside the rose-colored marble dwelling. How could she leave this place? Her heart ached at the thought.

After three hundred thirty sun cycles, a High Council had been convened. Representatives from all regions in the nation would gather today in the capital city to decide the fate of the great energy stones.

Una sat at her dressing table and applied her favorite fragrances: rose and lily. She dressed in the rich ivory linen robe with apple-green silk sash, colors of the healer and artisan orders. A large hood hung down the back of the formal robe required for the Assembly Hall.

She fastened the heavy necklace of gold, which proclaimed her rank as artisan of gems and healer, at the back of her neck. Seven inches wide, the edges reached to her shoulders. Centering the emblem over her heart, she gazed at the necklace in the glass. The green jet triangle and the blue lapis crescent filled her with pride.

Una was young for such achievements. Her work with stones and metals had received recognition throughout the island nation.

The priestess glanced at the sun clock, which cast a shadow from a metal rod onto a marble disk. Two solar intervals past dawn - the council would convene soon.

A twinge of fear grabbed her belly as she thought of the council session. They would discuss the fate of the great crystal, the Tuaoi Stone, used for countless years to generate energy for the country.

Zared and his followers wanted to set the range to maximum force. Turning it too high would be reckless and dangerous, she thought. Father is right to fight them. They underestimate the powers of the great stone.

Father said if Zared and his followers have their way with the great stone the land may be too unstable to remain in Poseidia. The enhanced power of the crystal could cause devastating subterranean earthquakes.

She bristled as she remembered the armed temple guards waiting outside. There were threats recently, and Father insisted they accompany her. She was outraged that a temple needed guards. The wrong people were gaining power, promising unlimited wealth with no restraint of physical gratification.

Una stood inside the doorway, fighting tears. It wasn't fair. Why couldn't everyone see her father's goodness and dedication. A priestess of the Healing Order did not show tears in public, and she could ill afford such weakness today. For her father's sake, and those who serve the One, she must radiate an implacable aura of serenity.

The Priestess breathed and recited the words of a mantra to regain her center. After a few moments, she mastered her emotions. A few more breaths, and her body was filled with energy. She was ready to face them.

She walked outside and nodded to the guards, signaling her readiness. A member of the priest's guard, dressed in the royal blue and gold uniform of his rank, stepped forward. He carried a weapon powered by the crystal, another witness to the sickness of the land. The power of the Stone, once used only for the highest spiritual purposes, now fueled implements of death.

The guard opened the hatch of the ovoid vehicle which would transport her to the Great Assembly Hall. Power was transmitted from the Tuoai Stone to vehicles such as this with crystalline storage cells. Even this basic form of transportation was threatened by Zared's madness.

Una filled her lungs with fresh air before she climbed into the car. From her home at the pinnacle of the mountain, the guard maneuvered the transport craft down the winding mountain road past homes and gardens toward the city center. Eclectic homesteads of stone, brick, wood or adobe were generously adorned by window boxes and terra cotta pots of petunias, daisies and snap dragons. Roses of every color climbed fences and trellises that were framed by a bright blue sky. An aching sense of loss threatened her equanimity. Sunny weather contrasted with the bleak feelings her trained will kept at bay.

The driver slowed his pace as they reached the outer limits of the city. He raised security shields on the clear areas of the car so they could see out but not be seen. Una knew he acted was for her protection, but the gesture rankled.

The city was designed as concentric circles of land constructed in a large sheltered bay. Bridges and waterways interconnected in a circular grid pattern. The market and temple complexes were at the center, and the residential areas lay in the outer circles.

The amphibious transport craft exited the street and entered a waterway. Una gazed fondly at marble and granite buildings. Una wondered if Poseidians carrying out their daily activities suspected a power struggle was being waged at the heart of their government.

The guard stopped in front of the main entrance of the Assembly Hall which faced the sea. He offered his hand and helped her out of the vehicle.

"Shall I accompany you inside, Priestess?" he asked.

"No," she said firmly. If a Priestess of the Healing Orders was not safe to enter the Temple, all was indeed lost. She gathered her forces and held her head high.

Feathery, bright purple blooms of flowering poinciana trees lined the avenue and filled the space above the street. Regal cypress and cedar trees surrounded the central park.

Colorful flags of all the provinces hung limp in an arc around the circular temple complex. The sea breeze had shifted; the air was cool and deadly calm. The atmosphere held the threat of a storm.

Constructed of pink granite and alabaster, the massive round structure occupied a city block. Eighty foot pillars, ornately carved with flowers and vines and inlaid with pearls, shells, coral and semi-precious stones supported the roof. The Priestess glanced up, reassured to see marvelous paintings of constellations and their stories covering the ceiling.

Sculptured statues of famous and revered Poseidians graced alcoves girding the central core of the Assembly Hall where the High Council would be held.

Una was outwardly composed as she walked along the marble hallway, her posture erect and commanding. Talking in small groups, people scarcely noted her passing.

She entered the magnificent Grand Hall. Designed like an amphitheater, rows of seats extended three fourths of the way around the room. Tall windows traversed the circumference between the last row of seats and the ceiling. Brilliant light filtered into the room from the east.

She moved toward the front of the hall where a large round dais was the focal point. Painted porcelain pots filled with white lilies and golden gladiolas bordered the circular area. Sandalwood incense burned in gold censers. Two high back chairs, with a speaker's podium in front of each, were the only furniture.

Una spotted the priest Kadir across the room, and her stomach fluttered. He was tall and bronze like most who lived in this land with straight black hair that touched his shoulders. She loved the look of his fine aquiline nose. How handsome he was in his sky blue robe. She swelled with pride to see the lapis crescent of the healing order around his neck.

Una walked toward him in what she hoped was a subtle manner. He saw her and gestured. She smiled as he walked toward her.

"Shall we take our seats?" Kadir inquired, extending his left arm.

"Yes," she answered, hooking her arm around his.

Choosing seats which afforded a good view of the stage, the young people looked around the room and soaked up the heady feelings of the occasion. The hall filled quickly with people dressed in their own colors, insignia and corresponding gemstones. The priests wore violet, the

musicians rose, and the merchants a deep green. The pale
yellow of the visual artists dotted the hall like daffodils. A
hushed excitement lay over the Great Hall. People were
silent or spoke in whispers. Una felt a mounting
anticipation.

"Whatever the outcome of this council, Poseidia will
never be the same," Kadir said, his handsome features set
in an expression of grim determination.

Una watched as the regal form of Hept-supht, Prime
Regent of all Poseidia, walked across the stage and
approached the speaker's lectern. Tall and dark, he radiated
the confident power of a high initiate. He grasped a brass
rod surmounted by a coiled serpent with studied familiarity.

The Prime Regent wore full regalia for the most
important occasion of state. An equal-armed cross inside a
circle hung from a thick gold chain around his neck. A
large diamond shone from the center, and the four arms of
the cross were studded with rubies, topaz, pearls and
emeralds.

Hept-supht wore a long white undergarment
covered by a vivid blue outer robe and an orange v-shaped
mantle. A simple gold circlet crowned his head. When
Hept-supht reached the stage, he positioned himself in a
beam of morning light which shone on the dais and
augmented his sharp features. He spoke without pretense
or posturing.

"Brothers and sisters, a High Council has been
convened after long silence. Thank you for coming on short
notice. Some of your have traveled far.

"Grave times are upon us. A sickness has befallen
beloved Poseidia. There is unrest in our great city.
Corruption and treachery threaten to rend the fabric of this
great land."

The Prime Regent was a skilled speaker. He moved
his hands and arms with measured emphasis to strengthen
the impact of his voice and words. Inflections were
choreographed to add force to his words. Carefully

executed pauses, pitch and modulation resulted from years of practice.

"We are here today to decide a matter of extreme significance," Hept-supht continued. "The fate of the great Tuoai Stone, and that of the priesthood who guard her sacred knowledge ,are in question." His voice reverberated through the hall.

He paused to let the significance of his words take effect. The assembled priests, artisans, merchants and politicians were motionless. The atmosphere in the hall was tense, like the stillness before a storm.

"Later today," he continued, "the teaching and healing orders will conclave to decide how to implement the decision you will make this morning. I implore you, consider your vote with utmost discernment and clarity of heart.

"I have asked Hierophant Iltar to open this council with an invocation," Hept-supht said.

A murmur passed through the hall as the imposing figure of Iltar approached the podium. As High Priest, he openly opposed Zared's scheme to usurp the power of the stone for purely material uses. Iltar's hood stretched halfway down his back. A gold tassel fastened to its tip glittered and swung like a pendulum as he walked in deliberate cadence to the dais. The three-tiered mitered crown he wore emphasized his tall stature and proclaimed his position as High Priest, a religious office equal to the civil role of Prime Regent.

Iltar wore a white silk robe reserved for the most solemn occasions. The sleeves and hem were trimmed in wide bands of gold and violet. His chest plate had twelve divisions, each containing a glyph and gemstone to represent the orders over which he presided.

He held an ornately carved staff of cedar inlaid with precious gems and metals. Grasping his staff in one hand and a golden censer in the other, he looked into the eyes of the audience. The fine features of his aristocratic face were inscrutable. The young priestess felt a painful mixture of pride and grief as she watched her father approach his task. She knew as few others did his uncompromising nature in spiritual principles. He was often accused of rigidity by the younger priests, even Kadir.

Iltar understood the magnitude of what was at stake - the survival of Poseidia. She knew the depth of the High Priest's concern came from a soul as pure as the snow on Mount Alta. Drawing herself to her full height, Una sent a wave of love and light from her heart to his. She was relieved her mother did not live to see this.

Hierophant Iltar stood at the center of the round dais in silence for a full minute, gathering power. He raised both arms and looked skyward. When he spoke, his voice was pitched to gain maximum resonance and volume, and the sound boomed and echoed in the hall.

> "O Thou, vast and almighty
> Infinite and omnipotent One,
> Whose everlasting embrace of Love and Light
> Brings forth countless manifest worlds.
> Purify our hearts to receive Thy Word.
> Illumine our minds to know Thy Will
> We invoke Thee, Unknowable, Invisible One.
> May we join Thee in the dance of eternal life."

Zared, the outspoken leader of the opposition stood in his place. A thin veneer of propriety could not conceal the blatant contempt on his face. Zared seemed a stark caricature of his race. His features were sharp and pronounced. His long, pointed nose, bent over a thin mouth that was stretched in a perpetual frown. He licked his lips habitually, like a reptile.

Cold, greedy eyes devoured others with their stare. He wore the violet hue of the priesthood, but it conferred no dignity. His spirituality had been consumed by greed and lust for early power. Una knew he hated Iltar.

"Step down, old man, you have outlived the wisdom of your hollow words. We don't need a dried up priest to pray to a useless god."

The audience gasped that Zared dared to attack the High Priest during invocation. But Zared had many supporters.

"Your feeble ways no longer serve the will of the people," Zared said, his voice louder. "We want the knowledge and power for ourselves. Your days of tyranny are over. We will take what we want."

Many in the hall murmured or voiced disapproval. A growing number cheered and called for Zared to come forward.

"Citizens of Poseidia, claim your rights," Zared shouted. "End this repression. The priesthood wants power for themselves. I say turn the crystal higher so we can have what we want. Stop wasting precious energy healing abominations which should be killed or used as our slaves."

A growing number in the audience applauded. Una watched in horror as hope of a peaceful solution dissolved in Zared's words of hate. Zared approached the stage as if to speak from the podium. He pulled a dagger from his robe. As he lunged toward Iltar, a young priest threw himself in front of the blade. The crowd erupted in a chaos.

"This is sacrilege!" one man screamed. "Murder in a holy place."

Una battled grief and outrage but remained composed for her father's sake. She would not disgrace him with weakness. Hept-supht and Iltar slipped out through the rear of the stage behind the curtains. Una knew there was a secret passage underground.

"We must leave at once," Kadir whispered in her ear and pulled her quickly to the door.

Una struggled with her feeligns. She knew Kadir was right. There was no choice but to leave Poseidia. The healers would not have time for a conclave.

Outside the sky turned dark, and a chill wind howled. Una and Kadir ran to the side of the building and stood against the wall, hidden from view.

A piercing shriek filled the air. She looked up. The orb of the sun was eclipsed by an enormous black bird of prey, circling high above her. The Condor sensed her gaze and dove toward her. The huge bird landed before them.

"You have no sword, and I am stronger now," sneered the dark feathered form.

"I have truth, a more powerful weapon," Una replied.

The Condor screeched. "We shall see." The beast spread its wings to a span of twelve feet and advanced toward them. All was dark.

She wanted to scream and run, but Una stood her ground and faced her attacker. Summoning strength, she spoke secret words of power and called upon the force of light. The priestess knew a moment of incandescence, then silent leaden blackness.

11
Recognition

Alex screamed and sat up in bed. She was soaked in perspiration, and her pulse raced. Crystal was surprised by her sudden movement and looked at her.

"That's the worst ever," she said. Crystal put her head in Alex's lap, and she hugged the dog a long time.

Swinging her legs over the side of the bed, she donned a blue chenille robe and slipped her feet into matching scuffs. She absently ran her fingers through her hair, removing curly red strands from her face as if that could clear her mind of fear.

"I'll make coffee and you can go outside." They padded toward the kitchen, and Alex let Crystal out the back door. The sky was the steel blue color between night and morning, and the day promised to be glorious. Savoring the early morning stillness, Alex breathed fresh air. She lifted and stretched her shoulders, trying to concentrate. She ground hazelnut coffee beans and poured cold water in the coffee maker.

Alex decided to shower while the coffee brewed. Turning the shower head on maximum pulse, she enjoyed the water pelting her skin. She worked up a lather of soap and shampoo, as if she could wash off the menace of the black bird that refused to recede from her consciousness.

Dressing in a colorful print skirt and cobalt blue blouse, she had a vague sense of preparing for battle. Alex brushed her russet hair and forced it into a barrette. She applied her makeup like war paint. Her jewelry was the final layer of protective coloration. She chose a gold sunburst necklace with a round cobalt blue center. Matching gold and blue suns dangled from her ears.

Alex stared at the mirror, and her awareness shifted. The mirror shimmered like water in a pond disturbed by a pebble, and the reflection changed. She felt the heavy robes she had worn in the dream. The face of the young priestess Una stared back at her from the glass.

Expressive ebony eyes, straight black hair and reddish brown skin provided a different raiment, but the soul in the mirror was her own. "What are you trying to tell me?" Alex asked.

The image passed, and her familiar reflection returned to the mirror. Alex felt profoundly moved and strengthened. She realized she'd been given a rare gift.

Shaking herself, she returned to the kitchen and prepared a large tray with mugs, cream and sugar, butter, honey and yogurt. She filled a large carafe with coffee and ground beans for another pot. Pouring a generous mug of steaming coffee, she stirred in cream and took a big gulp.

"Morning." A cheerful voice boomed behind her. "Smells like hazelnuts in here," Erik said, sniffing.

"Morning yourself," Alex smiled and turned to look at him. Erik wore navy blue slacks and a pale blue cotton sweater over a white polo shirt. Wet blond hair crowned a scrubbed boyish face. He carried Sheba in one arm and held a can of cat food in his other hand.

"Let's eat in the garden," she said. "Coffee?"

"Wonderful," Erik said, putting Sheba on the floor and claiming a ceramic mug.

Alex smiled inwardly and poured coffee into the mug. Caffeine addiction was common ground but not an ideal basis for a relationship.

Accompanied by an aria of meows, Erik opened the cat food and poured it into Sheba's bowl. They sat at the table to enjoy their coffee, and the doorbell rang. Exchanging martyred looks, they rose to answer the door.

Sheila stood on the porch, grinning like a Cheshire cat in red lipstick. She wore a white jogging suit trimmed in gold. Enormous white and gold bangles decorated her ears. Manicured hands clutched a large grocery bag and an insulated carafe.

"What's in there?" Alex demanded, licking her lips and peering into the sack. Sheila stepped into the foyer, handed her the carafe and scooped black hair across her head.

"Not before I'm introduced," Sheila said, staring at Erik and extending her liberated hand.

Alex laughed. "Sheila Goldman, Erik Anderson."

"Charmed, I'm sure," Erik said, bending at the waist. Clasping Sheila's extended hand, he looked into her eyes and gently kissed it.

Sheila stood, red fingernails suspended in air, staring at Erik. "Nice," she said, in a voice filled with sultry sarcasm. "I think Allie's mother may even like you."

"Is that good?" Erik wanted to know.

"I doubt it," Alex said, rolling her eyes. "Let's go outside."

They exited the back door, where Crystal planted muddy paws on the porch steps. Sparrows, cardinals and wrens chirped and called.

"Smells like the earth's been to the cleaners," Sheila said.

"That's a tufted titmouse," Erik said, pointing.

"You're making that up," Sheila said.

Alex laughed. "He's an opportunist but accurate. Gran adored birds, and they all love her garden."

They entered a red brick patio in the heart of the garden through an arched wooden rose trellis. Fragrant crimson roses climbed up the sides and over the top. A white wrought iron table with four chairs and a red and white umbrella marked the center of the bricked area.

Blossoms of multi-colored snap-dragons, black-eyed Susans, zinnias, golden yellow bachelor buttons and bright orange tiger lilies created a background like a Van Gogh canvas. Ardent honey bees drew nectar from redolent purple and white lilacs. Damp cedar chips added a woody scent to the fragrance of flowers and wet grass.

They wiped rainwater from the table and chairs. After claiming her seat, Sheila produced three plastic champagne glasses from the grocery bag. "Mimosas," she proclaimed, unscrewing the carafe and grinning devilishly.

"We have work to do," Alex objected.

"This is medicinal," Sheila said, in her best Jewish mother voice. "Champagne and orange juice are better for you than chicken soup."

After pouring three glasses of frothy orange fluid, Sheila extracted croissants, strawberries and whipped cream like a magician pulling rabbits from a hat. Alex tried not to laugh.

"A toast," Erik said, raising his plastic glass. "To chicken soup, may I never have it for breakfast."

"Here. Here." Sheila said.

"What other decadent surprises are lurking in that plain brown wrapper?" Erik asked.

Sheila raised her eyebrows like Groucho Marx.

"What's the secret word, little boy?"

'I give up," Erik said, laughing.

"That's it!"

"You two can play games all morning while I eat strawberries," Alex laughed. She selected a succulent red berry and scooped a generous dollop of whipped cream on the tip. Slowly lowering the ripe fruit into her open mouth, she closed her eyes and moaned.

Not to be outdone, Sheila picked a fat strawberry, dipped it in whipped cream and seductively licked white foam from the end.

"Stop, both of you, I'm not a saint." Erik giggled.

When Alex couldn't eat another berry, she sat back in her chair and pulled her feet up on the seat. She rested her chin on her knees and wrapped her arms around them. "Can I tell you about a dream?"

"I know that look; this is serious," Sheila said.

"Was there a raven in it?" Erik asked, smiling.

"A condor," Alex frowned.

Erik and Sheila exchanged looks.

"Uh oh," Sheila said.

"I lived in a beautiful place overlooking an ocean on an island called Poseidia. I was a priestess, dressed in official robes for an important occasion. My father was High Priest. His counterpart was called Prime Regent. They were good leaders, wise and honest.

"There was political unrest, a sense of impending crisis. Another man gained influence by appealing to people's greed. A High Council was called to vote on the fate of a huge crystal which was the power source of the country.

"There was a power struggle during the council. Zared, a very wicked man, incited the crowd," she continued after a period of silence. "He tried to kill my father, but someone jumped in front of him and was murdered."

Alex stopped speaking; her eyes filled with tears.

"My father and the Prime Regent escaped. I was with a young priest. We hurried outside and hid ourselves at the side of the large building.

"A gigantic black condor shrieked in the sky. The bird attacked us. The priestess summoned the forces of light. There was a brilliant flash, then total darkness. Then I woke up."

"Sounds like Atlantis," Sheila said.

"The conflict was about energy," Erik said.

Recognition dawned. "You're right," Alex said. "All their technology was powered by the crystal. When I dressed this morning, that priestess stared back at me from the mirror.

Alexandria looked at Erik and Sheila.

"I was that woman. Don Miguel will be here this afternoon, and I'm ready to do whatever it takes to solve this puzzle."

*   *   *   *   *   *   *

Crystal rushed to the door after the bell rang. She didn't bark and sat perfectly still until Alex opened the door. Don Miguel stood on the small porch, his handsome brown face illumined by a smile. He wore an elegantly tailored, taupe-colored suit of woven raw silk. His white shirt and bright floral tie were a perfect compliment to his graying temples.

Alex hugged him. "Come in," she said, grinning.

"It's good to be here. Your grandparents invited me many times. You look lovely, Alex," he said, his deep voice resonating in the hall.

Alex blushed. She'd thrown on a pair of white stirrup pants and a pale blue tunic. She'd asked Emma to French braid her hair and put on a necklace and earrings she made from rose quartz beads.

"The simplest clothing lets the inner beauty shine," don Miguel said, as if he'd heard her thoughts. He leaned back on his legs in a timeless Indian posture and placed one hand on Crystal's head and another under her chin.

"Crystal, I heard about you," he said, looking into her eyes.

Afternoon sunlight shone through the leaded glass panes of the front door, creating a magical space of shifting beams of light around Miguel and Crystal. They remained in that position for several minutes, locked in silent communion. Alex had never seen Crystal so still. Don Miguel stood after a few minutes and smiled. Erik approached with his right arm extended.

"I'm glad you're here, don Miguel. I hope you can help Alex."

"Thank you. You and I will both assist Alexandria in finding the answers within herself." Then looking at Erik's khaki shorts and bright Hawaiian shirt, he said, "I feel overdressed."

"I'll show you to your room so you can change. Then we'll have something to eat. You must be tired," Alex fussed.

Don Miguel smiled. "Please don't treat me like an old man. My work takes me on many trips. I would enjoy some tea, however."

*   *   *   *   *   *   *

Alex and Erik waited in the kitchen for Miguel, eying Emma's treats with active salivary glands. The aroma of fresh lemon bars filled the room.

"Couldn't we have a taste?" Alex pleaded.

"Absolutely not," Emma scolded. "You should be ashamed for asking."

"Where your cooking is concerned, we have no shame," Erik laughed.

"That looks more comfortable," Alex said, as don Miguel appeared in the doorway in time to prevent an international incident. He wore blue cotton slacks and a blue and white striped shirt.

"Don Miguel, I'd like you to meet Emma Manchester. You two have talked on the phone," Alex said, looking from one to the other.

"Yes," Miguel said, extending his hand. "It's a great pleasure to meet you, Emma."

Emma blushed, wiped her hands on her apron and extended her hand. She wore a yellow print house dress

under her apron. Her gray hair was pulled back in a twist.
Kind blue eyes sparkled over reddened cheeks.

"The pleasure is mine, Senor Piedra. I feel like I
already know you."

Don Miguel placed his other hand over Emma's and
smiled. "Please, call me Miguel."

Erik pulled back one of the wooden chairs. "Have a
seat, Miguel. Tea is served."

Relieved, Emma served hot and cold tea with sweets
worthy of high tea. Carrot cake, custard tarts, dark
chocolate fudge, lemon bars and Scottish shortbread were
symmetrically arranged on a silver tray.

"Ay! A banquet," Miguel said.

"I've been here three days. I've gained five pounds,
and my moral fiber has come unraveled," Erik said, patting
his mid-section.

Miguel, a consummate diplomat, took a small
portion of each delicacy and sampled them, pursing his
lips. He praised their various merits from the point of view
of an educated palette and made appreciative "hmmms'
and "ahs."

"You're too kind," Emma beamed.

Erik and Alexandria ate with abandon.

"Tell Miguel about the dream," Erik said.

"Let's go into the library," she said.

Alex was proud of the restored library. Bookshelves
were straightened and organized in pristine condition.
Mahogany shelves were polished and books dusted.
Striped burgundy and cream love seats and Queen Anne
chairs glistened. Polished mahogany reading tables shone.
The antique roll top desk and matching secretary looked
like museum pieces.

Pictures of Rose and Duncan, Philip, Amelia and
Alex were arranged on the tables and mantel. A mauve
and blue oriental rug lay between the chairs and couch in
front of the fireplace. An English pastoral scene in muted
blues and greens hung over the mantle. Afternoon light

shone through the diamond-shaped panes of the large leaded glass window, brightening fuschia roses and white lilacs which Emma placed in crystal vases.

An unabridged dictionary with yellowed pages and a worn leather cover lay open on a three-legged stand. A globe of the world rested in a walnut cradle in front of one of the bookcases. Don Miguel smelled the dictionary and tenderly ran his hand over the pages. He gently spun the globe, which rattled in its cradle.

"This is a wonderful room, Alexandria," don Miguel said, glancing around the library. "It smells like old books, my favorite aroma, dust and wisdom. I can feel Duncan and Rose in this place."

Alexandria's eyes filled with tears. "I miss them."

Don Miguel smiled, compassion in his eyes. "It's natural, but they are close by. You can be with them while your body sleeps. You have already done this.

"They hear us when we think of them. It's important to send strong and loving thoughts. It is painful for them otherwise." don Miguel said.

Alex nodded, sniffing and wiping moisture from under her eyes. She didn't trust herself to speak. Miguel offered her a handkerchief.

After a pause she asked, "How about a quick tour of Dr. Frankenstein's laboratory?" She tried to make light of it. Miguel cast her an appraising look, and she winced internally.

"That's not what I think," she sighed. "It's just so unsettling. Too many coincidences and surprises."

Duncan's secret room was transformed by Alex's scrutiny. Sparkling bottles and beakers lined clean shelves. Books and binders were dusted and upright. Halogen light poles brightened the dungeon-like feeling of the dark room. Miguel scanned the hidden laboratory, absorbing the contents.

"What do you make of it?" Erik asked. "Were you aware of Duncan's secret life?"

Miguel chuckled. "Duncan Stuart was a visionary and an iconoclast. He planted seeds where he thought they might germinate one day. I recall enigmatic statements he made about unlimited energy, controversial research that could have troublesome consequences. He certainly believed he was onto something transformative."

"Unlimited energy," Alex said.

"There's that word again," Erik said.

Alex had a sudden intuition and picked up the conference photograph of her grandparents and Selig.

"This is the man I saw at the cemetery. He was here yesterday demanding Grandpa's research papers,"

Don Miguel scrutinized the picture. "I have seem this man somewhere."

The three emerged from Duncan's private study.

"The dream," Erik said.

"Right," Alex related the dream, trying to capture details of the island country and the characters she recalled. Miguel listened with rapt attention. She finished and sat back on the love seat, exhaling.

"What do you think?" Erik asked.

"The images are vivid, and the people in your dream have names and personalities. Because of these details, it strikes me as memory rather than symbolism," Miguel said.

Alex nodded. "I agree. I want to continue the shamanic training. I need to get stronger and understand what's happening."

"We have two options," Miguel said. "I can teach you the next major tool of the shaman; the journey to the Upper World. Or, we can try hypnotic regression to investigate the significance of your dream," Miguel said.

"What do you suggest?" Alex asked, brow furrowed in a question.

"The purpose of a journey to the Upper World is to seek a teacher. The journey should serve to increase your power. I think that would be the best choice. Then we will work with regression," don Miguel said.

"Let's get started," Alex said, with a firm nod. "What do we need?"

"You'll need a place to lie down, a pillow and something to cover your eyes," Miguel said. It's best to have the room dark."

"Is this dangerous?" Erik asked.

"No more than the nightly journey the spirit takes during sleep. We die each night, but the breath calls the spirit back to finish its task in this dimension," don Miguel said gently.

"Can I help her? I'd like to know what she's experiencing," Erik said.

"I can't promise success, but if you lie next to her while she journeys you may get impressions. I have no objection if Alex doesn't," Miguel said.

"I like the idea," Alex said.

"The preparations are basically the same as for the lower world. I brought a cassette tape instead of my drum. Do you have earphones?" Miguel asked.

"Yes and another set of earphones with an adaptor so Erik can listen."

"Excellent. That will help him concentrate," Miguel said. "As you know, this physical dimension seems solid but is formed of atoms separated by immense distances. Solidity is an illusion. Shamans believe the other worlds are as real as this one. You must respect that in order to work in the other realms.

"Choose a place from which to ascend, preferably a high place like a mountain," Miguel continued. "As with your journey to the Lower World, it must be a place you know in this reality. Select a place in nature that inspired you and has special meaning. It is the doorway between the dimensions and aids your safe return.

"I know just the spot," Alex said.

12
Royal Raiment

Alex brought her sleeping bag into the library and spread it out on the floor in front of the love seat where Miguel and Erik sat. They looked like night and day to her. Erik's blond Scandinavian looks and Miguel's dark and mysterious Mayan appearance were a striking contrast.

She threw pillows and a blanket on top of the sleeping bag and procured scarves to cover their eyes. Kicking off her shoes, she removed her jewelry and placed it in a dish on the coffee table.

"I'm ready," she said.

"Please sit down while I explain the technique for reaching the Upper World," don Miguel said. "You went through a pool of water to reach the Lower World, which is the home of the feeling nature where healing occurs.

"To reach the Upper World, you must pierce a barrier which surrounds the outer layer of the earth itself. It is like a membrane which separates the dimensions of the Middle World from the Upper World, the mental realm of thoughts and ideas.

"It is important to state your purpose mentally as you begin this process. Have you selected a place to ascend?" Miguel said, leaning back in his chair.

"Yes," she said.

Alex picked a spot in a national park where she ventured off the footpath one day. Following where her curiosity led, she was rewarded with a primordial grove of elderly pines. The old trees grew in a circle and formed a sacred space whose center was a fragrant carpet of pine needles. Streaks of light danced through evergreen boughs as they swayed in a soft breeze.

Kneeling on the ground, she scooped up a handful of brown needles and watched them float back to earth through her opened fingers.

A boulder stood at the heart of the circle like a stone altar in a green cathedral. The large rock was surrounded by a random configuration of smaller stones and pebbles that tumbled down the mountain ages ago, before the trees grew around them. The roots of these ancient trees grew deep inside the earth, finding strength and sustenance. The branches climbed toward the sun in search of illumination.

"Once you can clearly see yourself in the place you've chosen, imagine smoke rising in the air, as if from a fire," don Miguel continued.

"Picture yourself rising on a current of air. The smoke, or mist, helps your visualization. Feel yourself become weightless. As you lift off the ground, mentally accelerate. Then fly," he said.

Alex and Erik lay next to each other on the sleeping bag and covered with the blanket. They hooked up the ear phones and plugged in the tape player. The final step was to cover their eyes.

"Raise your hand when you want me to begin the tape," Miguel said.

When she felt ready, she squeezed Erik's hand and lifted her fingers to signal don Miguel. She heard the primal, driving beat of the drum pounding in her ears. The sound seemed to come from inside her head and fill the whole world. Her body grew relaxed and heavy. Then her awareness shifted, and she no longer felt her body.

Alex visualized herself walking into her magical green circle. She felt the presence of the trees like conscious beings. She climbed onto the rock altar, spread her arms wide and mentally signaled Dolphin. She appeared in moments.

Dolphin swam through the air, moving downward in graceful measure, coming to rest beside her. As she had been taught, Alex imaged smoke which began as a swirling mist. White plumes circled around her. She willed it to spin faster and rise into the sky until she was surrounded by a whirling column of smoke.

She rose into the air, spinning slowly at first. Alexandria raised her arms above her head like a diver. She gained momentum as she felt a release from gravity. Dolphin was beside her. She felt the exhilaration of flight, speed and freedom.

Ahead of her was the membrane don Miguel described that separated the Middle World from the Upper World. Pointing her arms, she aimed and pierced the barrier. Suddenly, she moved through space. Blackness, bejeweled with myriad, sparkling stars surrounded her. She looked down and saw the earth, big and blue beneath her. Terrified, she nearly panicked.

"Dolphin! I'm going to fall."

She jerked around and was relieved to see Dolphin right beside her. Dolphin swam in a circle and came underneath.

"Ride on me for awhile, Little One."

Alex clung to her like a vise clamp, fingernails digging into her pliant skin. Dolphin made a clicking sound which resembled a chuckle. Relieved to be on Dolphin's back, Alexandria felt drawn in a specific direction.

"That way," Alex said, pointing to the right. Dolphin moved so quickly the stars looked like strings of light flowing past them. They traveled so far Alex thought they must be at the edge of the galaxy, perhaps the end of the universe. She fought the rising fear that she might never return to ordinary consciousness.

"Breathe, child."

Alexandria exhaled like air expelled from a balloon.

"What was your intention, Alexandria?" Dolphin asked telepathically.

"To learn the reason for recent events. To understand my purpose."

Alex tried to calm herself. She imagined her mind as a still mountain lake, perfectly reflecting the image of a snow-capped mountain. She deepened her breathing and willed the desire for knowledge of her purpose to permeate her being. I am safe. All is well.

She saw a green planet about the size of earth. Dolphin slowed her speed and reoriented her position. They closed in on the lovely green and white orb, descending through the planet's atmosphere into clouds. They floated through solid whiteness until Dolphin landed in a snow-covered field.

Crystal flakes fell softly, but the distant skylines were cloudless. An orange sun, three times the size of Earth's, hovered near one horizon looking like an enormous half circle. Fading golden-yellow and pink light illuminated the horizon around the sinking solar orb.

Skeletal winter trees looked like black sea fans against the pastel backdrop. Two full moons, one blue, the other starkly white, rose in the sky on the opposite horizon from the mammoth sun.

Alex leaped from Dolphin's back, overcome with the desire to make a snow angel. She fell on her back in the field, arms spread wide. Moving her arms up and down and her legs back and forth, she squealed with delight. Dolphin made a circle around her and pushed a big ball of wet snow with her snout.

Alex shrieked, "Let's build a snow dolphin!"

Dolphin whistled and brought lots of snow. Alex sculpted what she thought was a masterpiece. Dolphin's gray form rolled over in the powdery white snow amidst a cacophony of clicks and whistles. Alex scooped a handful of snow and took a mouthful. It tasted cold and pure, like ice from a mountain stream.

"I haven't eaten snow in thirty years,"

"A pity, dear. You're too young to be so old," chimed the kind voice in Alex's thoughts.

Alex was startled by movement at a distance. Something advanced toward them across the meadow. She thought she heard tinkling bells. Out of the gathering darkness Alex could barely make out a grand sleigh pulled by the largest white stallion she had ever seen. He appeared to be ten feet tall from head to hoof.

The proud steed and his alabaster sleigh stopped in front of them. The stallion whinnied in a loud voice and tossed his silvery mane. Steam jetted out of his nostrils and filled the air around his head.

Without hesitation, Alex climbed into the sleigh. Dolphin was already in motion, gliding along the top of the frosty surface like an aquatic snow mobile.

Alex covered herself with a thick rose-colored blanket. She brushed her hand across its exquisite softness. Snowflakes felt wet on her face, but the air was not cold.

The magnificent horse turned the sled, whinnied and raced across the field. Alex felt her hair blowing in the wind. Her breath made white wisps when she exhaled, but she was snug inside the magic chariot.

The sun was no longer visible, just a lingering golden-orange light beneath the receding cloud cover at the edge of the horizon. Twin full moons cast their light on the field, transforming the snow into a kaleidoscope of iridescent crystals.

They approached a chain of hills, and Alex noticed lights in the direction the sleigh was headed. Fixing her gaze on the source of the lights, she saw a colossal white castle built into the side of a mountain. Triangular flags flew from numerous turreted spires. In the moonlight, the castle looked like a fortress of abalone. The inviting scent of burning fire wood reached her nostrils.

The stallion slowed his pace to a high stepping trot, kicking up a flurry of snow. He stopped in front of a cave-like opening at the foot of the castle mountain. The white horse bobbed his powerful head and neighed. The sleigh trembled. Alex jumped from the sleigh and curtsied instinctively.

"Thank you for a thrilling ride."

The great horse snorted, reared on his hind legs and galloped off. Alex shook her head in wonder.

She entered the opening in the side of the hill where Dolphin waited inside in a warm dry cavern. Rock walls emitted a source of light. A chair, resembling a wooden porch swing, hung from a rock ceiling at the rear of the chamber.

A flax colored robe with a large hood and deep pockets lay on the seat. Comfortable looking shoes made of soft honey-colored material like fine tooled leather lay beside the robe. Alex removed her wet outer clothes, slipped the robe over her head and sat on the swing. She kicked off her shoes and pulled on the cozy slippers.

"I feel like Goldilocks."

Dolphin clicked, a merry sound, then leaped onto the swing, sprawling her huge body across Alex's lap. The swing rocked precariously. Dolphin squealed and clicked in what was unmistakably laughter. Alex giggled.

Without warning, the swing jerked like a Ferris Wheel seat and shot straight up inside the cavern. Alex thought they'd been fired from a rocket and was certain they would crash into the roof of the cavern.

Just as suddenly, the strange craft came to rest with a clunk in a chamber on a white marble floor. At the end of a long corridor of the same white marble, a doorway stood ajar. Dazzling light escaped into the hall.

Alex walked the length of the corridor with Dolphin gliding beside her. The wooden door was twelve feet high, six feet across and as thick as the length of her hand. A copper door ring, larger than her head, was at eye level. She stood at the partially opened doorway, heart pounding and legs shaking.

For the second time in her life, she thought she might faint.

"I can't go in there."

"Breathe, Alexandria," Dolphin signaled mentally.

Alex remembered the priestess from the dream and breathed the same way. Reluctantly, her pounding heart slowed. She pushed the door open wider and peeked inside. A fire roared and crackled in a monstrous stone fireplace, reaching twenty feet from floor to ceiling. Firelight was reflected in scores of diamond-shaped window panes.

She entered the room and gasped at the sight of two luminous beings seated on enormous carved wooden thrones. Here was the majestic purple-clad lady from her childhood dreams.

The magnificent goddess was seven feet tall and radiated awesome power. Shocking violet eyes that were full of compassion peered from a face the color of Russian amber. Her purple velvet gown was trimmed in silver brocade.

She wore a splendid coronet of silver filigree worked to look like lilies. The crown was studded with diamonds, pearls, amethyst and topaz. Eight silver points, surmounted by pearls the size of acorns, rose from the ornate band. A large alexandrite was positioned in the center of her brow.

In her right hand the goddess grasped the sword. Alex remembered its weight and felt the force of the blow that severed the raven's head. The glinting steel blade issued from the mouth of a gold dragon with blood-red ruby eyes. The hilt of the sword rested on the arm of the lady's throne.

Long curls of pewter-colored hair swept up through her crown and cascaded down her shoulders like a fountain. She wore a double strand of large pearls, with a rectangular amethyst at her throat. A piece of rose quartz rested over her heart, and a white crystal was set into her waist band.

Next to the magnificent lady sat a titan. Silvery white braids, woven with pieces of leather, beads and feathers hung to his waist on either side of a snow white beard. A silver diadem circled his head, and a large crystal sparkled at the center of his brow.

His red skin, hawk-like nose and high cheekbones contrasted dramatically with electric ice-blue eyes, shining from an ageless face. The giant wore a tunic and pants of supple white buckskin. A beautiful turquoise necklace was barely visible beneath his beard.

A colossal red lion, with a mane three feet wide, sat between the wondrous beings. The crimson beast stared at Alex, poised to pounce.

"Greetings, Dolphin," Lion said in a booming baritone. "You are welcome here."

"Well met old friend," Dolphin replied mentally.

The woman smiled, and her amythest eyes sparkled like the gems she wore.

"I am Alethia," she said, in a voice like wind through a canyon. Turning to the man, she said, "This is Dream Walker. We have waited long for you."

Alex sensed that nothing could be hidden from these beings. She felt her soul laid bare in their presence.

"I have come," she replied simply.

"It is well," Dream Walker said, in a kind voice like a babbling book in spring. "Kneel candidate, and receive the initiation of the Third Eye."

Alexandria knelt in front of the two thrones, and Dolphin floated beside her. The room was filled with a sensation of power and sparking electricity like the mounting energy of a spring storm. Alethia rose, and her presence filled the room. She placed a hand on Alexandria's head and raised the magical sword on high. The timber of her voice echoed in the large hall.

> "Time grows short. The hour approaches.
> A call to arms for the Spiritual Warrior.
> The day of reckoning is upon us.
>
> "Be not faint of heart.
> Fail not in your duty.
> Fear not the darkness.
>
> "Your sword is wisdom.
> Your shield is love.
> Your armor is truth.
>
> "Be valiant, server of the light.
> Yours could be the heart that tips the balance.
> Yours the choice that saves the world.
>
> "Choose Love.
> Choose Truth.
> Choose Power."

In the potent silence which followed, Alethia touched the hilt of her sword to Alexandria's forehead. Light exploded inside her head as billions of particles from the shattered obstructions of her mistaken beliefs and outworn habits were blown to the far reaches of space. Only brilliant light remained.

"Rise, Alexandria," Alethia said.

"The time has come to reclaim your power. You can no longer afford the luxury of the curious seeker. You must be about your business."

"What is my business? I came here to learn my purpose."

The goddess replied in a booming voice that rattled the window panes. The world seemed to shake to its foundation. Alex raised her hands and covered her ears.

"Remember what was forgotten.
"Unearth what was buried.
"Shatter long-held falsehoods.
"Vanquish an ancient enemy.
"Rejoice at finding what you feared was lost forever."

Inexplicable tears of recognition flowed down Alexandria's cheeks that seemed to originate from an exhaustless spring of grace and healing.

Dream Walker placed his hands on her shoulders and spoke in a gentle but powerful voice.

"An old enemy stalks you. He is alive again seeking false power. He has not learned; he still lusts for it. He does not know the source of his obsession and does not remember his prior bond with you.

"He knows the knowledge he seeks and will stop at nothing to obtain it. You already possess the key; you must find the lock. You will need courage, but you are supported. Align yourself with the angelic realms. We cannot intervene unless we are invoked.

"It is time for the portals between the worlds to open again. Many who lived before will respond to their own remembrances. You will assist them in reclaiming their history and inheritance. This is your purpose, a millennial promise about to be fulfilled. You are reunited with two others who share this destiny," Dream Walker said.

As he spoke, a vision flashed through Alexandria's mind of a great pyramid. She saw hieroglyphics and understood their message. Inside was a chamber with three doorways.

She held a silver key. Mysterious contents were protected by an electromagnetic field; only one who resonated at the exact frequency would be permitted to enter. Hiero-glyphics held the secret.

"I have a gift for you," Dream Walker continued. "Hold out your hand."

Alexandria did as she was instructed. Dream Walker placed three stones in her palm. They looked like green peas made of jade. She stared at them. "An unusual color."

"These beads are ancient," Dream Walker said. "They belonged to you in a distant epoch. Make them into a ring for your right hand. The stones will evoke memories, and the ring will be a strong talisman. Three green orbs, one for each member of your quest."

"Thank you, Dream Walker. My gratitude to you, Alethia. Your presence has always made a difference in my life. I will draw comfort from the knowledge of your existence here and my ability to contact you.

"I will do whatever is necessary to accomplish this quest. I vow to be worthy of your trust," Alex said in a strong voice.

"Farewell, Alexandria," Alethia said. Her unlikely coloring made her exquisitely beautiful, like a rare orchid.

"Remember your warrior nature. Call upon that focus of will, and summon the fire in your belly. The answers to everything you seek are within you," Dream Walker said. His eyes looked like blue flames.

He handed her a small silk pouch on a cord. "Keep the stones close to your heart until the ring is ready."

"Come onto the terrace, Child," Dolphin said mentally.

Alex followed her outside. A black swan, ten times ordinary size, sat on the large balcony. A seat was fastened around her. A rope ladder hung from the seat to the floor of the balcony. Alex climbed up the ladder and into the seat. Dry folded clothes lay beside her. She pulled the ladder inside the seat.

Swan gracefully lifted off the balcony, revealing a wing span of thirty feet. As soon as they were airborne, the swan picked up speed. Dolphin sailed alongside. Stars blurred into bright streams of light. When Swan slowed, beautiful blue planet earth came into view.

"This is your stop, dear," Dolphin signaled. "You must go back through on your own power, but I'll be right beside you."

Alex removed the comfortable robe and shoes and put on her own clothing. She was careful to place the pouch next to her heart; the silk felt soft against her skin.

She took a deep breath and stood at the edge of the seat, looking down at earth. Feeling a new strength, she dove out of the seat as if propelled from a diving board.

"Concentrate on your destination," Dolphin said. "Picture yourself landing gently on the rock. You control your speed and direction."

Alex pierced the barrier between ordinary reality and the upper world. The penetration of the membrane felt like diving through a waterfall. She entered earth's atmosphere and approached the surface. As she closed in on the circle of evergreens, she slowed her speed and turned around to descend feet first. She coasted to a standing stop on the rock altar.

Dolphin clicked. "Until next time."

Alex felt exhilarated. She threw her arms around the wonderful sea creature.

"Thank you for everything."

The tempo of the drums changed, signaling her return to ordinary awareness. She jumped from the rock and walked out of the circle of conifers.

Alex became aware of lying on the floor and felt the sleeping bag around her. After a few moments, the drumming stopped. She lay motionless on the floor, unwilling to move. She felt Erik stir and sit up beside her.

"Are you okay?" he asked softly.

She nodded and pulled the scarf from her eyes. Erik and Miguel stared at her. Reluctantly, she sat up. Her body felt heavy, but her mind was on fire. She touched the place where the pouch had been. It was silly to expect it to be there, but she felt a painful loss.

"I don't know where to begin," she said. "I feel as if I was gone a week instead of thirty minutes. I feel so emotional, I need time to think," Alex said.

"It's important to process the experience. You won't forget anything," Miguel said. "Now seems like the right time to give you something I brought with me."

Don Miguel reached into his shirt pocket and pulled out a silk pouch. He handed it to Alexandria, who had stopped breathing. Her hand shook visibly as she accepted the small bag. She exhaled and opened the draw string, pouring the jade beads into her hand. She gasped.

Alex touched the bright green stones in disbelief.

"I can't believe they're real."

"These ancient stones were found at Palenque. The color of the jade is quite rare," don Miguel said and put his arm around her shoulder. "These beads have been in my family for generations. When I saw your handiwork of the Cross of Palenque, I knew they belonged with you. I hope this gift will replace the necklace you gave to Chan Ka."

A torrent of pent up feeling exploded from a place deep within her. The emotion shattered the well of uncried tears still dammed up inside the broken heart of a twelve-year-old girl. That young heart mended enough to function but never healed.

"Oh, God," she sobbed.

Alex wept while Erik embraced her. She allowed herself to be comforted and accept the release of her long-buried grief. She suffered the tears to flow and permitted the aching sobs to cleanse her spirit.

Erik's arms felt strong and safe. The smell of his skin and cologne soothed her. Alex didn't resist when he stroked her hair. She clutched the priceless heirlooms tight in her fist, vowing never to be separated from them or the two people they represented. It would be all right, she wasn't alone anymore.

When Alex recovered her equilibrium, she stared at the wonderful contrasting men in her life. Ebony eyes radiated warmth and affection. Steel gray eyes emanated concern and protectiveness.

"Enough for one day?" Miguel asked.

"I have," Erik said. His face was drawn with concern.

Alex rubbed her nose on her sleeve and used the shirttail of her blouse to wipe beneath her eyes. She felt a little dizzy.

"I'll walk upstairs with you," she sniffed. "There's a heart-shaped locket in my old room that belonged to Gran. I want to put these stones in the locket right now until I can make a ring.

13
Romance

Don Miguel and Erik followed Alexandria up the spiral staircase. Four large bedrooms occupied the second story of the Victorian house. Miguel's room, decorated in Wedgewood blue with peach accents, was at the end of the hall next to the green and rose room where Erik stayed.

"I didn't realize you had an upstairs room," Erik said, looking at Alex.

"I moved downstairs when my father died. This is Gran and Grandpa's room," Alex said, changing the subject.

Rose and Duncan's room was across the hall from Miguel's. A deep turquoise and white color scheme imparted flair to the room. Tiny white roses dotted the fabric of the curtains and chairs. A priceless, walnut four poster bed stood between two windows.

"Grandpa called Gran his bride for the forty years of their marriage. He said she was the most pure and beautiful creature he had ever known, a perfect white rose. He always kept fragrant reminders of her namesake in their room," Alex said.

"That's beautiful," Erik said, staring into their room.

"Buenas noches," Miguel said as he approached his door. He turned to enter the room and laughed out loud. He motioned for Alex and Erik to join him in the doorway. Crystal was curled up on the carpet beside the bed. She opened one eye but showed no sign of moving.

Sheba was sprawled across Miguel's bed like Cleopatra on her barge. She glanced up, then turned away. Erik guffawed. "You're no one until you've been ignored by a cat," he laughed.

"Apparently I won't be sleeping alone tonight," Miguel chuckled. "I'm a lonely old man," he said in mock anguish. "I welcome the companionship."

Hand over heart, Erik backed from the room, acting stricken. Alex shook her head, rolled her eyes and walked toward her bedroom.

Gran created a fantasy bedroom in shades of purple for her only grandchild when she was three years old. The lavender room was a girl's dream, plucked from a fairy tale. A white canopy bed framed against deep violet carpet was the centerpiece. Matching white dressers, desk and shelves lined the lavender walls. A white cedar hope chest stood at the end of the bed, and a magical seat was built into a large bay window overlooking the garden.

Shelves were crammed with dolls, yearbooks, college mementos and photographs of young Alex with her parents. Thumbtacks held curled and yellowed pages of Alex's childish artwork on a bulletin board.

Erik picked up a jewelry box and opened it. A tiny ballerina popped up inside the lid. He wound the music box and set it back on the dresser. The dancer twirled as the little box played Skater's Waltz. "My sister had one of these," he said.

Alex looked at him. "That was a birthday present the year I turned seven. A cultured pearl necklace was tucked inside. Grandpa told me how pearls were formed. He said we should be thankful for our imperfections because overcoming them strengthens and improves our value like precious gems." She smiled. "I was thrilled. My birthday is December eighteenth. My family always tried to make it special since it's so close to Christmas."

Erik laughed. "Mine's January first. My birthday was lost between Christmas and New Year celebrations. My memories are mostly of adults with hangovers."

"How sad," Alex said. "We'll start a new tradition this year."

She opened drawers and looked inside boxes. "Thank heavens. I found it," she said, removing an antique heart-shaped locket and gold chain from a black velvet box.

Alex sat on the window seat and removed the silk pouch from her blouse pocket. She opened the locket and placed it beside her. Pulling the pouch apart, she carefully poured the beads into the locket.

"Perfect fit," she said, relieved. "Will you help me with the clasp?"

Erik joined her at the window. The padded upholstery seat circled the inside of the turreted bay window. A circular purple carpet covered the hardwood floor, and a round white table stood at the center. Frilly white lace curtains, tied with lavender satin sashes, draped across the windows.

Alex handed him the necklace and turned around so her back was toward him. He kissed her, and his breath felt warm on her neck. She gasped in surprise and shivered as goose bumps spread over her skin.

Erik lifted the necklace over her head and fastened the clasp. Alex put both hands around the heart-shaped locket. What an incredible gift the jade beads were, fated, predestined. She stared out the window into a clear, night sky. A silver slice of new moon hung against a starry background.

"I always expected Peter Pan to show up here, and I would take over for Wendy," Alex said, grabbing a white stuffed bear and sitting on the window seat. "I felt like a child in this room; I needed to leave to grow up."

She looked up at Erik. She wanted to touch his face and run her fingers through his blond hair. She needed to feel his breath on her skin, his arms around her.

Erik removed the stuffed bear from her grasp and deposited it on the window seat. He pulled her to her feet.

"It's time to bring some grown up passion into this little girl's room," he said.

She regarded those mesmerizing gray eyes, and her own eyes gave assent. They kissed. His lips were moist. She loved the smell of his breath. Erik's strong arms circled her waist and pulled her close. She put her arms around his neck.

He loosened his grip, took her hand and led her toward the canopy bed. He sat on the white bedspread and held both her hands. Erik took an unhurried look at her from her hair to her feet. He pulled her close and dropped her hands. She sensed that he intended to undress her, and the idea inflamed her.

He opened her blouse like a Christmas present. Every place his hands touched felt hot. When all the buttons were unfastened, he pulled the blouse off her shoulders and down her arms. It fell silently to the floor.

Erik pulled her close so that she stood between his legs. He unclasped her bra and removed it. She felt aroused and vulnerable simultaneously. Alexandria shuddered with the intensity of the sensation that was both pleasure and anticipation.

He sat back and looked at her. "You are so beautiful," he said, his voice husky. "Let your hair down."

She unfastened the barrette that imprisoned her mass of long hair, and red curls cascaded onto her shoulders. While he watched, she removed her jeans. He pulled her on top of him. Hungry mouths shared kisses. He rolled her over on her side. Erik pulled away and unceremoniously removed his clothes.

Alex remembered the beautiful body she had first noticed in Mexico. His waist was narrow, and a generous amount of hair covered his broad chest. She couldn't wait to touch it, to feel the texture against her breasts. She thought she would ignite from the fire inside her. The pressure was unbearable.

He climbed back on the bed and lay next to her. They kissed and eagerly explored each other's bodies with their hands. They rolled, limbs tangled together, craving everything now.

"I want to feel you inside me. I don't want to wait," Alex moaned. Erik lay on top of her, and she wrapped her legs around his waist as he entered her. She arched her back in pleasure and tightened the grip of her legs.

"You feel wonderful," Erik whispered.

They moved together in perfect rhythm until their pace increased. Erik's body stiffened in a paroxysm of ecstasy. Moments later Alex cried out as she found release. They collapsed breathless on the bed and clung to each other in a silent embrace.

He moved to her side, and they lay on their backs holding hands. Their bodies touched from foot to shoulder. Erik turned his head and looked at her. Profound openness showed in his gray eyes. Shields were torn away by intimacy. Alex knew that vulnerable look was in her eyes too. She longed to feel this close forever.

"You're a lot different to take to bed than my bear," she sighed, feeling content. "Hotter, for one thing."

"And you're a lot different to take to bed than my baseball glove," he laughed. His face grew serious. "I've looked for you a long time, Alexandria Stuart. Don't get any ideas about wandering off."

She nestled close to him and rested her head on his shoulder. She kissed his neck for emphasis. "You'd just find me."

"Roll over," he said, turning so her back faced him. He put his arm around her waist.

"I'm glad we didn't make love in my father's bed."

Erik kissed her shoulder.

"Don Miguel is in Dad's childhood room. When he reached his teens, he moved downstairs. He liked the independence. After he died, I slept downstairs. I felt closer to him there. Gran understood, but she kept the lavender room. I think she hoped I'd move back upstairs, especially after Grandpa died."

He held her and let her talk. Alexandria fell asleep feeling safe and protected for the first time since her father's death. She knew Erik would still be there in the morning.

*   *   *   *   *   *   *

Alex woke early. Morning light filtered in the bay window. For a moment, she was transported to her childhood. She recalled blissful summer mornings when she slept in this room while visiting her grandparents. She looked around the room at photographs, dolls, blue ribbons and drawings, reflections of her past.

Erik lay beside her. His boyish, blond hair was tousled and begged to be touched. She cuddled up next to his warmth, touching his body with hers wherever possible. Every point of contact felt like an electric charge. Memory of last night's lovemaking reawakened her desire. She closed her eyes and imagined.

Alex drifted back to sleep and was awakened later by the exquisite sensation of Erik sucking on her ear lobe. She moaned with pleasure and opened her eyes. He pretended not to notice and continued to gently kiss her ear and neck, slowly kissing his way down her neck and chest. He put his mouth over a nipple which hardened in response.

"I want to make love to you again," he whispered, "slowly this time."

"We should go downstairs. It must be nine o'clock," Alex said, struggling to concentrate while Erik continued kissing.

By the time his mouth reached her other breast, she couldn't remember her objection. She surrendered to the urge to kiss him, to touch his firm muscles and smell his skin. Nothing else mattered.

14
Regression

Showered and dressed in yesterday's clothes, Alex and Erik descended the spiral stairs. She was apprehensive about facing don Miguel, but the voice she heard in the kitchen eclipsed that concern.

"Good morning, Dear," Amelia Stuart said, in a voice as cold and stinging as dry ice. Her mother stood next to Emma at the kitchen sink. Her blond hair was brushed into a French twist, accentuating her lovely aquiline features. Sporty coral slacks and matching top coordinated with white and coral jewelry.

"I understand you slept in your old room." Amelia said, brushing her hand over her hair, smoothing stray strands of blond hair. "Rose would be pleased."

She didn't look at her daughter when she spoke, for which Alexandria was grateful. Alex turned a shade of red ordinarily reserved for fire engines.

"Good morning, Mrs. Stuart," Erik beamed. "What a pleasant surprise." Erik's charming demeanor didn't help Alex's embarrassment or anger. Crystal barked, sensing the tension.

Miguel pretended to be absorbed in the newspaper. Sheba, proclaiming mistreatment in pitiful meows, approached Erik and rubbed white fur on his pant cuffs.

"Pay no attention to her highness," Emma laughed, whisking gray hairs from her face with a soapy hand; "she's been fed." Emma turned back to the sink, sloshing dishes through soapy water.

"Coffee?" Erik asked.

Alex tried to become invisible in one of the chairs at the big table and lifted her mug in response.

Don Miguel looked dapper in a blue Madras shirt. His salt and pepper hair was neatly combed. He folded his newspaper and directed an appraising look at the couple. Inscrutable eyes sparkled like faceted pieces of black jet.

"The apple pancakes are decadent," he said, handing the platter to Erik.

"I'm ravenous," Erik smiled, patting his stomach.

"Did you sleep well?" Miguel inquired.

"Like an innocent babe," Erik replied, flashing his best boyish grin. "Must be the cool nights."

"What happens on hot nights?" Amelia asked.

Alex wanted to glare at her, but she decided to ignore her instead. She accepted the pancake platter from Erik, attention riveted on her plate. She felt as if a scarlet letter A was emblazoned on her forehead, and a sandwich board across her chest proclaimed, "I had sex with Erik."

"I slept well also," Miguel said. "As content as if my beloved Sophia were still alive and by my side. There's a lot of love in this wonderful old house.

"Of course, I did have two beautiful female companions in my room," Miguel said in a wry tone.

Amelia flashed him an outraged look.

Emma laughed out loud.

Alex looked at Miguel after he'd delivered his barb. She would have been able to keep a straight face if she hadn't seen her mother's expression.

"It's nothing to worry about, Mrs. Stuart," Erik said. "Crystal and Sheba chose to abandon their regular sleeping partners to be with don Miguel. There was no impropriety, and I was only a little jealous," he explained in his most appealing tone.

Amelia had the good sense to realize she was outgunned, and the air was cleared.

"Do you feel ready to try regression, Alex?" Miguel asked. "You had a remarkable journey yesterday. This process should not be rushed."

Alex was relieved to focus on something else. "Yes. Let's not waste time."

She lifted the gold locket from her shirt and looked at Miguel. "These beads give me a sense of destiny, as if there's a larger purpose. I'm impatient to know what it is. Alex smiled, "These pieces of jade remind me of peas; three peas in a pod. Can you imagine a more unlikely trio than us?"

Miguel chortled. "There is a similar expression in Spanish, 'parecerse como dos gotas de agua,' like two drops of water. We are the three drips," he chuckled. "Forgive me, I've amused myself.

"There are no coincidences," Miguel said. "Peas that grow within the same pod have a close relationship, but drops of water partake of a larger reality. When you place those drops into the same container they merge."

He lifted a spoonful of coffee from his mug and allowed some of the liquid to flow back into the cup. "It's a deeper metaphor for our spiritual relationship."

"I like that," Alex said smiling. "Three drips it is."

"Like water off a duck's back. I always go with the flow. How about three drips in the fountain? " Erik quipped.

"Enough," Alex said, pretending to glare. Don Miguel scowled, but his dark eyes twinkled.

"I've never been hypnotized," Alex said, furrowing her brow.

"Will she prance around the room like a poodle and beg for dog biscuits?" Erik chimed in, gray eyes twinkling with mischief under raised eyebrows. He petted Sheba, who had reclaimed her territory in his lap. His other hand held his coffee mug aloft between gulps.

"You'd like a trained pet, wouldn't you, Mr. Anderson? It would be a contrast to that cat," Amelia interjected.

Alex's eyes widened as concern over Erik's question registered. Miguel leaned his head back and laughed.

"I admit, that is an amusing image, but frivolity is for charlatans. We'll work with a technique called hypnotic regression. It's an effective means of remembering forgotten incidents or dreams."

Miguel placed his hand on top of Alex's. His presence radiated a quiet power his casual clothes could not mask. His confidence reassured her, and she relaxed.

"There's nothing mysterious or frightening about it," Miguel said, smiling. "It's actually a state of focused concentration. Your body relaxes, your mind concentrates, and your memory comes into clear focus."

Alex was reassured by his kind, honest eyes. She trusted him.

"The subconscious mind stores our experiences in photographic detail. People can return to the scene of a crime while in a hypnotic trance and read the license number of a fleeing car. They may have no conscious memory of seeing the license, but they see it clearly while hypnotized.

"I didn't realize that," Erik said. "That sort of information could be useful to an attorney."

"Regression data has been admitted as evidence in some legal cases," Miguel said. "I'd like to tape record the session, if you don't mind," he said, looking at Alex.

"Fine. Let's work in the living room," Alex replied. "The electronic stuff is there, and the couch is bigger."

Alex carried her dishes to the sink. "Can we get started?" she asked. "I don't want more time to worry."

"Certainly," Miguel said, standing.

"Enjoy yourselves, boys and girls," Amelia said as they left the kitchen.

Alex emitted a muffled sound like a growl. *She never quits.*

The living room beckoned like a French country cottage. Morning sunlight flashed a beam of radiance onto a white, baby grand piano. A white brick fireplace anchored the corner of the room next to the piano.

A colorful still life hung above the mantel. Huge sunflowers burst from a blue and white ceramic vase. Juicy-looking peaches, apples and cherries, piled in a hammered, copper bowl, begged to be picked from the canvas.

A couch of generous length with lots of ample pillows faced the fireplace. Blue and yellow floral print fabric covered the couch and comfortable chairs with ottomans that stood on either side. A white crocheted afghan was folded on an arm of the couch.

Floor to ceiling windows were covered by blue tie back curtains with valences. Sheer white curtains hung over the windows.

One wall was devoted to television, VCR and an elaborate stereo system. Shelves of video and audio tapes, along with a collection of phonograph records, surrounded the electronic equipment. An antique phonograph player stood next to the shelves. The beautiful piece of oak furniture still played seventy-eight rpm records. A valuable collection of the old black disks was carefully stored in a box on the bottom shelf.

"Glenn Miller, Tommy Dorsey Mario Lanza. I could spend a week listening to these," Erik said, tenderly examining the old records.

"What a charming room," Miguel said. "So different from the library but equally inviting."

Erik slid onto the piano bench. He lifted the keyboard cover and played a few chords, running his fingers over the keys, creating a harmonic background.

"We have two tape recorder options," Alex said. "Blank tapes too."

Alex arranged pillows on the couch, placing two where her head would be. She kicked off her shoes, plopped on the couch, fluffed and punched the pillows to get them right, and threw the white afghan over her legs. Her arms lay across her stomach, on top of the afghan.

Erik's random chording was transformed into the melody of a song. The tune was familiar, but Alex couldn't identify the title.

Miguel looked up from the tape recorder and walked toward the piano. "That's a wonderful old song, Erik. Before your time isn't it? How about starting over?"

"Of course," Erik said, commencing an introduction which spanned the keyboard with trills and flourishes.

Miguel sang the words to the old song in a pure tenor. Erik accompanied him as if they'd rehearsed for days. Alex was transported. The beauty of their music touched her soul and carried her spirit to a higher realm. They were a constant surprise to her.

"I'll be seeing you in all the old familiar places,
That this heart of mine embraces, all day through.
In that small cafe, the park across the way,
The children's carousel, the chestnut trees,
The wishing well.

"I'll be seeing you in every lovely summer's day,
In every thing that's light and gay,
I'll always think of you that way.
I'll find you in the morning sun
And when the night is new,
I'll be looking at the moon,
But I'll be seeing you."

As Miguel's triumphant voice reached the final chorus, a crystal clear soprano joined in harmony. Amelia's lilting voice provided the perfect counterpoint to Miguel's tenor.

Alex spun around to see if she was dreaming. She hadn't heard her mother sing in decades. Amelia stood in the foyer, eyes closed and chin raised. Her face was transfigured as if enchanted by the music.

Alex thought her heart would not contain the elation of this moment. A magic spell had been cast. Erik repeated the last verse. The rich voices raised to a crescendo and sang the final words with bitter sweet emotion. The last notes graced the air like a benediction from sacred temple bells.

Emma stood next to Amelia crying and clapping, a standing ovation of one. "I've never heard anything so beautiful. You couldn't have known, but that song was a favorite of Duncan and Rose," Emma spoke through tears.

Alex jumped off the couch and ran to her mother. She threw her arms around her, "I forgot how much I love to hear you sing. God, I've missed it."

Miguel approached and took Amelia's hand. "Thank you for joining us. Your soprano is celestial. What a joy to sing with you."

Amelia was white and shaking; her eyes were wet.

"Alexandria's father was a gifted pianist," she said with difficulty. "This house was filled with music once. Perhaps it can be again," she said, looking at Erik. Amelia squeezed her daughter's hand and walked back to the kitchen.

"I'm a sight, aren't I?" Emma said, sniffing and pulling a tissue from her apron pocket. "Make no mistake; you worked a miracle today," Emma said walking toward the kitchen.

Alex gaped at Miguel. "Emma's right, that was a miracle of major proportions. I could hardly believe the beauty of your duet, when I heard my mother's voice."

Alex wiped tears from her eyes.

" Mother hasn't sung a note since my father died. You reached inside her and brought the music back."

"Music is healing, Alexandria. This magnificent instrument has been silent too long. Your mother's exquisite voice needs to be used, even if it's in an empty room," Miguel said.

"I wish Dad and Gran were here," Alex said, her voice cracking.

"What makes you think they're not?" Miguel smiled.

"I'm selfish. I want to see their faces and touch them, not just imagine them in some vague hereafter."

"My dear Alexandria, the veil between the seen and unseen worlds is quite thin. Communication between the living and the so-called dead is a natural phenomena. If you will still your mind and open your heart, you will feel their presence. You've already met them in dreams and heard your father's voice," Miguel said looking into her eyes.

"You're right," she said, feeling chastised.

Alex walked back to the couch and collapsed like a rag doll. "I keep forgetting that. I'm sorry to be so self-centered. This is proving to be quite a day," she said.

"Are you sure you want to do the regression now?" Erik asked, sounding concerned. He rubbed his forehead as if his head ached.

Crystal's fluffy white form trotted into the living room and settled in front of Alex on the floor.

Alex sighed. "I'm better now that Crystal's here. I'm nervous, and my emotional reserve tank could use some fuel, but I want to do this now. What else could happen?"

"Don't ask," Erik said, pushing blond hair from his forehead. He donned his glasses and took charge of recording. Pulling a chair next to the coffee table, he readied a small arsenal of blank cassettes and extra batteries.

Don Miguel sat in a comfortable chair by the fireplace, placed his feet on the ottoman and positioned tablet and pen on his lap.

"I cannot predict if you will be able to access a prior life during the first attempt. Just relax, and we'll see what happens," Miguel said.

Alex reached under the afghan and pulled a kerchief from her jeans pocket. She tied it around her head and placed her head on the pillows, shifting position until she felt comfortable.

"Close your eyes and breathe easily," Don Miguel said in a soothing voice. "Don't listen to any sound but my voice. Pay attention to your breath. Each time you exhale, feel the tension leave your body. When you inhale, imagine breathing in peace and serenity.

"Begin at the top of your head and allow your muscles to relax progressively. Feel that calming sensation move slowly from your face and neck, down your body to the tips of your toes. Your whole body feels relaxed and peaceful."

Alex experienced the progressive relaxation. She felt herself becoming stone-like, starting at her head and moving down her body. Her breathing slowed, and her only sensation was heaviness. She experienced her breath as coolness moving in and out of nostrils, lulling her into deeper stillness. Her breath made a soft sound like a tropical breeze.

"Excellent; you are doing well, Alexandria. See yourself enveloped in a warm golden light. This light makes you feel safe, tranquil and relaxed. Let every breath take you into a deeper state of relaxation."

Alex lost the sense of heaviness. Her head seemed to float above and separate from the rest of her body. She felt buoyant, as if she was suspended in salt water. A fleeting thought passed through her mind that this sensation was better than nitrous oxide in the dentist's office.

"I'll count backward from ten to one," Don Miguel said, in the same reassuring tone. His voice sounded distant. "With each number you will go deeper. Concentrate only on my voice. Ten. Nine. Eight."

Alex's body ceased to exist. She became a faint breath moving in and out in a warm, safe place and felt content to float in this tranquil womb. Everything slowed; don Miguel's voice was soothing like a bubble bath.

"Three. Two. One. Imagine a place or time in your life where you were supremely happy. Visualize yourself there. Continue to relax and breathe."

Alex found it hard to respond, and there was a long silence while images came into focus.

"Can you tell me where you are?" Miguel asked.

"I'm home. It's Christmas," she squealed. "I got a new sled. Daddy and I are going outside to try it. It snowed a lot last night, and the hill in the back yard is white. Gran called it a white Christmas."

"How old are you, Alexandria?"

She paused to consider the answer.

"I'm eight years old."

"Look at your clothes and shoes. Can you describe what you are wearing?"

She looked at her feet, then her legs and arms.

"Mom made me wear leggings and boots that match my coat. I don't like them. They're heavy and hard to walk in. She made a string for my mittens so I won't lose them. She's tying a scarf around my neck because it's cold," Alex said, feeling impatient.

"What is happening now?" Don Miguel encouraged.

"This is fun." Alex giggled in a childlike voice. "I rode down the big hill in the back yard, the one that goes all the way to the fence. I got snow all over me. Daddy laughed and said I look like an Eskimo. He threw a snowball. It was cold. Some of the snow went down my collar," she laughed. "It made me shiver.

"Stanley's barking at the snow," she giggled again. "I'm going to pull the sled back to the top."

"Alexandria," Miguel said in a kind, firm voice, "go back a little farther to the time you were six years old. Can you recall your first day at school?"

Alex was quiet for a few moments. She didn't want to leave this scene; she felt so happy. She tried to resist, but her awareness shifted.

"I don't like Sister Mary Catherine. She's mean," Alex said crossing her arms and extending her lower lip in a pout.

"What else?" don Miguel probed.

"I met two friends today, Sarah and Elizabeth Anne. Sister won't let us talk. Elizabeth Anne says she's got dolls. We walked home from school together. They're nice."

"Good. I'll count to three, and I want you to go even farther back in your memory, to the source of your recent dream. You are calm and completely safe," Miguel said. "Continue to relax, and focus on your breath. One. Two. Three."

Don Miguel's voice sounded remote. Alex felt bathed in balmy darkness. She floated in comfort and silence for several minutes, just wanting to drift.

Alex was jarred by a wrenching wave of nausea. Her arms reached for something to steady herself. She gagged and choked as if vomiting.

"You are safe," Miguel said in a calm voice. "You are not in any danger. Relax and tell me what is happening."

The voice which spoke through Alex had a different quality, confident and in command.

"The sky is dark and full of evil clouds. We travel on a personal transport ship that tosses in a rough sea. I came on deck to get fresh air, but I feel no better. Nothing is left in my stomach."

She gagged again.

"Go forward in time until you feel better."

Alex breathed and became calmer. She was quiet for several moments.

"How are you feeling now?" Miguel prompted.

"I feel better, just weak. Three days have passed. I am still on the ship, but today the salt breeze is refreshing."

"Why are you on a ship, Alexandria?"

"I am Una Alana, priestess of the Healing Order," she said in a strong voice. "We sail west from our home land of Poseidia to the land known as Yu Ka Tan to begin a new life."

The timbre of her voice projected an aura of confidence and authority accustomed to royal stature.

"Why did you leave?" don Miguel asked.

A hint of condescension lay beneath the surface of her words. "Political circumstances forced our departure. Power shifted to different philosophical views, and it was not safe to remain. The land itself is in peril from an unscrupulous man. He endangers all life through his selfish plan to abuse our sacred energy source."

"What is that?" Miguel asked.

"The Tuaoi stone," she answered, as if surprised that he didn't know. "It is a large, crystalline stone which focuses and concentrates the energy of the sun to provide power for our country."

"What is your ship like?" Don Miguel asked.

"The shape is long and cylindrical, tapered at the front and back. The ship is a multi-purpose vehicle capable of flight, as well as travel on and below the surface of the water. The frame is constructed of lightweight curved metal bars and covered with layers of animal skins. The motive power is electro-chemical force."

"Do you recognize anyone from this time?" Miguel inquired.

She wrinkled her brow.

"You are here. Your name is Iltar. You are High Priest and my father. Erik is here. He is the priest Kadir."

In her hypnotic state, Alex felt no surprise at that recognition. It seemed a mere statement of fact.

"What do we look like?" Miguel wanted to know.

"The people of our country have straight black hair and bronze or coppery skin. You are considered handsome, Father. Your skin is reddish-bronze, and your blue-black hair reaches your shoulders.

"You usually dress in the white and purple robe of your office. A gold band circles your head and covers your forehead. A large blue jewel shines in the center of the band. Called Sky Stone, it aids understanding and opens the inner eye.

"You wear the thick gold chain necklace with a round pendant of Azurite and Malachite I made for you. I designed it to reflect your love of the earth.

"We left everything behind. I don't know if I will be able to continue my work. There may not be sufficient gems or minerals, and we may be unable to make metals."

"What are you wearing, Una? What do you look like?"

"My robe is made of sand-colored linen dyed using herbs, by making a tea. My hair is long and black like yours, twisted in a braid of four strands that hangs to my waist. I wear a large pendant with a light green, oval stone in the center called Sun Stone.

"My skin is darker than yours. I look like mother who died several years ago." She paused. "She was Rose, Alexandria's grandmother in your time."

"What period of history do you live in?"

She paused. "Thirteen thousand years before you."

"How do you measure time?" Miguel asked.

"Time is measured in increments of the Grand Cycle of stellar ages. Each age is measured by the apparent movement of the rising sun on the spring day of equal light and dark as it moves westward in the sky through the constellations. A Grand Cycle is one complete passage through the star pictures which takes almost twenty six thousand solar orbits.

"Our history spans two hundred thousand solar orbits. Two prior catastrophes devastated our land. Forty thousand orbits earlier than this time the surface of the earth shifted due to cosmic pressures from other planets and stars. An immense catastrophe resulted which changed our vast continent into a group of islands.

"A similar devastation occurred twenty-six thousand years from your time," Una's voice replied, like a teacher instructing a pupil. "Zared's scheme may trigger another inundation."

She inhaled sharply. "There are dolphins. What a glorious sight. Many of them jump in the air and splash into the water. Their clicking and whistling voices are musical. This is a fortuitous omen for our new beginning. I am grieved by this journey, but the dolphins ease my heart." She paused.

"Go forward in time five years," Miguel prodded. "Where are you now? Tell me what you see."

Breathing audibly, Alexandria deepened her trance. Her consciousness floated through time and space five years into the future. Peacefully drifting above earthly concerns, Alex resisted returning to awareness of Una.

"We have accomplished a great deal," Una's voice said. "The people welcomed us, and we built a strong community. Work on the new temple progresses as we prepare for a visit from Hept-supht from another of the colonies. He will travel over land and ocean in a transport vessel.

"I am married to Kadir, and we have a beautiful daughter. Her name is Mirari, which means miracle. Mirari is Amelia in the current lifetime," Una's strong voice said.

"Things in Poseidia continue to decline. Zared's crystal scheme caused subterranean earthquakes, volcanoes and violent weather distortions. We fear the island will soon be destroyed."

"Una, I want you to move ahead to the end of this lifetime. Where are you? Who is with you?" Miguel encouraged.

Her voice sounded peaceful but tired.

"Kadir is with me. He holds my hand. My children and grandchildren are gathered to say farewell. We will meet again. After three hundred solar cycles on this good earth, my body and mind are weary of the rejuvenation temple where we use the secrets of the stones to prolong life. It is peaceful; I do not suffer. My time has simply come. I tell Kadir, my dearest love, that he will join me soon. We can never be parted. Ours is an ancient bond."

There was a long silence. Her breathing was shallow and irregular. Alexandria's body became still.

"The spirit has departed the body. I float above, looking at my family. Kadir bowed his head beside me. I do not want them to feel sorrow. I am free of the burden of that aged body. I feel no pain, only lightness and joy after a long and fruitful life. Seeds were sown for the future which will flower many lifetimes from now. I am content."

She was silent, feeling surpassing peace. After a few moments a different voice spoke through the mouth of Alexandria. It roared from her throat with the potency of a lion.

"The priestess served well in that epoch, and she is called upon again to serve the great plan. A prophecy was encoded in the design of my ancient architecture. Hear and understand. The time of the Initiates is at hand.

"When great Ra ascends in the sign of the Water Bearer and smiles on the face of the Lion, the portals will open to the children of earth again. The long watch of the sentinel will end. The unending night of sleep will give way to the morning of remembrance.

"The eternal wheel of the ages will turn again toward light. Those who slumbered will awaken. The three who prepared will come forward to uncover the long guarded secrets.

"Isis will joyfully draw back her veil to the opened eye of Horus. Osiris is jubilant. Seth is vanquished.

"I, Thoth, in the dim mists of great Atlantis, conceived a plan to hold fast the initiatory energies of earth during the cycle of cleansing. Sacred Science was protected for those who would honor the Divine Heart and tread the path of enlightenment.

"I constructed a vessel to safeguard the eternal flame. The light never flickered through eons in darkness. The secrets were safe from the cleansing flood and chilling ice of purification. I proclaimed an aegis and it was so. The message has ever been declared in stone for those who passed the inner trials.

"Priestess of Light, destiny is upon thee. The resurrection of Osiris is at hand. Claim the joy that remembrance will bring. Come greet the dawn in ecstasy, daughter of Isis. Horus has risen before thee. Great Sirius rises with Ra."

Alex inhaled sharply, deeply, three times.

"What is happening now?" Miguel asked quietly.

Una's voice answered. "Master Thoth spoke from his dimension where he dwells in the stars of Arcturus. It is time for me to proceed on my way. The Priestess must heed his message."

"Thank you for your time with us, Una. Fix the state of peace and freedom you described in your mind. Bring that feeling back with you as the consciousness of Alexandria slowly returns to this time," Miguel instructed.

"I will count slowly from one to ten. You will return to ordinary consciousness one step at a time. When you awaken, you will feel rested and refreshed. You will remember everything you have experienced and nothing will disturb you. You will feel wonderful."

He counted to ten in a deliberate manner as she eased back to ordinary awareness. Alex climbed toward light on the surface of her consciousness as if rising from the bottom of the ocean.

"Open your eyes," Miguel directed.

Alex opened her eyes. Erik sat on the edge of the couch smiling. Tears filled his eyes. Miguel stood behind him, his face radiant. She sat up and hugged Erik fiercely. She felt a flow of energy between their hearts like liquid fire.

The three stared at one another in stunned silence. Alex exhaled. "I'm don't know who I am or which world is genuine. I'm straddling two realities."

"That is an accurate description. Time exists only in the third dimension. You've experienced that truth beyond an intellectual abstraction," Miguel said, handing Alex a glass of water.

"I've always taken past lives for granted, but I never thought about prior relationships. Una said Gran was my mother, and my mother was my child in that lifetime.

"I feel I reclaimed part of myself. Una was strong. She didn't have my weaknesses." Alex sat cross-legged on the sofa. "I want to hear her voice. I am blown away by Thoth. Did you get that on tape?" she asked, astounded.

"You sounded like another person when Una spoke," Erik said. "Your demeanor was different, almost imperial," he smiled. "The voice of Thoth felt like it was amplified through a speaker. It seemed impossible that sound could come from you."

"Don't be too hard on yourself," Miguel said. "Your ability to travel in the spirit realms is profound. Una's training as a priestess in that lifetime prepared her to live in alignment with truth. Her knowledge, which is your memory, is accessible to you now."

"When Una answered the questions, the information came as knowledge," Alex said. "It was like describing something from a history book."

Alex knitted her brow. "I need a phone."

"Now?" Erik asked in disbelief.

"I have to call a friend of Gran's, Aldora Blackstone.
I'm going to invite her to dinner. I didn't pay too much
attention before, but she and Gran talked about this stuff
all the time," Alex said. "They were in the A.R.E. together."

Erik handed her the portable phone, and she
punched in the numbers with her thumb. Aldora's raspy
voice echoed in the receiver, "Hello?"

"Aldora, this is Alexandria. How are you?"

"Alexandria, I feel guilty. I've meant to call you for
weeks. I don't know what happens to the time," Aldora
croaked.

Alex smiled. "Nonsense. I wouldn't bother you,
but I've had some unusual dreams recently along with an
amazing past life regression. I'd like your thoughts."

"That's up my alley all right," Aldora said. "I still
have some of your grandmother's books. Shall I bring them
by later?"

"Perfect. Some friends are visiting I want you to
meet. Come for dinner, and don't argue with me. Six
o'clock, Emma will do something wonderful," Alex said.

"Sounds like my kind of an outing, dear. I'll see you
after while," Aldora said.

Alex turned off the phone and looked at Miguel and
Erik. "I don't know if I can stand up." Erik helped her to
her feet. Alex lifted her chin.

"This priestess needs a nap before dinner," she said,
proceeding toward the spiral stairs. When she reached the
steps, she turned to see Miguel and Erik staring at each
other and laughing.

"Well?" she said to Erik, her eyes full of meaning.

"Duty calls," Erik said, nodding and winking at
Miguel.

Don Miguel guffawed.

15
Aldora

Emma opened the front door of the Stuart house dressed in a fresh blue dress and clean apron. Her gray hair was brushed tight in a prim bun. Alex and Crystal stood behind her. Fireflies twinkled in the twilight of a warm summer evening, and fading light cast long shadows across the darkening yard.

"Aldora, you're a sight for sore eyes. I've been meaning to call," Emma blurted.

Aldora Blackstone's infectious laugh echoed down the hall. "I don't know what happens to the time," she cackled. The two women embraced. Aldora hugged Alex. "You look like something is agreeing with you, young lady."

Alex blushed, and Emma smiled.

Aldora Blackstone was in her late seventies with coarse black, yellowish gray and white hair like the fur of a calico cat. The wiry multicolored mane grew around a full black face. Her generous mouth had permanent laugh lines. Brown eyes, the color of strong tea, were usually warm and stimulating like a cup of Earl Gray, but they could sting like iodine when she was provoked.

She looked equipped for any eventuality in khaki slacks, a plaid shirt and mountain hiking boots. Her shoulder bag resembled a backpack. A gold, Egyptian cartouche hung from a chain around her neck. She carried a shopping bag of books.

Crystal greeted Aldora enthusiastically. "Crystal, how are you, Doll-face? I've missed you too." Aldora rubbed behind her white ears and shook Crystal's head back and forth. She followed Emma into the library patting Crystal on the head and talking to her as she walked. She frowned when she entered the room.

"This place looks as sterile as a hospital. It's not natural," she huffed, "Your grandmother would be uneasy." She deposited the bag of books on the floor. "These are Rose's. I don't know where you'd like them under the circumstances."

Emma looked worried, and Alex stifled a giggle. Don Miguel and Erik stood to meet Gran's friend.

"We couldn't help it," Alex shrugged. "Someone broke into the library and emptied the roll top desk, secretary and book shelves onto the floor. We sorted through everything to see what was missing and organized papers for her will," Alex said, gesturing around the room.

Aldora looked hard at Alex while she spoke, as if assessing what she wasn't saying.

"I'd like you to meet two special people," Alex said, changing the subject. Don Miguel Piedra, this is Aldora Blackstone," Alex said. "You must know each other by reputation."

"Of course I've heard of you, Aldora. It is a pleasure to meet you," Miguel said. He extended his hand and leaned toward her. His black eyes shone. Small wrinkles at the corners of his eyes made his smile seem warmer.

Aldora nodded and smiled, and her eyes returned a wrm smile.

"Me too, Miguel. Rose was very fond of you; it's wonderful to meet you."

"This is Erik Anderson," Alex said, slipping her arm through his. "I met them both during a trip to Mexico," Alex laughed. "That sounds suspect, doesn't it?"

Aldora's expressive eyes appeared to double in size as she directed a look of approval toward Erik.

"This must be the something that's agreeing with you, child," Aldora said, sizing up Erik.

Alex fired a glance around the room that said, 'I dare any of you to mention my sex life.'

Erik's expression waxed cherubic. Don Miguel was as stone faced as Mount Rushmore. Emma vanished. Aldora didn't falter.

Sheba jumped onto the arm of the chair next to where Aldora stood. She meowed three times with inflections that sounded like words. Aldora laughed. "Who's this?" she asked looking into Sheba's eyes.

"Sheba," Erik said.

Aldora rubbed her head and scratched behind her ears. Sheba leaned against her and continued to make expressive sounds. "Sheba, Darling," Aldora said, "you might as well get used to it. Alexandria is going to be part of your life. Once things settle down, you'll get more attention than ever. I can tell you're capable of charm. Now's the time."

Sheba looked up at her, meowed in a subdued tone and jumped off the chair. "She actually talked to you," Erik said. "I've never seen her act like that."

"Cat's think I'm one of them. Has to do with an Egyptian lifetime," Aldora chuckled. "I hate preliminaries. Tell me about these dreams and regressions."

Alex laughed in spite of herself. "This dream had a different feeling, not the 'Alice in Wonderland' quality that most have. People and objects had more substance. I was inside the experience, not viewing it on a screen.

"Usually when I dream, impossible things happen," Alex said. "Cars fly, roads lead nowhere, scenes change suddenly, animals talk, dead people live, and it seems plausible. When you wake up, the dream seems 'curiouser and curiouser,' as Alice so aptly said."

Alex sat cross-legged on the love seat. She had changed into a tan skirt and peach cotton top with green turquoise and gold jewelry. The stones matched the color of her eyes which sparkled expressively while she related the story. Her red hair was partially pulled back from her face, revealing the chiseled lines of her jaw and cheekbones.

"I lived in a large seacoast city named Poseidia. The name of the island country was also Poseidia. I had a sense of a storm brewing, a crisis building."

"Did you say Poseidia?" Aldora asked.

"Yes. I was a priestess, and my father was High Priest. My name was Una, and he was called Iltar. The people in the dream looked like American Indians dressed in ancient Egyptian-type clothing."

"I see," Aldora said, nodding. Her face was intent, her brow knitted in concentration as if working out the solution to a puzzle. She grasped the arms of her chair.

"A high council was convened to decide the fate of a giant crystal known as the Tuaoi Stone. The crystal provided the major power source of the land, and there was a controversy about its use.

"Iltar, and another man named Hept-supht, who was Prime Regent, were at odds with an evil politician named Zared. He wanted to exploit the stone by tuning it to its highest setting. Many believed it was dangerous.

"The dream felt like a past life, so don Miguel suggested we try hypnotic regression. We taped it, and I'd like to play it for you.

"Are you kidding? Crank that puppy up," Aldora laughed.

Erik pushed the play button on the recorder. He sat back and held Alex's hand. As she listened to the tape, she experienced the feelings of surprise, love, loss and gratefulness that seemed disconnected while she was hypnotized. Tears filled her eyes.

Erik put his arm around her. His touch comforted her. The bond that existed between them in the past returned to conscious awareness.

When the tape was finished, Erik turned off the recorder. Alex looked at Aldora and waited for her to speak. Tears ran down Aldora's cheeks, and she pulled a handkerchief from the pocket of her plaid shirt.

"I'm overcome," Aldora said. "Are any of the names familiar to you?"

"Not consciously," Alex said.

Aldora sat back in her chair, brown eyes wide and intense. She ran her fingers through her calico hair and stared at Alex.

"This may be a bombshell. I don't want to rush this discussion, but it may save time for juicier topics. According to Edgar Cayce, Poseidia was the last vestige of once-glorious Atlantis. The original continent was broken up into islands in stages over thousands of years. The misuse of the Tuaoi Stone, the great crystal you described, caused the final destruction of the island about thirteen thousand years ago." Aldora paused.

"You're saying the information in my dream and regression matches Edgar Cayce? Alex asked, surprised.

"That's exactly what I'm saying."

Alex walked to the library window. She stood with arms folded and looked at the stars. Feeling the eyes of the others on her, she turned to look at Miguel, Erik and Aldora.

Aldora joined her at the window and put her arm around Alex's shoulders. "I've been in the A.R.E. forty years. Some members would give both arms and a leg for this experience."

"But what does it mean?" Alex asked, exasperated.

Aldora shook her head. "I'm not an expert on the Atlantis aspect of the work, but Edgar Cayce said America is the reincarnation of Atlantis. He said many souls from that time are reincarnated now. Those who caused devastation and those who worked for good have returned

to play out their dramas. Cayce said we'd face another
challenge to our survival and have another chance to get it
right."

"I hate to interrupt, but can you continue your
discussion over dinner?" Emma queried from the doorway.

"Your food is not an interruption," Erik laughed.

They adjourned to the dining room. Emma created
a Mexican theme for dinner. She chose a red table cloth
with napkins of assorted primary colors. Five candlesticks
of different sizes formed a centerpiece.

Heaping platters of vegetable enchiladas wrapped
in blue corn tortillas and covered with cream sauce were
surrounded by concentric circles of avocados, tomatoes,
cucumbers and pico de gallo. Generous bowls of black
beans, corn masa, guacamole and corn chips rounded out
the bounty.

Don Miguel assisted Aldora with her chair.

"Alexandria, did you know that your grandparents
had readings from Edgar Cayce?" Aldora asked.

"No," she said, surprised. "Gran never mentioned
it. When did that happen?"

"Around 1939, Duncan developed serious health
challenges from a crippling disease akin to arthritis. He
worked his way through a cavalcade of medical doctors.
Not one of them could help him.

"Rose heard of Cayce and some of the remarkable
successes his trance remedies had achieved. She convinced
Duncan to get a reading," Aldora laughed conspiratorially,
her face alight with humor.

"That was no small accomplishment. Duncan Stuart
was a show-me-the-evidence scientist. No hocus pocus.
She told him there was nothing to lose and everything to
gain. Eventually, he agreed."

Erik raised his eyebrows. "Trance remedies? What
happened during the readings?"

"Edgar Cayce was given a hypnotic suggestion,
generally by his wife in the earlier years, and he went into

a deep hypnotic trance. He never remembered a word he said when he came out of it."

Aldora laughed, an endearing cackling sound.

"We didn't have tape recorders in those days. A stenographer transcribed every word and typed them up. Mr. Cayce did fourteen thousand readings over the course of his lifetime. They're all in three-ring binders in the association's library in Virginia Beach. The binders take up two walls."

"Gran talked about the potential for healing humanity that his work represented. I wonder why she never told me about the readings," Alex frowned.

"Duncan's health reading indicated a weakness in his thyroid or pituitary and recommended a homeopathic remedy. Duncan was skeptical, but Rose had it made up anyway and cajoled him into trying it. His symptoms were completely gone in a month.

"Duncan ordered a health reading post haste for Rose. They had what they call life readings for both of them in 1940. Those readings talked about past lifetimes in Atlantis and Egypt.

"It was a stretch for their beliefs in those days, but after Duncan's healing, they were more receptive. His reading talked about crystals and power sources and said he was a priest who worked on the Tuaoi stone in Atlantis. Your grandfather was obsessed with energy sources. That reading was the beginning of his conscious fascination with crystals," Aldora nodded.

Alex and Erik looked at each other. "Energy," she said.

"Free energy," he said.

"Speaking of tape recorders, I read recently they put all those readings onto a little phonograph record that you play in a computer. All fourteen thousand readings fit on one little record. Land sakes alive, I can't fathom such a thing."

Erik laughed out loud with delight.

"How would we get the disk, Aldora?" Alex asked, nearly falling off the edge of her seat.

"I can give you the phone number in Virginia Beach. I read about it the monthly association magazine," Aldora said.

"You said everything was transcribed. Did the person who had the reading get a copy?" Alex asked, struggling to contain her excitement.

"Yes. I read your grandparents' readings. It's been fifty years, but I'll bet there here somewhere. Duncan never threw anything away. If he had anything to do with it, they were neatly cataloged and filed. Rose might have held onto them, but they would have been lost in one of her ubiquitous stacks," Aldora laughed. "Those two were mighty different."

Alex couldn't wait to get into the secret room and search the file cabinets. She felt she was finally on the trail of Gran's intention.

"I've got to find those readings," she said.

Aldora's laugh burst forth full force. "The game's afoot, Watson," she chortled.

"I like this lady," Erik grinned.

"It's been a full evening, and I'm an old woman," Aldora croaked, her warm eyes bright with mischief.

"You are barely in your prime," don Miguel smiled.

"I love that Latin charm. Help me up, Miguel."

He rose to assist Aldora.

"I need to talk to Emma before I leave. I'll let myself out. Keep me informed, young lady."

Alex gave her a big hug. "Thank you for coming. You've been an incredible help. I promise to call when we know something," Alex said.

"I'm certain our paths will cross again soon. Until then, vaya con Dios," Miguel said.

"That goes for me as well," Erik smiled.

"Elementary," Aldora quipped and walked down the hall toward the kitchen.

Alex, Erik and don Miguel looked at one another as Aldora Blackstone's sturdy footsteps echoed down the hall toward the kitchen. The grandfather clock ticked in the foyer and chimed the quarter hour.

"Is anticipation fatal?" Alex said, crossing her arms in frustration.

16
Readings

"I can't wait to search those files now that I know what might be there," Alex said. "I wouldn't mind if Emma or Aldora knew about the secret room, but I'm not sure it's safe. Shall we have brandy and cigars while we wait?"

"Smashing," Erik said, raising his chin and attempting to mimic a British accent.

Alex put her hands on her hips and rolled her eyes.

"Perhaps one can search, and two can stand guard," Miguel suggested. "If anyone returns while you're inside, we'll pretend you went to the bathroom, Alexandria."

Alex grinned. "Create a diversion if necessary. I'll report back if I find anything juicy."

Erik rubbed his hands together and blew into his palms as if he was about to roll dice. He put his ear to the bookcase, pretending to listen to tumblers in a lock.

"Erik!" Alex said, curling her hands into fists.

He smiled wickedly and pushed the place on the bookcase that looked like an ordinary whorl in the wood. The wall receded into the darkened room. Alex entered and tuned on the lights.

"Close the bookcase. I'll knock on the wall when I'm ready," she said.

Once the eerie ingress to the secret room became a blank wall, Alex headed straight for the antiquated army-green file cabinet. The heavy drawer resisted her attempt to open it and creaked as she wrenched it out of the ponderous steel cabinet.

Alex craned her neck to see inside the drawer. She combed through faded manila folders, eagerly scanning the curled and yellowed typewritten labels. Some came loose from the folders and fell to the floor.

The top drawer contained folders labeled atomic energy, crystals, energy sources, lasers, navigation, propulsion systems, solar power and ultra sound. She closed it and wrenched the second drawer open. About halfway back in the drawer she spotted a file whose tattered label read 'E.C. - 1940.'

She yanked the folder out of the drawer. Adrenalin rushed through her body, and her stomach churned acid. Her hands felt weak as her eyes drank in the half century old documents.

The folder contained five readings given to the Stuarts by Edgar Cayce. Each bore an identification number which rendered the document anonymous for research purposes and protected the identity of the client. There were the health and life readings for Duncan and Rose and a life reading for her father.

Alex was momentarily paralyzed. She held her breath. She wanted to read every word right there and controlled the urge with difficulty. She took another look in the drawer and noticed a plump folder behind the one she just removed. The label said 'E.C. Data.' Inside were correspondence and excerpts from readings. Alex removed the folders and pushed the drawer closed. It seemed like enough for the moment.

She felt a flash of anger. Why hadn't Gran told her any of this while she was alive? It would have made things a lot simpler and saved a lot of time and effort. Then she remembered Selig. There must be something potent in here.

Clutching the folders like priceless treasures, Alex went to the spot where the bookcase opened and tapped on the wall. Nothing happened. She wondered if they had company in the library or just didn't hear her rapping. She waited a few minutes and knocked harder. This time she heard the mechanism engage and watched as the wall opened, and the bookcase swung into the secret room.

She turned off the light and stepped into the library. Erik pushed the lock, and the entrance to Duncan's hermitage became an ordinary bookcase.

"Coast is clear, but we had a near miss when Aldora left," Erik said, waving her into the room. His eyes were eager. "Emma came to the doorway to see if we wanted anything just as you knocked the first time. Miguel and I acted as if we didn't hear anything. I held my breath and prayed you wouldn't knock louder. We told Emma we were fine, and she left."

"Find anything?" Miguel inquired, eying the file folders she carried.

Alex stood dazed in front of the bookcase. Her cheeks were flushed, and her palms felt clammy. She clutched the folders to her chest.

"Five readings, including a life reading for my dad. I also found this file called 'E.C. Data' which looks like correspondence between Grandpa and the A.R.E. He visited there at least once."

"Well?" Erik asked with impatience, motioning her to sit next to him on the love seat.

"Sorry," Alex apologized, sitting beside Erik. "It appears Grandpa requested additional information from the A.R.E. that pertained to his reading. There are excerpts from other readings, along with newspaper clippings and letters. Most of the information relates to crystals."

She opened the file that contained the Stuart's readings. "Let's divide and conquer. Erik, you take

Grandpa's readings, and don Miguel, here are Gran's. I want to read my father's."

Don Miguel assumed his regular seat in front of the fire place. Her eyes raced over the pages. Her silent reading was punctuated by nods and hums. Alex looked up when she finished.

"Listen to this," Erik said, leaning forward and placing his elbows on his knees. "This sounds like your regression; I'm paraphrasing from reading 813-1."

> "Before that we find the entity was in the Atlantean land, when there was much turmoil and strife from the rejections by many of those laws and tenets of One; when the upheavals began that made for the egress of many from that city of the Poseidon land - or in Poseidia.
>
> "The entity dwelt among those where there was the storage of the motivative forces in nature from the great crystals that so condensed the lights, the forms, the activities, as to guide not only the ship upon the bosom of the sea but in the air and in many of those now known conveniences of man as in the transmission of the body, as in the transmission of the voice, as in the recording of those activities in what is soon to become a practical thing in so creating the vibrations as to make for television -- as it is termed in the present."

"The syntax and phrasing are difficult to follow, especially in my second language, but the information is startling," Miguel said.

"This is about the Tuaoi stone," Alex said, eyes bright with excitement. "I can't believe I'm actually seeing this in print. My dream and regression experiences seemed real, but it's uncanny to have them corroborated this way." She shook her head as if to ward off doubt. The session conductor asked a question while Edgar Cayce was in trance," Alex continued.

"This is reading number 2072-10 from Grandpa's correspondence file."

> "Question: Going back to the Atlantean incarnation -- what was the Tuaoi stone? What shape or form was it?'
>
> "Answer: It was in the form of a six-sided figure, in which the light appeared as the means of communication between infinity and the finite; or the means whereby there were the communications with those forces from the outside. . .
>
> "It was set as a crystal. . . It was in those periods where there was the directing of aeroplanes, or means of travel; though these in that time would travel in the air or on the water, or under the water, just the same. Yet the force from which these were directed was in this central power station, or Tuaoi stone; which was as the beam upon which it acted. In the beginning it was the source from which there was the spiritual and mental contact."

Alex stopped reading and looked at Erik and Miguel. "The principle of ultra sound technology works by directing an electrical current through a crystal to create sound waves. Seems similar to the principle of the Tuaoi stone. Did Grandpa invent or remember?"

"When did Duncan die?" Erik asked.

"Nineteen-ninety. He collected his minerals and crystals, his rock pile Gran called it, over a forty year span," Alex said.

"What does Philip's life reading say?" Miguel asked.

Alex felt an inexplicable familiarity with the words of reading number 1215-4.

"The entity then was not only one skilled in aircraft and in water craft, as an aviator and a navigator, but made great strides in keeping in touch with other lands through the forces of nature in the experience.

"Hence those things of nature that have to do with communications become a part of the entity's experience. The imaginations of tales of travel, the activities, that have to do with strange lands, strange people, strange customs, become as a portion of the innate forces.

"And from those very influences there may arise later in this experience those activities that may bring again renown to the entity in this experience."

"That's remarkable, considering your father's distinguished career as a pilot during the Korean war," Miguel said. "Your grandparents said he was one of the youngest pilots in that conflict since most flew in World War II."

"Dad used to say all he ever wanted to do was fly. Funny that he became a Navy pilot, flying planes that took off and landed on ships. Aircraft and water craft, like the reading said. I still don't understand how he survived a war and crashed during a routine flight."

"There could be many reasons, Alexandria. Some karmic, some mundane. Perhaps it was just his time," Miguel said kindly.

"How old was your father at the time of the reading?" Erik asked.

Alex glanced at the date typed at the top of the page. "Ten," Alex replied. "I wonder if he knew about this reading? No one mentioned any of this to me until Aldora," she frowned. "How about Gran's reading, don Miguel?"

"According to this reading, number 3253-2, Rose also went to the Yucatan," Miguel said.

> "The entity was among those that chose to enter as leaders in what is now called Yucatan. The entity aided in establishing the temple through which there was hoped to be the appearance again of the children of the Law of One, as they listened to the oracles that came through the stones, the crystals, that were prepared for communications in what ye now know as radio. For ye may tune again to things afar off, if ye set thyself in order and attune to the infinite."

"The language is arduous, but the content is stunning," Erik sighed. "That also sounds like the regression." He leaned back on the love seat, put one foot across the opposite knee and cupped his hands around the back of his head.

"They read messages from the crystals; that reminds me of Chan Ka and the stones of light," Alex said.

"What do you make of it, Miguel?" Erik asked.

Miguel rose from his chair by the fireplace and walked to the leaded glass window. "If you accept the premise of this material, it certainly explains my connection with Rose and her love of Mexico."

He turned and looked out at Rose's garden.
Our collective past is coming into focus. I'm eager to see what we find in the computer disk when we search for the names. We need to know the purpose underlying these messages," Miguel said.

"The plot thickens?" Alex asked.

Erik groaned and rolled his eyes.

"Excuse me," Emma said from the hall.

"I don't mean to interrupt." Emma's body was illuminated from behind and her wispy hair looked other-worldly framed by the hall light. Her form darkened the doorway, and she seemed to speak from another dimension.

"Aldora phoned. A friend of hers has the computer disk you want and will loan it to you for a couple days. She'll drop by in the morning," Emma said.

"Fabulous," Alex said.

"I'll order the CD tomorrow. Meanwhile, we can start searching in the morning," Eric said, rubbing his hands together and raising his eyebrows.

"Shall we call it an evening?" Miguel said.

Alex looked at him. "That's not like you. Are you all right?"

"Just tired," Miguel smiled.

"I'm not. I feel like I'm on fire. I'll take the folders with me." She leaned over the table and scooped up the files like a college student hoisting textbooks on her way to the library. "I'll read this technical stuff as a sedative," Alex laughed.

"I'll see you both at breakfast," Miguel smiled.

Alex stopped by the kitchen to call Sheila and invite her to join the CD-ROM session. She procured a half-empty bottle of Chardonnay, collected two wine glasses from the cupboard and went upstairs to join Erik.

Once inside the bedroom, Alex removed her clothes and threw them in a pile on the floor in an uncharacteristic gesture. She donned an emerald-green night shirt. The silky fabric clung to the curves of her body. Unfastening her barrette, she shook her red hair loose.

Erik lost no time in stripping down to his cotton boxer shorts. He stretched out on the bed and smiled his approval from a supine position.

"You are so beautiful, like a precious emerald. Your night gown shimmers like the facets of a rare jewel."

"Aren't we poetic? Does an ulterior motive lie behind those fancy words, Mr. Anderson?" Alex smiled.

"As unbelievable as it seems, I think I'm too tired to make love," he said, rolling on his side to look at her. "Come here, and we'll discuss it."

She joined him on the bed. He kissed her. They embraced and tangled their limbs together. Erik ran his hands over the curves of her body and caressed her through the smooth fabric. She felt the telltale response as he pulled her to him.

"Pity you're too tired," she teased, kissing his neck. "I hoped you'd rise to the occasion. Shall we have wine instead? I couldn't carry the pretzels."

"Funny," he whispered into her ear, "All of a sudden, I'm feeling inspired."

They made love with the fervor of long separated lovers, each eager to please the other. Afterwards they held each other close. Alex felt love flowing between their open hearts. She looked at his face and ran her fingertips over his mouth. He kissed her palm. She touched his cheeks and eyes. She marveled at the magic of their union. Tenderness engulfed her, and she responded with a gentle kiss.

"Want some wine?" she asked.

"I'm spent," Erik sighed.

"I still can't relax. Will it bother you if I read? "

"I won't be aware of a thing. Tell me everything in the morning."

He punched the feather pillow to achieve the right shape and indentation for his head. Erik turned out the light on his side of the bed and settled into the covers with his back to her. In minutes she heard his rhythmic breathing and envied his ability to shut his brain off as quickly as his computer.

Alex poured a glass of wine and attacked the contents of the folders. She felt close to her father and grandparents as her eyes devoured the material. She couldn't imagine why Gran had never shared this secret and wondered if her mother knew.

The files contained numerous excerpts from other readings, mostly scientific in nature. All were numbered in the same way. Most applied to crystals. Some readings referred to television, then an infant technology, and hinted at other revolutionary discoveries on the horizon.

She learned that the Tuaoi Stone was originally under the control of the Atlantean priesthood and used to commune with what the sleeping Cayce called 'the forces of light' for spiritual guidance. She wondered who or what were the forces of light.

The priests focused the rays of the sun through the great stone to amplify solar energy. This allowed them to regenerate their bodies so they lived hundreds of years. Over a period of thousands of years, the stone's capability to capture and store solar energy was modified for more mundane purposes such as transportation to distant parts of the island realm.

The energy of the crystal, later called the Firestone, was directed through polished granite spheres positioned at remote locations, or on ships and planes, to capture the energy and distribute it locally.

As the fame of Atlantis spread, the capital city of Poseidia became a target for invasion. An aspect of the great crystal was modified to be used as a defensive weapon. Called the death ray, the device was similar to a laser. The weapon was meant to be used only as a last resort if the city was attacked.

The ultimate test of the weapon emerged in an unexpected manner. Outlying mountainous regions of the large island reported increasing attacks on wildlife and people from wild beasts roaming the wilderness areas.

A heated controversy arose between those who followed the spiritual leaders and those who were focused on materialistic values regarding the use of the death ray to eliminate the animals. Political turmoil resulted as the citizens aligned on opposing sides of the issue. Alex shivered as she remembered the council session in her dream and the powerful charisma of Zared as he swayed the Atlanteans to turn the crystal to a higher setting.

The stone was tuned to its highest setting and directed at the animals. The high frequencies resulted in earthquakes which caused the complete destruction of the land. Many people left before the earthquakes and underground volcanoes created the final cataclysm which caused the island paradise to sink beneath the ocean waves.

She thought of her grandfather's work on the atomic bomb. Unlimited free energy and weapons. Then she thought of Selig. Was Selig after weapon technology?

When she finished the last page, she glanced at the red numbers of the digital clock. Two:twenty. Her head ached. She crawled out of bed to take some pain medication and realized she was stiff. She was so absorbed she hadn't moved the entire time she was reading. Alex swallowed the pills with a glass of water and stretched her muscles in exaggerated feline movements. She turned off her table lamp and nestled into Erik's back, putting her arm around his waist. She smiled as he responded to her touch with a soft moan. Alex dozed off as the pain in her head subsided.

17
Aris

High Priestess Aris approached the Temple of Healing. The pyramidal shape eclipsed the lush grove of palm trees which grew along the river behind the building. Chilly morning air was filled with cries of heron eager for breakfast. The compelling aroma of baking bread escaped from brick ovens, and her stomach grumbled. She would deal with her hunger later.

Aris squinted as she gazed east. The brilliant representative of the great god Ra climbed from the horizon heralding a new day. In two weeks the festival of the beneficent star Sirius would celebrate her rising with Ra on the most propitious day of the year. Droves of people requested rites of purification in preparation for the new year celebration.

The priestess sighed, weary from many long days of healing work in the temple. Today another endless stream of supplicants would present themselves. She prayed that an early start might give her an advantage. Aris entered the empty temple and breathed deeply as the blessed stillness caressed her.

The healing temple culminated preparatory work in six initiatory temples flanking the Nile from south to north. Each temple focused on one spiritual center in the body and the work of unfoldment required to raise the light along the spine. Fiery energy lay coiled like a slumbering serpent at the base of the spine, waiting to emerge from latency.

Initiates worked through expressions of survival, procreation, power, love, speech, wisdom and immortality. The current of the longest river in the world flowed south to north as the energy of enlightenment was intended to do once the Kundalini force awakened in the body.

Aris walked around the circular hall that surrounded the dome of the central healing chamber, passing seven stations which encircled the main chamber. Fine beeswax candles, cradled by brass sconces and covered with translucent alabaster globes, hung on the wall outside the seven rooms. Seven hallways bordered the rooms like spokes on a wheel and opened to the outside to admit light.

Within the seven rooms around the circle, the initiates fine-tuned the energies they mastered in the preparatory temples and completed advanced training for the priesthood. Seven symbols carved into the stone above each doorway represented the work of that stage: a red coiled serpent, orange cockerel, yellow scarab beetle, green equal armed cross, blue gateway, violet hawk with wings spread, and over the seventh doorway was the brilliant white crown of mastery.

Each room's furnishings corresponded to the color and energy of the center to be aligned. Corresponding gems, incense and metals were utilized to intensify a particular vibration. Gold jars inlaid with precious gems and metals, bowls of precious oils, vials of healing flower essences and carved alabaster lamps graced the initiatory chambers.

Aris recalled her rigorous training to be a priestess in this sacred healing temple. Her progression through the initiatory rites of purification and consecration was swift, and she was installed as High Priestess at the young age of thirty-eight summers.

The priestess removed clean cotton towels from storage and spread a fresh cloth of pure white linen on the large rectangular altar in the central chamber. Carved from a single block of pink granite, the altar was free of ornamentation but polished to a high gloss.

She organized incense and bowls of fragrant oils, arranging crystals and sacred gem stones on the altar cloth around them. The stones were used to focus sunlight during the rituals to amplify healing energies.

Aris configured a seven-pointed star of candles in the colors of the rainbow. When she was satisfied, she lighted a globule of frankincense resin; smoky aroma filled the sacred space.

The High Priestess tied back woven wool rugs which covered the windows during the night. Each rug was a work of art, hand loomed from threads of vivid colors depicting scenes from temple life. White gauze curtains, covering the windows underneath, responded to the chill morning breeze that gained admittance to the temple. The cool air drifted through the openings and caused graceful plumes of white incense to dance around the room.

Although temple attendants would arrive soon to perform the routine tasks, the High Priestess carried clean towels into the baths. She experienced these tasks as a meditation. She removed jars of bath oils and cleansing herbs from overnight storage and poured them into alabaster bowls in the bathing rooms. Attendants would light fragrant oil lamps and place fresh flowers from the garden into glazed pottery vases.

They would stoke the fires, banked just hours ago when laundry workers left, adding dung and coals. Water for tea and bathing flowed into the temple through masonry viaducts from nearby irrigation canals. Ceramic pots of water would soon warm on the fire.

Aris finished her preparations in time to have tea. She walked out to the temple garden to gather additional herbs and flowers and plucked sprigs of fresh mint, chamomile and lemon grass. She selected delicate lotus and hyacinth blossoms from the pool to place on the altar.

She admired the varieties of cactus and touched them lovingly. Some were small and fragile; others were spiked and forbidding. Delicate flowers of brilliant orange, fuschia and gold burst from spiny crevices. Other plants crawled along the ground like beached sea serpents. Birds of paradise, calla lilies and bromeliads bloomed. The magical white blossoms of the night flowering cactus, which opened only in moonlight or starlight, had withdrawn for the day.

Three cheerful temple cats greeted her. They enjoyed regal status as sacred symbols and kept the temple free of bothersome rodents. The cats followed her into the kitchen, and she gave them water while she waited for hers to boil. When she poured boiling liquid over the fresh herbs, their wonderful scent was released. Closing her eyes, she inhaled their essence.

The High Priestess returned to the garden and sat under a large date palm, its green fronds framed by an azure sky. She sipped tea and nibbled bread and honey.

When her mug was empty, the priestess went to pay homage at the shrine of eternal fire burning in the holy of holies at the heart of the temple. Aris cleansed and anointed herself and donned ritual robes and copper breast plate. The ceremonial piece was formed of three pyramids. Two white crystalline triangles pointed downward and looked like wings beside the green triangle pointing upward in the center.

She wore the diadem of her personal emblem on her forehead; a seven pointed star, symbolizing the seven spiritual centers. Each point of the star was set with a gem stone in one of the seven colors of the rainbow. Ruby, amber, topaz, peridot, lapis, indigo tourmaline and amethyst. A clear quartz crystal shone from the center of the star.

Aris left the preparatory alcove to join the other priests and priestesses in meditation. The High Priestess led the small group in prayers of invocation. She read a Hymn to Hathor from The Book of Coming Forth by Day.

"Blue-lidded daughter of dawn, golden lady of the mountains, carrier of her father's wisdom, let an old man rest in your arms. Let him look last on love's face, breathing love's breath. I live in light a million years. The sun rises or sets now--it matters not. Here is ecstasy in death and certainty in life. We are gods in the body of god, truth and love are our destinies. Go then and make of the world something beautiful, set up a light in the darkness."

She rose and entered the central healing room. The chamber's circular shape represented a sphere of pure white light whose protective essence would envelop the healers and the one being healed. The center of the ceiling was a retractable dome like an astronomical observatory. When the cover was opened, sunlight shone through a large crystal onto the table beneath.

White light, refracted by the crystal, was transformed into the seven hues of the visible spectrum. A rainbow enveloped the person's body with red at the head and violet at the feet.

The first supplicant of the day lay on the healing table. A white linen robe of the finest cotton covered a disfigured body. Much of the work of the temple dealt with these tragic beings, angelic spirits who watched the earth with fascination and desire for physical sensation.

These souls projected curious thoughts into materiality, inhabiting the bodies of plants and animals. In the beginning, they were able to move between the physical dimension and the unseen realms with ease.

They grew careless, driven by desire, and became imprisoned in the physical forms. Many of these unfortunate souls sought release from their physical chains. Some had tails, feathers, or claws, incongruous mixtures of human and animal characteristics.

To prepare for today's ceremony, the candidate fasted three days, eating nothing and drinking only fresh water and teas of medicinal herbs to cleanse the system. Temple attendants treated each supplicant with love and respect regardless of appearance. They were bathed and massaged with fragrant healing oils and ointments to facilitate the removal of poisons from muscles and organs.

Incense and candles burned. Three healers took their positions and formed a triangle. The High Priestess stood at the head. She selected gemstones according to their color and energy properties and placed them on the patient's body over areas which needed strengthening and purification. Gently, she placed rose quartz over the heart, malachite on the throat, amethyst on the eyes, dark lapis over the joints and a white crystal on the brow.

A temple musician struck gongs and a lyre tuned to the frequencies of colors and energy centers in the body. The healers chanted tones corresponding to the seven energy centers. They looked at the color which aligned with that center, and the light of the Kundalini fire was raised along the spine.

The healers focused their minds to draw energy from the sun through the great crystal. They acted as transformers and modified the amplified solar power like lightning rods before the energy entered the one on the table.

The rainbow of light shimmered with power as the potent energy in the room increased. The gems on the patient's body seemed on fire from within as the stones worked in conjunction with the refracted light of the crystal, harmonizing and strengthening the energy currents.

When the High Priestess signaled the conclusion of the healing session, grateful tears flowed from the sightless eyes of the supplicant. His spine was straightened, and his skin looked more natural. He was still blind, but the opaque material which covered his eyes had cleared.

"Your desire for light was strong," the Priestess said.

The man placed his palms together and bowed.

She touched his arm, and he eagerly clasped her hands. He looked up toward the light as tears ran down his cheeks. The Priestess smiled; humble tears glistened in her eyes. Such moments made the work worthwhile.

At the end of the long procession of suffering people, the priestess left the pyramid of healing and emerged into a darkening evening. Her eyes were drawn up to a sky full of stars. She hailed Orion and his companion, wondrous Sirius, brightest star in heaven and great benefactor of the land of Khem. Her heart lifted. She smiled and whispered a prayer of gratitude.

Aris gazed at the Lyre, her favorite constellation, and at bluish white Vega, the star which anchored the poles of the earth. Orange Arcturus twinkled from its place in the Herdsman. She admired the imposing form of the Dragon.

Her consciousness shifted, and she was startled as an unseen force lifted her from the ground. The priestess rose into a star-studded night until she was above the earth. The circle of the zodiac was visible around her. The star pictures were transformed into living beings.

Recognizing them, she saluted each in turn. She smiled at the Virgin and gazed past her to the Scales. She greeted the forbidding looking Scorpion. The ominous form of giant Serpent Bearer had one foot in the circle and the other on the Scorpion's claw. Towering above the circle, the patron of healers moved to stand between Scorpion and Archer. The other constellations shifted as their starry companion took a more central role on the belt of the ecliptic.

Leviathan serpents of stars writhed in the strong arms of Imhotep, patron of healers. Aris was transfixed as Serpent Bearer closed his eyes, and the giant snakes coiled around him. His body became the central pillar of a fiery caduces.

The priestess shielded her eyes from the blinding light. When she looked again, she stood in front of the Pyramid. She turned to face the river. The ground in front of the great lion was open, and workers filled underground chambers with artifacts and tablets. They prepared for the dedication of the master initiation temple and the final sealing of the Hall of Records.

Her own resting place was being prepared in an underground chamber. Several honored individuals would be entombed in burial chambers with the records and artifacts.

Aris held a star clock she designed to include with the other buried treasures. Similar to a sun dial, the clock was divided into sections for the constellations of the ecliptic. Serpent Bearer stood between the Scorpion and the Archer in the circle.

She designed a carving of two star maps with her own likeness between them. One chart showed the night sky in her time. The other showed the positions of the stars thirteen thousand years in the future. The coded message of the monuments was written in stone, stars and legends.

Aris knew that far into the future, on the other side of the aeonian darkness, she would once again hold the star clock, gaze upon her own ancient remains and remember this time.

Storm clouds approached from the west, harbingers of the long night. As a wall of gloom gathered on the plateau, a shadow crossed the Lion's face. Two huge doors slammed shut over the storage chambers.

Serpent Bearer's incandescent form burned within the white-hot flames of the caduces. His voice reached her from the fire.

"As the mill of heaven grinds the wheel of cosmic ages, light will slumber through the cycle of darkness. At the appointed time, dawn will bring the morning of remembrance, and a new humanity will be born. You must carry these memories in your heart."

He was consumed in the flames.

"Don't leave!" she wailed. Her cry stretched to the end of the galaxy.

18
CD-ROM

Alexandria became aware of a dim voice calling from a vast distance across light years. She couldn't make out the words. She focused to comprehend the meaning, but it was an immense effort to respond. Someone shook her arm.

"Alex, wake up. You're crying in your sleep."

She felt another nudge. Alexandria opened her eyes, feeling disoriented. Tears rolled down her face.

"Were you having a nightmare?" Erik asked.

"Another unbelievable dream," she said, sitting up in bed and blinking. Alex rubbed the spot between her eyes with her thumb and index finger, trying to clear her mind. She snatched a tissue from the bedside table and blew her nose.

"This was Egypt, a long time ago," she said.

"Who were you talking to?" Erik asked.

"A constellation came to life like Frosty the Snowman," she said with a sardonic grimace. Erik's confused look made her smile. "Forgive me. I need to start at the beginning. Before I do that, I want to write the dream down to etch the details in my brain. I'll read the dream at breakfast so Miguel, Aldora and Sheila can hear too."

"Fair enough. I'll bring coffee after I shower," Erik smiled.

"I'll hurry," she said.

Alex recorded the details of her dream in a spiral notebook. The first part of the experience felt real, but the second part seemed surreal. She knew it was significant but couldn't decipher the meaning. The image of the Serpent Bearer was burned into her awareness as if she'd been marked with a branding iron. She felt an excruciating sense of loss, as if everything that mattered had been buried in those storage chambers.

Erik brought coffee and handed her the mug. She drank the hot liquid as she poured the words of her dream onto paper. When she finished, she showered and dressed in a pastel print sun dress. She twisted her wet hair like a rope and secured it to the top of her head with a barrette.

The doorbell rang as Alex galloped down the spiral stairs two at a time. "Coming," she shouted. Aldora and Sheila stood on the porch. "I had another dream," she announced without prelude and hugged them. "I'll read it at breakfast."

Aldora's tricolor hair was awry. She wore wrinkled khaki walking shorts and an oversized white camp shirt. Sheila's straight black hair was brushed back in a barrette. She wore a long red dress and big silver earrings.

The three women walked into the kitchen and found Erik setting up his computer on the round wooden table. Don Miguel fed Sheba, and Crystal watched Erik with interest.

"Who wants coffee?" Alex asked.

Four hands went up like eager school children.

Alex poured coffee into ceramic mugs and gobbled raspberry scones, washing them down with cold milk. Fortified, she washed her hands and poured another mug of coffee.

Alex stood in front of the sink, framed by a halo of sunlight. Her friends sat around the table in silence. She recounted every detail of her dream experience, glancing up when she finished to assess their reactions.

"I've studied dream symbols for years," Aldora said. "That was no ordinary dream. The Una dream was certainly Atlantis. This sounds like a subsequent lifetime in Egypt, combined with a prophecy.

"The Cayce information refers to a Hall of Records underneath Giza," Aldora continued.

"I didn't know that," Alex said.

"Cayce said information and artifacts are buried under the Sphinx. I didn't realize people might be buried there," Aldora said in a breathless tone.

"The legend of a Hall of Records exists in several mystery schools," Miguel observed, black eyes dancing. "Khem is the ancient name of Egypt. The Khema were the Pleiades."

"I read an article about Serpent Bearer in an astrology magazine recently," Sheila said. "Ophiuchus, Greek for Serpent Bearer, is a thirteenth zodiac sign reaching into the ecliptic between Scorpio and Sagittarius, the Scorpion and the Archer. I'll have to find that issue. You've plugged into something here, Sweetie. This is cutting edge stuff."

"The Greeks borrowed Asklepios from the great Egyptian healer Imhotep, Alex. The cult of Asklepios was always connected with serpents. Asklepios was such a great healer, his patients did not die. When Asklepios tried to revive Orion from a fatal scorpion sting, Hades convinced Zeus to kill him. He didn't like the implications of an empty underworld."

"There's Orion again," Alex said.

"Hermes gave Asklepios the caduces in recognition of his skill," Miguel continued. " Asklepios, or Imhotep, was placed in the sky as a constellation to honor his achievements. He stands next to the Scorpion, on the opposite side of the sky from Orion, to prevent further trouble. The two constellations are never visible at the same time."

"In your dream, you said Vega anchored the poles of the earth," Erik said. "Vega was the pole star twelve thousand years ago."

"Really?" Alex asked in disbelief. She walked to the table and sat in a wooden chair.

Erik nodded. "I have some nifty astronomy software that moves the stars backward and forward in time. Robert Bauval, who realized the relationship between the pyramids and the belt of Orion, uses the program. Bauval, and his co-author, Graham Hancock, discovered that the Giza monuments mark a precise moment in time.

"On the spring equinox sunrise in 10,500 BC, the three pyramids of Giza perfectly mirrored the three stars in Orion's belt. Also at that epoch, during the astrological age of Leo, the Sphinx looked due east at the sign Leo. John West believes the Sphinx was originally a lion," Erik said.

"According to Edgar Cayce, the great pyramid was built between 10,400 BC and 10,300 BC," Aldora said.

"If the Sphinx looks due east at the equinox, and he saw a lion in the sky during the age of Leo, he will see the Water Bearer rise at the dawn of the age of Aquarius," Sheila said.

"Those two constellations are one hundred eighty degrees opposite each other. If Orion was on the southern horizon in 10,500, your friend the Serpent Bearer would be north," Sheila continued. "Orion is with Taurus, the bull. The four points of the astrological fixed cross."

"Why go to all that trouble?" Alex asked. "What's the message?"

"As I have said before, all the cultures I have studied use the movements of the stars and planets to create a reference point, a star clock, if you will," Miguel said. "Star pictures are turned into creatures and planets into gods. Stories are created and remembered through myth and legend."

"Wait a minute," Aldora said. "The lion, bull, man and eagle. Aren't those like the animals from Ezekiel's vision in the Bible?"

They all stared at her. "You're saying there's a prophecy?" Alex asked.

"Many traditions predicted the time period circa two thousand AD would be paramount," Miguel said. "The fifth sun of the Aztec calendar, the Hindu Kali Yuga and the close of the age of Pisces conjoin. Is it possible the constellation of the Serpent Bearer returning to the zodiac could signal the revelation of hidden knowledge, the return of the Christ to the twelve disciples?"

"If Giza is a coded astronomical message, a star clock, something should trigger the alarm," Alex said, shaking her head.

"Let's fire up the CD and see what we can find in the readings," Erik suggested. "We can check out SkyGlobe later."

Donning his reading glasses, Erik installed the program from the floppy disk onto his laptop hard drive to run the CD-ROM.

Alex loved the professorial look his glasses gave him. She wanted to ruffle his hair but scooted a chair next to him instead. She wanted to see everything first-hand.

The others gathered around the table. When Erik inserted the CD, the computer whirred and clicked as the processor read the disk. The main screen came up, and the word SONAR flashed on the screen.

"This is slick," he said, "Okay folks, we're live. Give me a word or phrase to search."

"Atlantis," Alex said.

Erik typed Atlantis on the keyboard. The computer continued to hum and click as it searched. A dialog box appeared on the screen showing the search process. After a few seconds, another box appeared.

"Atlantis, thirteen hundred ninety three occurrences in nine hundred seventy three documents," Erik laughed.

"Whoa," Alex giggled.

"We could spend hours just looking at the Atlantis references," Sheila said.

"Oh my," Aldora said. "I had no idea there were that many. No wonder people marvel at the internal consistency of the information. Considering the number of references and the time span they were given, it's unbelievable."

"Try Poseidia," Miguel suggested.

Erik keyed in the word, and a few moments later the screen reported sixty-two occurrences in fifty documents.

"How about Yucatan?" Alex asked.

"One hundred forty six occurrences in one hundred twenty four documents," Erik reported.

"This could take forever. Try something more selective," Sheila suggested.

"How about the Tuaoi stone?" Aldora asked.

Erik typed the words.

SONAR reported fifteen references in seven documents. Alex scanned the references as they appeared in sequence on the screen. "These are all in Grandpa's files I read last night. Cayce called the crystal a Firestone. He described the stone as a large cylindrical opalescent crystal with six facets used in the Atlantean sacred temple.

"The crystal was an unlimited energy source. Eventually they used the power as a weapon. They set the frequency too high which caused massive earthquakes. What I read was very similar to my dream about Atlantis."

"What next?" Erik asked.

"Shall we try 'Iltar'?" Miguel asked. "I am curious to see if the High Priest is there."

"Four references in one document, reading number 5750-001" Erik said. "That's promising. Let's have a look."

The name Iltar appeared highlighted in a sentence. Erik scanned the screen. "Let me print this. I think Miguel should read it."

Three sheets emerged from the printer. Erik handed them to Miguel, and his bright eyes raced over the pages. His clear and beautiful voice filled the room.

'Then, with the leavings of the civilization in Atlantis (in Poseidia, more specific) Iltar - with a group of followers that had been of the household of Atlan, the followers of the worship of the One, with some ten individuals - left this land of Poseidia and came westward, entering what would now be a portion of Yucatan. And there began, with the activities of the peoples there, the development into a civilization that rose much in the same manner as that which had been in the Atlantean land.'

Alex put her coffee mug on the table and gaped at don Miguel. "I have chills," she said. "Don Miguel, I believe you were Iltar. I can almost see it, like my dream and regression. What else does it say?"

"The first temples that were erected by Iltar and his followers were destroyed at the period of change physically in the contours of the land. That now being found, and a portion already discovered that has laid in waste for many centuries, was then a combination of those peoples from Mu, Oz, and Atlantis. . .

"In which pyramid or temple are the records mentioned in the readings given through this channel on Atlantis, in April 1932?

"As given, that temple was destroyed at the time there was the last destruction in Atlantis. Yet as time draws nigh when

changes are to come about, there may be the
opening of those three places where the
records are one, to those that are the initiates
in the knowledge of the One God.

"The temple by Iltar will then rise
again. Also there will be the opening of the
temple or hall of records in Egypt, and those
records that were put into the heart of the
Atlantean land may also be found there - that
have been kept, for those that are of that
group. The records are one!'

Don Miguel's silver and black head bowed. He held
the papers in his hands and continued to stare at the printed
words. His brow furrowed, and his lips pursed. He seemed
deep in thought, transported to another time.

"Imagine, reading about your own past life," Aldora
said.

"We're supposed to find the records," Alex said with
an intense shiver of recognition.

"We were there when they were buried. This is our
purpose."

The group sat in stunned silence as the implications
of Alex's revelation sank in. Their reverie was shattered by
pounding at the front door.

Crystal growled in a menacing tone and raced past
Alex who headed toward the front of the house. The
animal's behavior alarmed Alex. She opened the front door
to see Officer O'Reilly accompanied by Rudolph Selig and
another police officer. She noticed Selig's obsessive
grooming, as if extreme fastidiousness would free him from
moral degradation.

"Sorry to trouble you, Miss Stuart, but we have a
search warrant," O'Reilly said, cocking his head toward
Selig with unconcealed distaste.

"I'll oversee the search. We'll do our best not to
disrupt your house."

Alex accepted the envelope O'Reilly handed her. Removing the thick document, she unfolded the pages and pretended to read the warrant. The words blurred.

"I told you earlier, this is a waste of time. My Grandmother donated everything to the university," Alex said with forced bravado, silently blessing Grandpa's foresight for creating the secret room.

Selig glared at Alex. Malice dripped like icicles from frigid, beady eyes. Inwardly she recoiled, but she held his gaze.

"It's futile to resist, Miss Stuart."

"Wait out here, Selig," O'Reilly ordered. "We'll be careful, Miss Stuart."

Selig waited on the porch. He looked like a greedy vulture perched on a tree branch, waiting for prey to become carrion. He didn't have the courage to hunt and kill himself. He left the dirty work for others so his talon-like fingernails remained pristine.

Crystal stood inside the door, eyes riveted on Selig. A low growl echoed in her throat. Alex stood beside her. Selig lit a pencil thin cigar and placed his lips around its plastic tip.

"Your dog is an excellent judge of character," O'Reilly said, scowling. Alex looked at O'Reilly. She was glad he was there.

She was sure the police could hear the thunder of her heart as they searched the house. She stopped breathing while they searched the library, terrified they would accidentally trip the mechanism to the secret room.

Selig was desperate for Grandpa's files, that was clear. Alex felt her stomach turn as she recalled the Cayce files she'd taken upstairs last night. She breathed a silent prayer of thanks that she stuffed them under the bedspread so Emma wouldn't notice.

Don Miguel joined Alex and Crystal at the door.

"Don't let him upset you," Miguel said, placing his strong arm around her shoulder. She relaxed a little. Miguel moved behind her and rubbed the muscles in her neck and shoulders with his powerful hands. She hadn't realized she was so tense.

"Call upon your strength, Alexandria. Fill your being with power. Selig merely acts out his role in this drama. Don't be too concerned," Miguel said.

Alex breathed deeply and felt a shift like an opening. She sensed an overshadowing presence. Calmness, peace and strength washed into her consciousness. Crystal relaxed but did not reduce her vigilance. The search lasted forty-five minutes but seemed like hours to Alex.

"We're finished," O'Reilly said, walking toward the front door. "We didn't find anything resembling the material he's looking for. Mr. Anderson said the computer belongs to him."

Alex nodded. "I don't think my grandfather computerized anything."

"Hello, Miss Goldwoman," O'Reilly said as Sheila joined them in the foyer.

"Hello yourself, O'Reilly," Sheila smiled. Miguel's eyebrows furrowed in amused curiosity.

O'Reilly opened the leaded glass door.

"What did you find?" Selig demanded.

"Nothing," O'Reilly said.

"This is not over, Miss Stuart," Selig said. Anger revealed a slight German accent.

"I know you have the records in your possession. I can feel it. If necessary, I'll confiscate the contents of this library and tear each book apart page by page until I find what I'm looking for."

Alex felt like he'd thrown acid in her face. "I told you, my grandmother got rid of everything," she lied.

Selig turned his venomous stare toward Miguel. "Duncan ventured far afield. He had difficulty discerning significance and had a strange obsession with dusty relics, human and otherwise." He directed a look of loathing toward Miguel.

"That's enough," O'Reilly ordered. "We'll be in touch if there's anything else, Miss Stuart. Thanks for your cooperation." He pulled the big door shut as he left.

"I will make you a cup of strong herb tea," Miguel said.

"Who was that nasty looking man?" Aldora wanted to know when they walked into the kitchen. "There's something familiar and decidedly unpleasant about him. I think I've seen him at an A.R.E. event."

"I can't believe that," Alex said, as she collapsed into a chair. "His name is Rudolph Selig. He claims rights to Grandpa's research data. There was no mention of him in the will, but he trumped up a phony document and managed to get a search warrant." She felt nauseated.

"This may sound crazy, but he reminds me of Zared in the Atlantis dream," Alex said. "You said the good guys and the bad guys are back, Aldora."

"The plot thickens?" Miguel said.

They all laughed.

"Let's get back to work," Alex sighed. "I want to get my mind off that awful man. My goose bumps have goose bumps."

"Listen to this," Erik said, looking at the screen, "from reading 486-1."

> "Hence we find the entity then, Ax-Ten-tna, as would be said in the present, was the first to set the records that are yet to be discovered, or yet to be had of those activities in the Atlantean land, and for the preservation of the data, that as yet to be found from the chambers of the way between the Sphinx and the pyramid of records."

Try searching the word 'capstone,'" Alex said.

Erik keyed in the word. When the first of four references came up, he scanned reading 440-5.

"This is interesting.," he said.

"As to describing the manner of construction of the stone, we find it was a large cylindrical glass (as would be termed today), cut with facets in such a manner that the capstone on top of same made for the centralizing of the power or force that concentrated between the end of the cylinder and the capstone itself.

As indicated, [See 996-12] the records of the manners of construction of same are in three places in the earth, as it stands today: In the sunken portions of Atlantis, or Poseidia, where a portion of the temples may yet be discovered. . . under the slime of ages of sea water -- near what is known as Bimini, off the coast of Florida. And in the temple records that were in Egypt, where the entity later acted in cooperation with others in preserving the records that came from the land where these had been kept. Also the records that were carried to what is now Yucatan in America where these stones (that they know so little about) are now during the last few months - being uncovered."

"What's the date of that reading?" Sheila asked.

"December 20, 1933," Alex sighed.

"Selig could know about this if he spent time with Duncan. If he hung around the A.R.E., he knows what's supposed to be buried there," Sheila said.

"Knowledge of the crystal as a power source is buried with the records," Erik said, removing his glasses and rubbing his temples.

"A volatile irony to be sure, knowledge of free energy buried in the middle east."

"Free unlimited energy and powerful weaponry, a deadly combination in the wrong hands," Alex said.

"Enough to kill for?" Aldora asked.

"Has anyone searched in Bimini or Mexico?" Miguel asked.

"I think there have been expeditions to Bimini. I don't know if anything was found. I don't know about Mexico," Aldora said.

"What was that other name? Hep something?" Erik asked.

"H-e-p-t-s-u-p-h-t," Alex spelled.

"Fifteen references in six documents." Erik printed the Hept-supht references, and Alex read the materials.

"There's a fair amount about the construction of the Great Pyramid," she said, "and more about the records. The syntax is more unwieldy than usual."

"God, no," Sheila said.

Erik smiled and read from number 378-16.

"In the record chambers there were more ceremonies than in calling the peoples at the finishing of that called the pyramid. For, here those that were trained in the Temple of Sacrifice as well as in the Temple Beautiful were about the sealing of the record chambers. For, these were to be kept as had been given by the priests in Atlantis or Poseidia (Temple), when these records of the race, of the developments, of the laws pertaining to One were put in their chambers and to be opened only when there was the returning of those into materiality, or to earth's experience, when the change was imminent in the earth; which change, we see, begins in '58 and ends with the changes wrought in the upheavals and the shifting of the poles, as begins then the reign in '98, as

time is counted in the present, of those
influences that have been given by many in
the records that have been kept by those
sojourners in this land of the Semitic
peoples.'"

"It is worse," Sheila said.
"Patience," Erik said, raising his index finger.
"Listen to this question."

"Give in detail what the sealed room
contains?

"Answer: A record of Atlantis from
the beginnings of those periods when the
Spirit took form or began the encasements
in that land, and the developments of the
peoples throughout their sojourn, with the
record of the first destruction and the changes
that took place in the land, with the record of
the soujournings of the peoples to the varied
activities in other lands, and a record of the
meetings of all the nations or lands for the
activities in the destructions that became
necessary with the final destruction of
Atlantis and the buildings of the pyramid of
initiation, with who, what, where, would
come the opening of the records that are as
copies from the sunken Atlantis; for with the
change, it must rise (the temple) again.
"This in position lies, as the sun rises
from the waters, the line of the shadow or
light falls between the paws of the Sphinx,
that was later set as the sentinel or guard,
and which may not be entered from the
connecting chambers from the Sphinx's right
paw until the time has been fulfilled when
the changes must be active in this sphere of

man's experience. Between then the Sphinx
and the river . . .

"Am I the one to receive directions as
to where the sealed room is and how to find
it?

"Answer: One of the two. Two, with
a guide. Hept- supht, El-ka, and Atlan. These
will appear.'

"Bloody hard to listen to," Sheila said, exhaling.

"The same records in three places," Alex said,
aquamarine eyes on fire. "A connecting chamber from the
Sphinx's right paw. We know Hept-supht connected with
Cayce when he was alive. Who are El-Ka and Atlan? Didn't
the Iltar reading talk about the house of Atlan?"

"Alexandria," Miguel said, grasping her hand, "if
your dream is correct, your former incarnation as High
Priestess lies buried in the Record Chamber in Egypt."

"But the man who was Hept-supht died in nineteen
fifty- four," Alex said.

"Souls can assist from other dimensions," Miguel
said.

"We might find the star clock you described," Erik
said, whistling through his teeth.

"The star charts you described would prove their
antiquity," Sheila said.

"We are at the center of the fulfillment of the
prophecy," Aldora said in awe.

"Try record chamber," Alex said, consumed by the
need for answers.

"Here's a good one," Erik said. "reading number
5748-6."

"With the storehouse, or record house
where the records are still to be uncovered,
there is a chamber or passage from the right
forepaw to this entrance of the record

chamber, or record tomb. This may not be entered without an understanding, for those that were left as guards may not be passed until after a period of their regeneration in the Mount, or the fifth root race begins."

"Those who were left as guards," Alex said, frowning.

"What's the fifth root race?" Erik asked.

"The next evolutionary step for humanity," Aldora said.

"I agree," Miguel said. "The doctrine of root races is common to eastern, western and indigenous traditions."

"Don't the Hindus use a symbol like a caduces to represent the energy flowing through the body?" Alex asked.

Miguel nodded.

"I think Serpent Bearer has something to do with the fifth root race, something about immortality. Like Moses raised the serpent of brass in the wilderness," Sheila said.

"The Sanskrit word Kundalini means sleeping serpent. The Eastern mystery schools speak of raising the serpent energy, like raising the light in your dream, along the spine. Enlightenment, the ability to regenerate the body and immortality is the result," don Miguel said.

I'm detecting the glimmer of a pattern here," Erik said. "Limitless energy, powerful weapons and immortality. Selig is probably not acting alone," Erik said.

The group was silent. Alexandria walked to the kitchen window and stared outside. She turned to face her companions.

"When do we leave for Cairo?" Alex asked.

19
Flight Into Egypt

Alexandria sat on her suitcase in the foyer of Gran's house, resting elbows on knees and cupping her chin in her palms. Afternoon sun light pierced the leaded panes of cut glass, creating patterns of light on motley pieces of luggage marshaled at the entry. Sheba crouched across Erik's bags like a sphinx. Crystal sat at Alex's feet, looking forlorn.

We're going to Egypt.

Alex reviewed her checklist for the hundredth time: pants, long skirts, sun hat, water bottles, flashlight, film, camera, video camera, protein bars and sunscreen.

Satisfied, she relaxed and extended her right hand toward the light. Alex twisted her hand, admiring the ring she made in the midst of the manic week. The three jade beads were arranged in a sterling triangle. An ornate silver snake coiled around the green orbs like a serpent in the sun.

She found an exquisite, apple-green peridot shaped like a pyramid. She was delighted with the radiant central star. She bartered with a friend and procured two triangular diamonds. The finished gold amulet reproduced the image of the three pyramidal stones from her dream. The green triangle pointed up, and two diamonds looked like wings on either side. When she placed the finished necklace around her throat, she felt a curious rush of familiarity. She touched her breast bone where the talisman rested beneath her shirt and remembered the cross of Palenque on Chan Ka's neck in Chiapas.

"Ready?" Erik queried from the hall, hands on hips and feet apart. He wore long khaki pants and hiking boots. A beige vest, with a dozen pockets in various sizes and combinations of snaps, flaps and Velcro, covered a white cotton camp shirt. Alex thought he looked like a movie poster of "Indiana Jones."

"As ready as I can be, considering the whirlwind preparations," she replied, brushing russet hair from her forehead.

"I can't wait to get to Egypt," he said. "Mohammed will meet us at the airport."

Alex smiled. His excitement was contagious. Outside a horn signaled Sheila's arrival. "This is it. Where's Miguel?" Alex asked.

"Here," Miguel said, appearing behind Erik. He looked distinguished in dark brown slacks, woven leather belt and white shirt. He wore caramel leather haraches and beige silk socks. Silver hair showed at his temples under the brim of his white Panama hat. His black eyes danced.

Emma and Crystal followed them onto the porch. Alex hugged Emma. "Be careful," Emma pleaded. "Come back in one piece. Your mother is beside herself with worry." Emma's forehead wrinkled, and her blue eyes clouded.

Alex dropped to her knees and put her arms around the fluffy white dog she adored.

"Don't worry, you two. I'll be home soon with exotic presents." Crystal attempted to wag her tail, but her brown eyes looked sad.

Alex kissed her on the nose. "Take care of Emma."

Outside, Sheila stood next to a borrowed van like a scout master. She was dressed in a coordinating khaki outfit with matching hat.

"All aboard," she said.

The three questers piled into the vehicle like children off to camp. Erik crammed luggage into every available space, then climbed in front with Sheila. Alex sat in back with don Miguel and felt a pang of guilt when she looked at Emma and Crystal on the porch.

As Erik and Sheila chatted in the front seat, Alex became lost in her own thoughts, recalling her trip to Mexico. Sheila drove to Kennedy airport and dropped the travelers outside the Egypt Air check-in location. She administered a fierce hug to each of them.

"Always a bridesmaid, never a bride. You guys better call me before you rewrite the history of the world," she admonished. Moist eyes belied stern words.

"We will," Alex promised. She gave Sheila's hands an affectionate squeeze and kissed her on the cheek.

They entered the terminal and joined hundreds of travelers crowded into a small area in front of the Egypt Air ticket counter. A noisy throng of impatient people clamored for seat assignments on the booked flight.

After two hours of administrative machinations, travelers funneled down narrow aisles of the Boeing 747 like an ant colony on the move. Passengers squeezed into tight rows of bright gold upholstered seats for the overnight flight. Attendants distributed plastic packs of earphones, travel slippers and ear plugs, offering pillows and gold blankets to the travelers.

Alice glanced at Don Miguel, who looked serene in the window seat. He stared into the darkness, watching the ground crew stow luggage into the bowels of the huge plane. He seemed unaffected by the press of humanity.

Erik drank two double scotches at the airport and was already asleep in the aisle seat. Alex felt like the occupant of a tin of salted fish sandwiched between them and squirmed like a child resisting a nap.

The pilot finally taxied the plane to the end of the runway and revved the powerful engines. When he accelerated for take off, the plane labored on the runway like a gigantic duck-billed platypus lumbering down the beach in a comic attempt to fly.

The engines thundered, and the overhead luggage carriers shook and rattled. At the point she was certain they would abort take off, the behemoth was airborne. The pilot banked the plane in a wide arc, revealing a million diamond lights of the Manhattan night skyline. Alex leaned across Miguel to look.

"It's breathtaking," he said.

Alex sighed, crossed her arms and sat back in her seat. She stared at the electronic map on the bulkhead that plotted the progress of the trans Atlantic flight. The computer flashed periodic weather reports. She glanced at her watch and did a quick calculation. Six a.m. in Cairo. They were scheduled to arrive at five the next afternoon.

Miguel looked at her. His eyes twinkled with affection. The corners of his mouth turned up slightly. "I suggest you take measures to relax and use this time to advantage. Otherwise, it will be an unpleasant night."

Alex blushed. "You're right." She kicked off her shoes and pulled on the royal blue acrylic slippers that reminded her of baby booties. She positioned blindfold and ear plugs, readying her cassette player on auto-reverse. She inserted a favorite tape of electronically generated thunderstorm sounds designed to synchronize the hemispheres of the brain.

Alex willed herself to relax. Breathing deeply, she allowed the sounds of the synthesized rainfall to lull her consciousness into an altered state. With each intake of breath, the cramped discomfort of her third dimensional surroundings melted away. She drifted into a dark, dreamy calmness and imagined the vast waters of the Atlantic ocean far beneath her.

Alexandria entered the realm of dreams and found herself at the intersection of four paths in the midst of a large forest. She stood at the crossroads of an impossible juncture. Each quadrant of the wood expressed the quintessence of one of the four seasons.

Scarlet tulips and buttery daffodils danced in the spring wood. Chartreuse new leaves burst from trees and bushes. Fragrant pink cherry blossoms, white apple trees, goldenrod, vivid fuschia quince and rose azalea proclaimed their awakening from winter sleep.

The trees of the summer wood were heavy with the weight of fully grown leaves. Insects hummed in hot, heavy air. An ibis bird fed in the shallow waters of a pool.

A fiery canopy of towering golden oaks, yellow elms and red maples crowned the autumn quadrant. Pine and spruce trees provided a green contrast to the glory of the flaming trees.

A white mantle blanketed the winter realm. Large flakes fell onto a crystal carpet which covered the forest floor. Stillness pervaded the slumbering woodland.

Alex gazed at the archetypal representations of spring, summer, fall and winter; the simultaneous expression of birth, death and resurrection. A path led into each seasonal landscape from her vantage point at the center of the wheel of four directions. She chose the autumn path.

The trail beneath the vibrant trees curved along a rippling stream. Sunlight filtered through colored leaves and created sparkling diamonds of light on cascading water.

Dry leaves cracked beneath her feet as she walked, and the pungent aroma of decay reached her nostrils. Brilliant leaves drifted to the ground as tall trees released their magnificent raiment and covered the ground in a gentle, maternal gesture. A patchwork quilt of red and gold prepared earth for the long winter night.

Alex inhaled and filled her lungs and diaphragm with pristine alpine air. A sapphire sky was dotted with wispy white clouds. Industrious squirrels chirped as they gathered nuts. Noisy birds flew in formation high overhead, rehearsing their southern flight. Tears of gratitude welled up in Alexandria's eyes. She saw the exquisite interplay and balance of the cycles of light and dark.

Alex walked for a mile along the edge of the cheerful brook until she caught the scent of burning wood. The path took a sharp turn, and she spied an ivy-covered cottage nestled at the edge of the stream. An inviting plume of white smoke rose in a welcoming spiral from a stone chimney. She smelled fresh bread and realized she was ravenous.

Alex approached the small wood and stone cottage. Orange Marigolds, deep crimson, white and purple Chrysanthemums surrounded the house and walk. Blue and yellow pansies spilled from window boxes. A grove of old apple trees grew behind the cottage. Their branches bowed to ground, laden with a heavy crop of round, red fruit. Her mouth watered, and she ached to pluck one.

The door opened, and a man emerged from the small cottage wearing a gray hermit's robe. Brilliant blue eyes smiled at her. Her own eyes filled with tears of joyful recognition.

"Ra Ta!" she cried.

He extended his arms. She ran to him, and they embraced. "It is a long while since our work in the temple, young Aris," he smiled as he motioned her inside.

Overcome with wonder and emotion, Alexandria stepped into the welcome warmth of the cabin. She sat in a wooden chair where a place was set in front of a stone fireplace. A cheery fire of pine logs burned and crackled, the aroma of smoke was like incense. A woven flax cloth and a pottery vase of fall flowers cheered the simple carved table. Beeswax candles burned on either side of the flowers.

A black cat, sleek as a panther, slept by the fire with her tail wrapped around her. When Alex sat at the table, the cat opened her eyes. She stretched and assumed a posture like an Egyptian cat deity. Her regal demeanor contrasted with the simple surroundings. The cat meowed a greeting.

Ra Ta laughed. "Forgive Bastet. She seldom has visitors. I'm afraid she tires of my company."

The hermit served her a pottery mug of hot spiced cider and a plate piled high with warm baked bread, honey, cheese and cold sliced apples. She bit into a cold piece of apple and a slice of cheese. The sweet juice filled her mouth, and the tart cheese made her pucker.

"This is the best food I've ever eaten," Alex said.

Ra Ta smiled and watched her eat.

When she finished, she sat back in a rocking chair in front of the fire. Bastet jumped into her lap. Alex stroked the shiny fur of the elegant feline, and Bastet purred in response. Alex felt a pang of guilt. She never petted Sheba. She looked into Ra Ta's startling blue eyes. He seemed to read her thoughts.

"If you're ready," he said, "we must take a journey. Someone waits for you."

"Of course," Alex said without reservation. "Should I lie down?"

"No. Close your eyes. I will be your guide."

Alex did as he instructed. She cradled her arms around the soft body of Bastet and willed herself to realx.

With a swiftness that astounded her, they rose into space. A luminous temple shone like a magnificent beacon against the darkness of the starry background. Alexandria stood next to Ra Ta at the entrance.

"Where are we?" she asked.

"Shambala, dwelling place and school of masters of wisdom which exists on the etheric plane," Ra Ta replied.

"All spiritual traditions have saints or masters. This is their abode."

They entered the city of light and walked into a grand foyer. The enormous space was filled with beings of light. She could not distinguish physical features, but she was aware of their individualities. Alex recognized Alethia and Dream Walker and experienced their power. They extended a silent greeting.

One being's light burned brighter than the others, and she was drawn to his intense fire like a moth to a flame. She approached the radiance of his presence and felt impelled to genuflect.

"Do not kneel, Priestess of the Light," he communicated with thought.

"You have known me in many guises in many lifetimes. You experience me now as Thoth, as I appeared in Egypt and Atlantis."

An aura of love, power and authority emanated from him like brilliant sunlight. In her mind's eye, she envisioned a handsome man with dark auburn hair and eyes like pale translucent amber. Alex sensed a compassionate smile.

"It is a momentous time," Thoth continued. "Humanity is poised to enter a new dimension, an expanded universe. This is the moment of your collective initiation. Earth herself prepares for initiation. You must surrender judgment and learn compassion. Move into your hearts and reclaim the stars.

"The universe is a vast, multi-dimensional reality. Earth has been isolated because the realm of the third dimension is the laboratory of choice. There are no rewards or punishments, only consequences. Humanity learns through endless repetition not to repeat unpleasantness. Souls have a right to the outcome of their choices."

Alex saw the blue planet from space. Conflict was invisible from this perspective.

"In this classroom," Thoth continued, "you have studied the lessons of the heart. Look closely at the words "earth" and "heart." The last letter of "earth" is the first letter of "heart." Using the same letters, we have "terah," or "terra," earth with an opened heart, a fourth dimensional sphere. This is the next evolutionary step for humanity.

"A path of return has always existed for those whose aspiration drew them inward and upward to a more actualized state. They listened with the heart and heard the music of the celestial spheres, felt the harmonies of the divine symphony.

"I drew the constellations in the sky in a distant epoch. The star pictures portray the blueprint of humanity's unfoldment. The story endured throughout the ages through myth and legend. Teachers and way showers were sent as guides.

"The pattern of completion is encoded in humanity's DNA. The number and kind of linkages determines the level of expression. Compassion opens the heart and forms new linkages in the helix. Existence is holographic. As individual units expand their capacity for divine expression, the projection of the whole expands."

As Thoth's words echoed in her mind, Alex saw the stars as if she were inside a cosmic planetarium, viewing the starry canopy from inside the celestial bowl. The ancient depiction of the star pictures were revealed to her in their true significance. She grasped the stories they were intended to tell.

"The Orion nebula is a galactic birthplace of stars, a place of generation," Thoth said. "Orion, the great hunter, with brilliant Sirius behind him in the stars of his hunting dog, stretches his bow and aims his arrow across the sky.

"See how he pursues the seven sisters of the Pleiades, who appear to flee before him, as he chases them into manifestation. Just as your body's maturation is tied to secretions from the endocrine glands, your spiritual development is related to the movement of life force in your chakras, the centers of spiritual force.

"Across the celestial bowl, Serpent Bearer holds the key to the doctrine of immortality. He is the image of Horus

Bedehty, who rose to heaven on falcon wings, overcoming death and avenging his father. The serpent coils up and around to mastery when the energy reaches the crown above his head. The constellation marks the ascension point, doorway to the next evolutionary step."

Thoth placed his hand on her head. Knowledge and memory filled her consciousness.

"It is your privilege to perform a service for humankind. You and your companions must perform the ancient ritual of the soul's journey through the Duat, as did the initiates of old in the Great Pyramid. This structure was built under my direction as a temple and school ten thousand years before I took the final stages of initiation with John in the same temple," Thoth said.

"The long awaited alignment of stars has culminated. As it is above, so it will be below. You are messengers, sent to carry the ancient message to this time." Alex had a vision of robed initiates in different chambers of the pyramids.

"The upward pointing triangle of the pyramid represents fire. The pyramid of records is deep in the earth, under a canal, representing the downward triangle of water. Fire from the sky and water from the earth must be equilibrated. Awaken the energies which have been quiescent for millennia and anchor the timeless symbol of union of opposites."

Alex imagined the great pyramid interlocking with another pyramid pointing deep inside the earth, forming a colossal hexagram.

"Your genetic patterns were encoded into the monument thirteen thousand years ago. The ritual will activate the pattern in your chakras and form new linkages in your DNA helix. If you are successful, you will trigger the next root race. The Hall of Records is protected by Atlantean technology. After the ritual, you will be able to pass those left as guards at the portal of the record chambers. They will recognize your genetic signatures."

As Thoth's message permeated her consciousness, Alex saw the celestial sphere surrounding earth. Soaring through space, she viewed the milky way above the spiraling arms of the galaxy.

She climbed higher so that her perspective included the family of galaxies orbiting the colossal black hole which magnetizes the super-galactic center. Her awareness touched the vast Oneness which encompasses all that is. She was enfolded with a profound love so unconditional she thought her heart would break. Joy pierced her soul like a sword. Transcendent love filled her being, then radiated back in reciprocity to the universe of which she was both a tiny cell and everything at once.

Thoth's voice echoed in her consciousness like a triumphant chord at the close of a majestic symphony.

"Let the plan of Love and Light work out, and may it seal the door where evil dwells."

20
Giza

Alex woke on the plane with a brutal headache. She'd slept for seven hours. When she removed her blindfold, bright light assaulted her eyes like Persian daggers.

"How do you feel?" Miguel inquired.

"Nauseous," she said, rubbing her temples. "I have to go to the bathroom."

When she emerged from the cramped lavatory, flight attendants distributed stale crackers, processed cheese and canned fruit cocktail.

"That was disgusting. Everyone on the plane's been in there five times," she said.

Erik smirked. "Full flight."

Alex drank a bottle of water and swallowed three aspirin. Rubbing her temples, she looked at Miguel and Erik.

"I'm beginning to recognize that expression," Erik said. "Another dream?"

She nodded. "More like a journey. I found myself at a crossroads. Each path led into a woods that embodied one of the four seasons."

"Cool," Erik said.

"Which path did you choose?" Miguel asked.

Alex smiled. "Autumn."

"Matches her hair," Erik said, eyes twinkling.

"I met a hermit named Ra Ta who I recognized from Egypt. He took me to a place called Shambala."

Miguel's dark eyes widened.

"Everything was made of light," Alex said, her eyes dancing. "An incredible being of light, who said he was Thoth, spoke to me telepathically." Her cheeks reddened.

"He told me we are to perform a special ritual in the Great Pyramid. He will be our guide. We are to stay in the pyramid from sundown to sunrise, reenacting an ancient rite of initiation. If we are successful, the ritual will alter our DNA."

"Regeneration in the mount," Erik said.

"Fifth root race?" Miguel asked.

"My thoughts exactly," Alex said.

"What if we're not successful?" Erik asked.

"Thoth said the Hall of Records is protected by Atlantean technology that we programmed to recognize ourselves thirteen thousand years ago. We have an appointment. If we're not successful, it could be fatal."

"That's good motivation," Erik said.

"How do we manage to be alone in the pyramid?" Miguel asked.

"No problem. Money can buy anything in Egypt," Erik said. "Mohammed can make the arrangements."

"Thoth said we must follow the journey of the great Neter in his barque through the underworld during the twelve hours of night."

"That sounds like the *Book of the Dead*," Miguel said.

"The name is actually the *Book of Coming Forth into Light*," Erik said. "The words were written on papyrus rolls and placed near the deceased's mummy."

Alex pushed her red curls away from her face. "Thoth said the ritual depicted the sun's apparent movement around the earth and the cycle of the seasons. He said the soul undertakes a similar cyclical journey through successive incarnations until final liberation is attained.

"He told me the sun had four aspects to the Egyptians; Khepher, the scarab beetle at dawn, Re at noon, and Atum in the evening. At night, while traversing the Dwat, the name is Iwf, which means flesh."

"So earthly existence is the underworld?" Miguel said. "I read Thoth was in charge of the journey even though Anubis was guide and Osiris was lord of the underworld," Miguel said.

"Thoth said there was a choice of two ways to leave the pyramid," Alex said. "The soul could go south toward Orion to be reborn in the physical, or north toward final liberation and eternal life."

"Resurrection or ascension," Erik said.

"After long silence, the initiates are returning to the temple," Miguel said in a hushed tone.

*   *   *   *   *   *   *

The jet-lagged travelers disembarked the plane and entered the crowded Cairo airport. Hundreds of people waited in ticket lines, at baggage claim, or greeted arriving passengers.

Alex was amused by a slogan in Arabic letters printed next to a six foot bottle of Coca Cola above the ticket counter. The familiar symbol of the universal solvent was a welcome anchor in the unfamiliar sea of Moslem culture.

A dark, handsome Arab man, dressed in jeans and jogging shoes, approached with arms wide. "Erik," he said, grinning.

"Mohammed, it's good to see you." The two men embraced.

"How was the flight?"

"The best kind, uneventful," Erik said.

"You must be Miguel," Mohammed said.

"A pleasure to meet you," Miguel said, shaking his hand.

"This is Alexandria Stuart," Erik said.

"I suggest you cover your fiery hair to avoid attracting attention," Mohammed said and turned toward baggage claim.

Alex bristled and started to reply, but Erik touched her arm and shot a warning glance.

"When in Rome," she said.

Alex shoved her red hair inside her sun hat and put on her sun glasses on to hide her annoyance. She thought it was hypocrisy that women should bear the burden of male weakness, covering themselves so men wouldn't be tempted.

After claiming their luggage and clearing customs, Mohammed led them out of the airport to a white passenger van. The driver bowed and presented Alex with an exquisite pink rose tied with a white silk ribbon.

"Thank you," she said, blushing.

The driver helped her into the van and gave each of them a bottle of water.

"Drink plenty of water, even if you don't feel thirsty," Mohammed instructed.

When they were underway, Mohammed relaxed and looked at Alex for the first time. "This is a Moslem country. We live with the constant threat of violence from religious fundamentalists and political terrorists. Children carry assault rifles. My behavior is for your protection. Do your best to blend in."

"She will," Erik said.

Alex chose the diplomacy of silence.

"Things are heating up," Mohammed said. "The antiquities department digs in secret and covers up whatever they find. Naturally, I have sources. The existence of multiple chambers has been confirmed, but they have not breached the portal."

"Those who were left as guards may not be passed until a period of their regeneration in the mount," Alex said softly.

Mohammed directed an appraising look at Alexandria, and she held his gaze. When he looked away, she turned her attention outside the false calm of the van to the teeming streets of Cairo.

The kaleidoscopic crowd of vehicles, humanity and animals ignored traffic signals but moved without collision in an inexplicable cadence. Carts bound for market rolled along the road's edge, overflowing with green produce. Mules were dwarfed by the size of their heavy loads. Hundreds of people walked or rode bicycles.

Women in long black dresses and scarves balanced baskets or pottery vessels on their heads and moved through the crowds with ancient grace. Older men wore traditional long galabiya robes and woven head wraps. A growing number of young men and boys wore western clothing.

The narrow ribbon of fertility reached life giving fingers of moisture into the parched sand of the desert. Sailboats cruised along the river. For thousands of years Egyptian civilizations lived in spiritual reciprocity with the annual cycle of the river's life-giving flood and the archetypal gods who embodied that relationship.

They drove over a bridge. "We have crossed the Nile and entered the city of Giza on the western bank where deceased pharaohs resided before their resurrection," Mohammed said.

The streets of Giza were less crowded and were lined with shops selling papyrus, essential oils and perfumes, gold jewelry, hand blown glass artifacts and clothing.

The driver pulled off the main road and drove through a large wrought iron gate which looked like black lace against the vivid blue desert sky. Alex thought she'd stepped into a tale from the Arabian nights. The oasis of the Moorish Mena House hotel sprawled across a twenty acre complex. Fifty foot palm trees, their trunks wrapped in white cloth, formed perfect rows along paved drives. Flower pots, brimming with red, yellow and pink hibiscus lined emerald lawns.

"Get plenty of rest," Mohammed said. "Tomorrow will be busy. I will make the necessary arrangements."

The travelers checked into spacious rooms with balconies overlooking lush manicured grounds. Tall palms provided relief from the unforgiving sun.

Alex walked outside and discovered their room had a view of the pyramids. She stood in the shadow of the greatest monuments in the world and experienced the same haunting sense of familiarity she'd known at Palenque, coupled with an aching sadness.

I can't believe I'm in Egypt.

Mingled smells of automobile exhaust, cooking odors and flowers reached her nostrils. She tried to absorb the grandeur of the sand colored pyramids framed by tall palms against the bright blue sky.

Alex closed her eyes, and a different image flashed before her mind's eye. The great pyramid stood amidst a verdant garden oasis, painted brilliant white and crowned with a glistening gold capstone. Thousands stood in silence. Many wept. Several robed figures stood below the north entry.

She opened her eyes, and the fleeting vision passed. Erik joined her on the balcony. They held hands and watched the angle of the sinking sun cast angular shadows on the huge stone structures.

"This is home," he said.

"We've come home together to fulfill our ancient promise," she said, looking at him with eyes like fiery opals.

Alex frowned. "I don't want you to go crazy, but I felt someone watching us in the airport."

A scowl formed on Erik's face.

"You don't think Selig and his cronies will let us waltz into the hall of records without a fight do you?"

"Did you tell don Miguel?
"I didn't have to. I'll talk to Mohammed tomorrow."

*   *   *   *   *   *   *

Alex woke cradled in Erik's arms. They were scheduled to meet Miguel and Mohammed for breakfast at six-thirty. Mohammed promised sunrise on the Giza plateau was worth the effort. She felt like a child on Christmas morning. She'd dreamed of visiting Egypt her whole life.

Alex gently extricated herself from Erik's embrace and put on the clothes she laid out the night before. When she brushed her teeth, Erik wandered into the bathroom looking sleepy and disheveled.

"What ungodly hour is it and in what time zone?"

"You're the morning person," she said, mouth filled with toothpaste.

Erik scowled.

After they dressed, they walked through the dark hotel grounds to the restaurant. Without the sun, the dry desert air was chilly. Palm trees looked like ghostly wraiths. The aroma of baking bread beckoned.

Don Miguel and Mohammed were already in the restaurant, drinking strong Egyptian tea and laughing. Both wore khaki pants and shirts.

"Good morning," Mohammed said, his face brightened by a broad smile.

"We need coffee," Erik said.

Mohammed laughed. "When you are ready, we'll take my favorite approach to the Giza plateau, from the east through Mena village. You will thank me when you see the sun rise on the face of the Sphinx."

"I had difficulty sleeping last night," Miguel said. "I read the beautiful translation of 'The Book of the Dead' by Normandi Ellis. I believe the words for our ceremony are contained there."

"I trust you to make that choice," Alex said.

"Ditto," Erik said.

The group finished breakfast, followed Mohammed out of the hotel and boarded the white van. Camel drivers in caftans and colorful head wraps readied brightly decorated camels to hawk rides to captive tourists on the street.

The van driver came to an abrupt halt. The three travelers emerged from the vehicle and fell in line behind Mohammed. They walked between buildings, bazaars and private homes, emerging onto an open space.

The first rays of sunlight deepened the creases on the stone face of the great Sphinx. The three pyramids loomed like shadowy stone mountains in the background. The companions stared at the last remaining wonder of the ancient world.

"The resurrection of Re-Kepher," Mohammed said, pointing toward the rising sun.

Alex was rooted to the spot. "My God," she said. The fleeting vision she saw from the hotel balcony returned with Technicolor intensity, and she was transported to another dimension.

Thousands stood in reverent silence on the Giza plateau in predawn darkness. The High Priest intoned the sacred sounds chosen for this profound occasion. With heavy heart and deep purpose he sealed the record chambers for the last time, safeguarding the knowledge.

Lord Thoth conceived a mighty plan to mark the time forever. The precise moment of the ceremony was coded by the stars into the stone monuments. Silent sentinels would carry the message through eons of time.

The leonine form of the great Sphinx gazed east into the sky at its starry likeness. The multitude looked east and waited to glimpse the rebirth of the golden orb of day over the Nile. As the sun rose on the spring day of equal light and dark, Re-Khepher smiled on the countenance of the lioness. The faces of the faithful were illumined.

To the south at the moment of sunrise, the stars of Orion's girdle were mirrored on the ground by the awesome white pyramids whose gold capstones glistened in the dawning light.

To the west, the Water Bearer waited in darkness for the wheel of ages to bring his time of ascension, when the Sphinx would welcome him. To the north the giant Serpent in the Sky, mastered by the healer and tamer, held the prophecy.

"Thirteen thousand years from now the plan will unfold on the other side of the darkness," the High Priest said. "The long watch of the sentinel will end. The aeonian night will give way to the morning of remembrance. Isis will deliver the keys to unlock the buried treasures and open the gateway to the stars. The time will come for humanity to return home."

The High Priest intoned a series of chants. Alexandria felt the vibration from his powerful voice inside her head. A stone slab moved shut at the base of the lion's right shoulder.

"Alex?" Erik asked.

Tears of remembered grief mingled with hope streamed down her face. She looked at Erik and Miguel. "I had a vision of the sealing ceremony. I saw thousands of people gathered here. That's the moment the alignment of pyramids represents."

"Ah," Miguel said, a smile of understanding spreading across his face.

"Maybe the opening is coded too," she said, wiping her nose on her sleeve.

"What is she talking about?" Mohammed asked, glaring at Alex.

"I'll explain later," Erik said.

Mohammed frowned. "Follow me, please," He walked toward a vantage point in front of the Sphinx. "This area is closed to the public because of repair work on the monument. We'll get as close as we can.

"You can see the famous stela of Tutmosis IV, who lived around fourteen hundred BC," Mohammed continued. "Ancient Egyptians believed their land was ruled by the gods themselves. One day after hunting, Tutmosis fell asleep in front of the Sphinx, which was covered in sand to its neck. The Sphinx spoke to Tutmosis in a dream and promised if he cleared away the sands, he would become king of all Egypt. "

"Did that happen?" Alex asked.

"There is the stela to prove it," Mohammed said.

"The Sphinx temple was built from limestone blocks removed from solid bedrock in the Sphinx enclosure when the statue was carved from the living rock," Mohammed said. "The blocks weigh two hundred tons each. How the ancient Egyptians accomplished this feat is a mystery. Modern technology can not match this achievement.

"The architecture of the Sphinx and Valley temples are unlike anything else in Egypt, except the Oseirion temple in Abydos. Mammoth blocks are devoid of any decoration or markings. The Oseirion is now below the water level. Flood waters and silt have covered the temple over the centuries, perhaps millennia."

Alex noticed the magnitude of restoration. Her eyes were drawn to the right shoulder of the Sphinx where scaffolding covered repair activity. Cold chills enveloped her.

Between the Sphinx and the river.

Miguel followed the direction of her gaze. "What is happening there?" he asked Mohammed.

"That area is constantly being repaired," Mohammed said. "For some reason it is unstable."

Mohammed discreetly pointed out the spot where the antiquities department entered in secret.

Alex looked at Miguel and Erik. "Those who were left as guards," she whispered.

"Let us proceed to the pyramids," Mohammed said.

The three friends followed Mohammed up the sixteen hundred foot causeway toward the pyramid of Khafre. The path was set at an angle of fourteen degrees from due east.

"Bauval and Hancock believe the half buried position of the constellation Leo on the celestial horizon represents the half buried body of the statue viewed from the same perspective," Erik said. "Another clue to the as 'above so below' message of the whole area."

Alex nodded. She found it hard to concentrate, the notes of the High Priest's chant echoed in her ears.

"Forgive me," Mohammed said, "I feel compelled to provide tourist information."

Miguel laughed. "I'm delighted. Visiting Egypt has been a dream of mine."

"Excellent," Mohammed grinned and warmed to his topic. "The great pyramid covers thirteen acres of land and is oriented to the cardinal directions. The pyramids sit at the base of the Nile delta and the center of the world's land masses. The corners are perfect right angles. It is an extraordinary achievement. Modern buildings do not match this accuracy."

They followed Mohammed around the base of the geometric marvel which gave mute testimony to the wisdom of the ancients.

"The structure is estimated to weigh six million tons and contain two point three million limestone blocks. The three pyramids were originally covered with white limestone casing stones, weighing ten tons each and polished like mirrors. Imagine the awesome spectacle of these giant diamonds shining in the desert, visible for miles. Tragically, they were removed to rebuild Cairo after an earthquake.

"The King's Chamber is constructed of red Aswan granite, obtained five hundred miles to the south. The sarcophagus is carved from black diorite, one of the hardest minerals. Controversy rages how that was accomplished with stone age tools."

Alex stared at the massive structures. "Photographs can't prepare you for the colossal scale," she said, shaking her head.

"A message we left to ourselves," Miguel said.

Mohammed's expression became serious. He stared into Erik's eyes. "The arrangements are made for your overnight stay. Do not enter the subterranean chamber under any circumstances."

"Yes, sir," Erik said, saluting and clicking his heels.

Mohammed frowned. "This is not a matter for jokes, Erik." He turned and walked toward the van.

They climbed into the white vehicle and rode to the rise above the Giza plateau. Street vendors descended like a swarm of locusts. Leathery brown faces sculpted by the harsh desert climate peered from cotton head wraps. Cotton galabiya robes brushed the sandy ground.

Even children peddled post cards, small stone scarabs or cheap scarves with cord so tourists could masquerade as Arab sheiks. Erik bartered for stone scarabs like a native, feigning outrage at the asking price and countering with an outrageous figure of his own.

A young Egyptian boy pushed articles at Alex. "I give you good deal lady. How much you pay?" Round, brown eyes betrayed hunger for American coins.

Alex shook her head. "Not today." She felt bitterness. Poverty engendered no respect for the gift to humanity the great monuments represented, only a means of profit.

The travelers stood on the rise overlooking the expanse of sandy plains containing the pyramids. Riders, with colorful robes draped across their horses, galloped across the vista like sheiks from the Arabian Nights, kicking up sand in their wake. Tied head wraps blew in the wind. Alex expected to see a magic carpet rise from behind the pyramids and soar skyward.

When she could speak without being overheard, Alex turned to Miguel and Erik.

"I saw the Sphinx as she was created."

"She?" Erik asked, raising his eyebrows.

"The original statue was a tawny lioness crowned with a reflective orb with a cobra at the top of her forehead. Her eyes were bright blue.

"In my vision, She looked east as a bright star hovered on the horizon. I knew in a matter of days Sirius would rise, blazing white, just ahead of the sun. Then the floods would come."

"You've described the goddess Sekmet, the powerful" Erik said.

"The lioness smiled," Alex said. "Her fiery blue eyes were beautiful and terrible. When she opened her jaws and roared, the ground trembled. I believe the sound of the lion's roar later became the name of the god Ra."

Erik laughed out loud. "That's perfect. The hieroglyphs are phonetic."

"I read the Egyptians loved puns," Miguel said. "The Mayan language is also filled with puns and homophones."

"When Sekhmet roared, a stone slab closed at the base of her right shoulder. The voice of the lion closed the entrance. But what sound opens the door?"

Alex looked at them. "I know this is illogical, but the star I saw wasn't Sirius but one that rose before Sirius."

"That would be Procyon," Erik said. "The name means before the dog. Sirius is the dog star."

"Gentlemen, we have work to do."

21
Heart of the Matter

Erik hunched over the computer at the makeshift desk in their hotel room, frowning at the colored lines and dots of the SkyGlobe program. His reading glasses perched precariously on the bridge of his nose. Don Miguel poured over reference books spread across the round table. Outside the air-conditioned room, the blazing desert sun climbed in the sky.

"That completes the report to home base," Alex said, placing the telephone receiver in its cradle. "Everyone sends regards."

She sat cross-legged on one of the double beds. Removing the elastic band from the red braid at the napeof her neck, she twisted the strands and replaced the blue band. She pushed a few stray hairs from her face.

"Shall we discuss the plan?" she asked, blue green eyes sparkling with excitement.

"Certainly," Miguel said, with a formal nod and a twinkle in his black eyes. "According to your instructions, we must spend the night in the Great Pyramid, preparing to enter the Hall of Records."

"Without being vaporized," Erik said, looking up from the computer.

"We're supposed to honor the ancient rites of initiation," Alex said. "But Thoth said we'll be doing something unique. We will experience a group initiation."

"I've scanned the Cayce CD for further clues," Erik said. "I spotted a couple intriguing references to the entrance of the Great Pyramid and an alignment to Polaris."

"There is a reference in this book to Procyon," Miguel said. "Procyon sounded the advance warning of the annual inundation. As Erik said, 'before the dog.' When Sirius rose ahead of the sun, the flood was upon them."

"I think astronomy is the key to this puzzle," Alex said, placing her index finger on her mouth. "Sheila and Aldora conducted some research of their own. Turn's out we're in Cairo at an important time for ancient Egypt."

"There are no coincidences," Miguel said.

"Sheila said the annual flood came when the sun was in the sign Leo," Alex said. "The sun moves into Leo in a few days. She also said the moon will be full tomorrow night. Among the stars, stones and legends the ancient wisdom dwells," she said in a dramatic tone.

"Aren't we waxing poetic?" Erik smiled. "Since the construction of the Aswan damn, Egypt no longer has the annual flood. I'll check the computer for other alignments."

"Speaking of waxing, Sheila said the fixed star Sirius is roughly fourteen degrees Cancer in the Tropical zodiac. Since the sun is still in Cancer, she said the moon will oppose Sirius as it waxes toward full."

Erik rolled his eyes, pushing his glasses upward with his middle finger. "I'll check the time."

The telephone rang.

"That's odd" Erik said.

"'Hello," Alex said.

A man's voice spoke through the receiver in halting English. "Am I addressing, Alexandria Stuart?"

"You are. Who is this?"

"One moment please."

After a pause, a woman spoke in flawless English. "Alexandria, forgive the subterfuge, but it is necessary. I speak on behalf of Her Grace, Sekhmet Montu and the people of the faith."

Alex felt cold chills of confirmation spread over her skin. She imagined the face of the lioness she had seen, feeling the keen gaze of ice blue eyes and the discernment of a pure heart.

"The time has come for the ancient ones to fulfill the prophecies. Our spiritual warriors will watch over you. Be brave, my sister."

"Thank you," Alex whispered.

"Goodbye for now," the woman said.

Alex heard the dial tone.

"Who was that?" Erik demanded.

A knock at the door preempted further discussion. Erik opened the door and Mohammed entered. The scowl on his face threatened like a desert sand storm.

"I believe your pursuer is in Cairo. More guards will be required, but my people will keep a close watch on his activities."

Erik frowned. "We expected this."

"Are you certain you want to go through with your overnight stay?" Mohammed said.

The three men looked at Alexandria.

She met their stares.

"This is our purpose."

"I don't like it, but I agree," Erik said.

"Initiates took lifetimes preparing for these rituals. Many did not survive the tests and trials," Miguel said.

"We will be guided and protected," Alex said.

"I can't explain my feeling," Mohammed said, "but I believe that you will be."

"I have chosen several selections from the hauntingly beautiful translation of *The Book of the Dead* by Normandi Ellis for each hour of night," Miguel said. "Look at this diagram of the interior of the Great Pyramid. Here are the places I suggest we recite the prayers."

Miguel pointed to the chambers, passages and junctures and read the words he selected.

"You chose well," Erik said.

Alexandria walked to the window. She stared through the glass at the Great Pyramid. The midday sun created a haze on the horizon.

"The speeches are exquisite, but something about the sequence is not quite right," she said.

"What do you mean?" Erik asked.

She turned to look at them. "Thoth said we are to learn the lessons of the heart."

Alex walked back to where they sat and pointed at the diagram. "You said an ancient name for the King's Chamber was the chamber of the open tomb, and the Queen's Chamber was called the chamber of second birth. The Queen's chamber is directly under the apex. That feels like the heart of the pyramid to me.

"I think we should perform our meditation in the King's Chamber at midnight and enter the Queen's Chamber afterward."

"She makes a good point," Mohammed said. "The heart was the most important thing to the ancient Egyptians. The heart lived on Ma'at, the principle of truth and divine justice."

Alex noted that Mohammed spoke of her in the third person. She smiled inwardly.

"The stellar alignments Bauval and Hancock discuss also link Sirius to the Queen's Chamber," Erik said.

When Alex spoke again she was transformed, as if the spirits of Una and Aris were united in her consciousness. Her voice was filled with ageless wisdom.

"The shafts from the Queen's chamber aren't open to the outside," Alex said. "Perhaps they represent the final integration of initiatic energies. The niche on the eastern wall could have five steps to symbolize the completion of the fifth root race, the regeneration in the mount Cayce mentioned."

Miguel stared at her, probing her expression.

"When the astronomical alignment was right, starlight shone down the shaft and was refracted through a crystal, illuminating the dark chamber," she said.

Don Miguel smiled. "In Egyptian temples, and later in the temple of Solomon, the holy of holies resided at the innermost center and the darkest place of the sanctuary.

"Thoth replaced the left eye of Horus, the full moon, which represents the perfect reflection of divinity. That act restores the feminine to a world which sadly needs her, most fitting, my dear."

Alexandria's eyes filled with tears. Her own heart was filled with awe and humility. She walked outside to look at the pyramids. The shaded balcony protected her from the full force of the desert sun. The stone structures seemed to shimmer in the midday heat.

When Mohammed left, Alex looked at her beloved companions.

"Well? Erik asked.

"I can't tell you about the phone call yet. You will have to trust me."

Erik frowned. "I don't have to like it."

They spent the next two hours rehearsing the ritual and speeches Miguel chose, then slept to prepare for their twelve hour vigil.

22

As Above, So Below

Miguel phoned and woke Alex at five-fifteen. The late afternoon sun cast long shadows on the lawn outside their hotel room. She showered, dressed in comfortable clothes and gathered the items they chose for their overnight stay in the pyramid. Alex and Erik met Miguel in the Mena House lobby and waited for Mohammed. Her stomach growled from hunger and apprehension.

"Final check," Erik said. "Flashlight? Batteries? Blanket? Food? Water? Candles? Flowers?" Alex held up the items as he named them, nodding to the scout master.

Don Miguel carried a serpentine wooden staff with a forked tip, signifying snake defense. He wore a brightly colored woven belt and a white head band.

Mohammed arrived at five forty-five and drove them the short distance to the Giza plateau. The three companions climbed out of the van and followed him to the north side of the Great Pyramid. The Sphinx was in shadow. The descending sun hung huge and orange between the pyramids, gilding the edges of the sand colored monuments.

Alex squinted at the sun and remembered the reflective disk she had seen on the head of the goddess Sekhmet.

"You will be undisturbed between sunset and sunrise as you asked, Erik," Mohammed said, his jaw set in a firm line. "I will wait in the van until morning."

"Thank you, my friend," Erik said.

Alex gasped. She thought she caught a fleeting glimpse of Selig.

"What is it?" Erik asked, frowning.

"Just an active imagination. I'm a little nervous."

Mohammed scowled at her. "I warn you again to be careful. There many eyes in the desert tonight, not all of them are friendly."

"You have my word," Erik said, grasping his arm.

The men stared at each other. Mohammed nodded.

Alex looked at the artificial mountain of two and a half million limestone blocks, looming like Everest.

"I feel like an ant contemplating the ascent of a camel," she said.

"A seven hundred and fifty foot camel," Erik said.

Mohammed led the way as they clamored up the steps chiseled into the ten ton stones on the north side of the Great Pyramid. They climbed toward Caliph Al Mamoun's point of entry, forced open in the ninth century. They stopped outside the place known as Mamoun's Hole. Alex shielded her eyes and looked up toward the gabled stones of the original entrance at the nineteenth course of masonry.

"Time to bid farewell to Re-Atum, the dying sun," Miguel said. "We are ready to recite the first selection from Normandi Ellis's translation of the Book of the Dead. Will you join hands with us, Mohammed?"

"Very well."

Alex trembled in anticipation of what faced them during the next twelve hours as Miguel's beautiful voice spoke the first words.

"May we come and go in and out of
heaven through the gates of starlight. As the
houses of earth fill with dancing and song,
so filled are the houses of heaven. I come in
truth. I sail a long river and row back again.
It is joy to breathe under the stars. I am the
sojourner destined to walk a thousand years
until I arrive at myself."

Mohammed closed and locked the gate. Armed
guards were posted around the four corners of the pyramid.
He leveled at fierce stare at each of them. Alex knew
concern and affection lay beneath his angry countenance.

"We are blessed to have you as our friend," Miguel
said.

"Good luck," Mohammed said, whirled around
and headed down the northern face of the pyramid.

"Show time, folks," Erik said.

Alex smiled at Miguel, then looked at Erik. "I love
you both. Whatever happens tonight, never forget that."

They stepped inside the dim cavern of limestone
blocks. Alex touched the large stones and ran her hand
across their scarred surface. They seemed like living
presences.

"How long have these stones stood in silent
testimony of their makers genius?" she asked.

The three stood inside the north entrance and faced
west. Miguel's face was transformed by concentration and
dedication. His voice was strong, but the stone passage
absorbed the sound as he spoke the second prayer."

"May the light shine through us and
on us and in us. May we die each night and
be born each morning that the wonder of life
should not escape us. May we love and laugh
and enter lightly into each other's hearts.
May we live forever. May we live forever."

> "We spend our lives preparing for
> death, for the moment when we offer up our
> days and labor, our sayings and doings, the
> sum of ourselves, and beg the gods to call it
> good."

They advanced horizontally through the artificial
tunnel created by Mamoun until the path joined the
descending route. The junction marked his entry into the
descending passage and access to the off-limits
subterranean chamber. The route toward the original
entrance was barred by a steel door. On the western side,
two elephantine granite plugs masked the junction of the
descending passage.

"How could anyone believe this awesome structure
was built only as a tomb?" Alex asked. "That seems as
arrogant as believing the earth is the center of the solar
system."

When they reached the juncture of the gate of assent,
Alex made herself comfortable and tried to relax. They
rested until seven o'clock.

At the second hour of night, Miguel positioned
himself at the juncture of passages and recited the next
speech.

> "I know the future for us all and it is
> death. When you've reached the lips of the
> great devourer, you are staring into the jaws
> of creation."

> "Like the sun at day's end, we pass
> west through the gap in the mountains. We
> go quickly or slowly toward Amentet, the
> stony plateau. It is only the darkness before
> light, the hidden place, the house of
> transformation."

"You chose the words well, don Miguel," Erik said.

"There's no chance I'd ignore Mohammed's warning and go toward the subterranean chamber," Alex said, shivering.

The three travelers stooped over, bending at the waist and entered the ascending passage. The path was less than four feet square and stretched one hundred and twenty-nine feet upward in a twenty-six degree incline. They progressed ape-like through the cramped space toward the bottom of the Grand Gallery.

Alex recoiled as a dark form scurried into the corner. She recalled the majestic vision of the pyramid covered with gleaming white stones and crowned with a shimmering gold capstone.

"How can they let this happen to these incredible monuments?" she asked.

"If the officials cared, we wouldn't be here," Erik said. "It's a perverse paradox, but the politics have protected the secrets."

"Please calm yourself, Alexandria," Miguel said. "Conserve your energy."

"I'm sorry." She blushed and tried to slow her breathing.

When they emerged from the ascending passage, Alex felt dizzy and nauseated. She leaned against the wall to catch her breath and steady herself.

A choice of ways presented themselves. Straight ahead lay the horizontal route to the Queen's Chamber. Behind a steel covered door was the second access to the subterranean chamber; a nearly perpendicular passage dropped toward the base of the structure.

They took the steps which led to the bottom of the Grand Gallery. The breathtaking vista from the foot of the architectural masterpiece spread upward before them.

"Magnificent, the hall of truth in light," Miguel said. "I have seen pictures, but I never imagined such beauty."

"The gallery is one hundred fifty-seven feet in length and twenty-eight feet high, with seven courses of limestone masonry," Erik said.

"I don't think I can make the climb," Alex said, sitting on the floor. "I feel sick."

"You must," Miguel said in a gentle but firm voice.

"We have forty-five minutes until our next prayer," Erik said, handing her a water bottle. "We'll rest here."

Alex extracted a protein bar from her pack and peeled back the foil wrapper. She washed down the chewy peanut butter flavored bar with a generous swallow of water.

"No ornamentation or inscription speaks of the intent or significance of this masterful achievement," Miguel said.

"Which is out of character with other Egyptian monuments," Erik said.

Alex closed her eyes and tried to gain control of her uneasiness. She breathed and called up the memory of the priestess Aris.

A few minutes before eight, Erik passed a bottle of water to each of them. Alex savored the cool sensation in her mouth and throat. Alex and Erik stood beside Miguel and gazed upon the assent to the King's Chamber. At the third hour of night, Miguel stood erect and spoke.

"Hail Thoth, architect of truth, give me words of power that I may write the story of my own becoming. I stand before the masters who witnessed the creation, who were with Ra that morning the sun rolled into being, who were with Osiris in the grave as he gathered himself together and burst from the tomb white with heat, a light and shining god."

Alex sighed and looked once more at the long gallery. They began the arduous ascent at eight-twenty. She clung to hand railings inserted into the limestone ledges and climbed the slatted wooden ramp which lay over the polished stones. Alex recalled the stations of the cross from her childhood, the reenactment of the crucifixion of Christ. The memory strengthened her resolve.

They reached the top at ten minutes to nine and turned to look back. Her chest hurt from the rapid pounding of her heart, and she was soaked in perspiration. Removing a water bottle from her pack, she swallowed a generous helping. They rested for several minutes. At nine o'clock Miguel spoke.

"I am an Osiris, a man waking in the night, listening to the varied voices of stars. The gods speak through me and I am one of them. Yet, at times, they seem to shine so far away from me . . .

". . .Truly, I strive to carry the load without noticing the burden, to be on this hot earth a cool jug of water, to stand in the wind like sturdy sycamore branches, a place where birds rest, where cattle gather, where sap rises, wherein earth and sky are home."

The three friends clamored onto the limestone ledge known as the big step. They leaned against the stone wall of the pyramid.

"We should rest here for one hour," Miguel said.

"I agree," Erik said.

"Thank you," Alex said. "She closed her eyes and slept without dreams.

*   *   *   *   *   *   *

"It is time," Miguel said, looking at his watch. "Ten o'clock."

Alex felt stiff from sleeping on the stone surface. The three friends stood and faced the opening leading into King's Chamber.

"I am Ra, from whom time began, rising, a red feather in the wind, tuning, turning. I am the hub of a wheel, a day star hovering over an endless sea. I am not the harvest; I am the seed. I am not the lyre I am the song. I will not pass away. I will not pass away."

They stooped and crawled inside a low passage where the substance of the pyramid changed from alluvial limestone to igneous granite. When they entered the antechamber they stood. Three deep grooves were carved into the walls. Alex glanced above her head and noticed a pair of granite leaves set into the grooves.

"What are these?" she asked.

"The mainstream theory is that three huge portcullis stones were lowered to protect the chamber, a common practice in Egyptian burials," Erik said. "How that happened is this tight space has been the subject of heated controversy. No trace of the stones was ever found."

"Seems like a lot of detail and effort if there's no meaning," she said.

"Grist for the mill for pyramid scholars and cranks," Erik said.

"We are at the threshold of the chamber of the open tomb," Miguel said. "Shall we begin the next prayer?" Alex nodded and quieted her mind as Miguel spoke.

"When the time comes, I give up life without regret to feed a spirit greater than mine. I shall die, a small thing become part of the larger world. May we live forever and forever."

They bent over and negotiated the final short passage between the antechamber and the King's Chamber. They timed their approach to enter at ten-thirty. Inside the chamber, Alex drew a deep breath.

"The room feels like it's vibrating," she said.

"People often compare the feeling to a hydro electric power plant," Erik said. "There's an acoustical resonance which causes sounds to echo above your head."

"The ancient Maya builders possessed such knowledge," Miguel said.

They gathered around the empty black sarcophagus and stared into the empty coffer. Alex touched the surface of the cool stone.

"I read the coffer has the same ratio of proportions as the arc of the covenant," Miguel said.

"The opening we crawled through isn't large enough to accommodate this coffin," Alex said.

Erik smiled. "That's one of several mysteries. Diorite is an extremely hard substance. How the Egyptians carved a single block with such precision using stone age tools is unexplained. Modern drilling tools can barely manage the job."

"The rest of the pyramid, as far as anyone knows, is constructed of limestone. This chamber is built from red Aswan granite, quarried five hundred miles to the south," Erik said.

"Granite is an igneous rock," Miguel said. "This chamber must represent trial by fire."

Erik pointed to the five courses of masonry forming the walls. "There are exactly one hundred blocks in this room; the nine monoliths in the ceiling weigh fifty tons or more."

"What's this?" Alex asked, pointing to an opening on the southern wall.

"One of the infamous air shafts," Erik grinned.

"With the infamous astronomical alignments?" she said.

"Exactly."

"This place is incredible, even if the Egyptologists are right about the date. Whether this monument has stood for five thousand years or thirteen thousand years, it's magnificent," Alex said.

They selected a spot near the center of the room to prepare for their ritual. They placed a white votive candle in the center, arranging lotus blossoms and papyrus leaves around the flame. Miguel grasped his shaman's staff. Alex pulled her necklace from under her shirt and lovingly touched the three interconnected triangles.

The three initiates positioned themselves in a triangle, embodying the archetypal trinity of Osiris, Isis and Horus, father, mother and divine child.

They sat on the floor and lighted the candle. They closed their eyes and joined hands, beginning their meditation. Alex felt the pulsing vibration of the pyramid's energy as the mammoth structure responded to their ritual.

Each entered a place of silence and power to enact their appointed role as messengers from the past to the future. At midnight, when the sun was at the nadir, Miguel spoke.

"The candle's only purpose is to shine in the darkness. Bread is meant to be ground to pulp in the teeth. The function of life is to have something to offer death. Ah, but the spirit lies always between, coming and going in and out of heaven, filling and leaving the houses of earth. A man forgets, but his heart remembers -- the love and the terror, the weeping, the beating of wings."

Fiery astral light stirred into wakefulness in the granite chamber, stimulating the energy centers at the base of their spines. Alex rocked back and forth as the potency of the force uncoiled.

She experienced a jolt of power as the unbridled energy rose into her solar plexus. Her heart chakra opened in an exquisite and piercing sensation of oneness. The fiery wheel of the throat center spun as the word of life prepared to emerge. They spoke in unison as they had rehearsed.

> "I am a phoenix, a soul sparking, a tongue of fire burning up flesh. I consume myself and rise. I am light of the Light, keeper of the book of my becomings: what was, what is, what will be. I am Osiris, a god and the ashes of man. I am the skin he takes on and sheds. I am the cord that binds him from this world to the next."

Brilliant white light exploded in incandescence inside Alexandria's head and pulsed like a heartbeat of light at her brow. Molten consciousness streamed into the crown of her head, burning her awareness. Energy moved up and down her spine, forming a caduceus of spiraling light.

Alex opened her eyes and saw light emerging from the black sarcophagus. Swirling incandescence moved in two steams of twisting light. The currents spun faster around each other until they merged. The twirling lights became a giant black serpent twenty feet in length, slithering from the crypt.

Alex tried to scream, but her mouth made no sound. She wanted to run, but her body had turned to stone. The serpent Apophsis, nemesis of Osiris, approached. The huge snake advanced across the chamber and stopped in front of her, coiled like a King Cobra ready to strike.

"I am death and immortality," the snake said in a rasping voice. "Adversary and redemption. To survive, you must embrace me."

The chamber's resonant quality caused the sound
to reverberate above her head. The serpent's forked tongue
licked the air like a red flame. Faceted jewel-like eyes bore
into her skull. The room reeked with menace.

"Summon   your   power," don   Miguel's
communicated telepathically. "This is your purpose,
Alexandria."

His presence strengthened her. She breathed to still
her heart and called upon the memory of Aris and Una.
She thought of Dolphin.

"I claim your power for my own," she said to the
black form.

"That is well," the snake hissed. Alex thought the
serpent smiled. "Journey with me, Priestess."

The snake uncoiled and arched its back. Alex willed
herself to move but was frozen to the spot. Her
consciousness left her physical body, and her astral form
climbed onto the back of the serpent Apophsis. They rose
through the ceiling of the King's Chamber, out of the apex
of the pyramid into an indigo sky. A billion suns burned
across light years like bright diamonds in the darkness.

Feeling disoriented, Alex looked for familiar
constellations. She recognized the belt of Orion and the
brilliant star Sirius. The luminous Milky Way stretched
across the celestial canopy. A bright star on the opposite
side of the great river in the sky seemed to form an
equilateral triangle with Sirius and the brightest star in
Orion, in his right shoulder.

"What is that star?" she asked the snake.

"Procyon, the star of Horus," the Serpent said.
"Orion, the hunter masters the energies symbolized by his
sword, but that is not enough for salvation. The ultimate
victory of the divine son, Horus, results from raising and
utilizing those energies throughout his being. Horus
becomes the Serpent Bearer. He claimed my power for his
own."

Alexandria searched the skies for the zodiacal constellations. Above the Water Bearer a small group of stars formed the astral shape of a dolphin. As she watched, her friend emerged from the twinkling configuration.

"Dolphin!"

"Pay close attention to what you see, little traveler," Dolphin said telepathically.

The giant serpent climbed higher in gentle undulating movements toward the circumpolar constellations. Alex saw a multidimensional cube formed by shining alpha stars The snake stopped at the constellation Cepheus, the King. Alex was amazed to realize that three of the central stars were in the same positions as the chambers in the Great Pyramid.

"This is the destination of the soul," the serpent said. "The eternal castle in the sky. The work in the pyramid on earth prepares the soul for immortality. The chambers are gateways to other dimensions."

The serpent flattened its form, and Alex stepped off. She stood at the place of Polaris, on the axis of the world and gazed upon the silvery garment of the galaxy. The great snake moved to take its place in the constellation of the Serpent Bearer. Rasalhague, brightest star in the head of the snake charmer, shone like a beacon.

Alex noticed the constellation Serpent Bearer stood between the Scorpion and the Archer, directly across the sky from Orion and Taurus, the Bull. The Lion and the Water Bearer formed the other arms of a cross in the sky. She understood the precessional wheel of ages had turned, fulfilling a cyclic destiny.

Sirius outshone all the other stars. As Alex watched, the Shining One became an enormous cow with a brilliant blue-white star between her horns. The sacred cow opened her mouth, and the sound of her bellowing moo filled the skies. The faint echo of Miguel's voice called Alexandria's soul back to the King's Chamber.

"He gathers the sand serpents to his
breast. He fears no living thing. He made
them, what is known and not known. He
speaks their names and takes their venom.
The snake who gobbles the world enters Ra.
Burned in fire, he vomits the evil he has
spoken. His words are smelted into gold.

"With a kiss, Ra turns poison into
magic. He twines the snakes about him. Now
death lives on his forehead, side by side with
light. Let breath come and go. Let the great
world change. Let men see that serpents
entwine the god as the light of god entwines
each man. It brushes his lips with sunlight,
with kisses of life, kisses of death, kisses of
joy, kisses of poison and magic."

The three messengers became a mystical caduceus.
Erik and Alexandria were the male and female currents
spiraling around the central pillar of the shaman. Spiritual
lightning electrified their cells. Alexandria could see inside
their bodies and perceived the double helix of their DNA.
The spiral strands shifted and formed the new linkages and
connections of a spontaneous genetic mutation.

When Alexandria opened her eyes, the chamber
seemed illuminated. A halo of light surrounded her
companions' heads. She felt a blissful oneness; the same
emotion seemed to be reflected from the faces of her
companions.

"We were with you," Erik said. "We experienced
everything."

With tears of joy in her eyes, Alex spoke the lines of
the ritual she'd memorized.

"Do you know magic? Can you utter
the name of your soul and bring yourself back

to light? Can you speak your destiny, create
life for yourself from yourself as Temu created
Ra? From the light of your works do you
know who you are?"

They gathered their belongings and left the King's
Chamber in a state of reverence. It was nearly two a.m.
They crawled through the low passage and antechamber
and emerged at the great step overlooking the Grand
Gallery. They leaned against the wall and drank more
water.
"We will rest again," Miguel said.

* * * * * * *

At three o'clock, the ninth hour of night, Miguel
called out, his voice echoing down the long expanse.

"Hail Thoth, architect of truth, give me
words of power before gods and goddesses
and creatures of light and the messengers of
heaven. Grant me unity of the heart, mind
and spirit. Grant me love and light, an
everlasting body. Grant me the words of
transformation and the will of the flesh to
make things happen. I wait to come forth by
day again."

Alex and Erik followed him down the long ramp,
holding onto the rails. When they reached the foot of the
Grand Gallery, she glanced at the sealed entrance to the
narrow shaft, leading to the grotto.
They turned and proceeded once more in ape-like
fashion along the cramped horizontal route to the Queen's
Chamber, one hundred twenty seven feet in length. The
passage was less than four feet high.

The floor dropped abruptly two feet at the opening into the Queen's Chamber, which Thoth called chamber of the second birth. They entered the room and stood.

Miguel looked around the chamber. "The King's Chamber is a place of fire and radiance, this place is like a cool lake or mirror, intended for the perfect reflection of divine essence."

"That's true," Alex said, smiling.

"The chamber is constructed of plaster over limestone walls and appears to be intentionally unfinished," Erik said.

"Regeneration in the mount?" Alex asked. "There are five steps in the niche, five courses of masonry in the walls of the King's Chamber."

"And five levels in the relieving chambers above the King's Chamber," Miguel said.

"The shafts are also on the north and south walls. The niche is just south of the center line on the eastern wall," Erik said.

"East for rebirth, or the birthing of a new creation," Alex said.

They rested awhile to prepare for the next ritual. Alex placed a mirror on the floor as she'd seen in her vision and arranged a crystal and a lotus blossom on the mirror.

"The flower of life," Miguel said.

At four o'clock they took their places. Erik and Miguel stood on the northern and southern walls, in front of the shafts. Alex stood in the niche, symbolic mother of humanity's next evolutionary unfoldment, represented in ancient times by the child Horus. Erik spoke first.

"Now I seize darkness by its arms and
shake it. The souls of ancient swallowed gods
fall out of the belly of obscurity. The old, the
few and the forgotten walk back into being
with me. I am bringing home the world. I
am triumphant."

The shaman raised his staff on high toward the apex of the pyramid, now directly overhead.

> "Then the will of Osiris rose up and spoke to its body. His heart beat and Isis rejoiced, then Horus was born in the body of spirit. Osiris united with heaven and earth. I too am a man longing for unity. I too am a soul opening unto light. I wait to come forth by day in Restau, the passage unto god."

Alexandria spoke. "May our hearts be weighed and found as light as the feather of Ma'at."

The three initiates had returned to the temple in fulfillment of their ancient promise. They drew energy from the stars which passed through them and the ancient temple of initiation into the earth. They became a living chalice of liquid flame.

In a loud voice they chanted, "Ah Men," the name of the ancient hidden God of many traditions. Three times their chant echoed in the chamber.

Terra responded to the ancient call, and reciprocal energy moved back up the pathways and out the shafts of the great temple. A blinding flash of light rushed from the top of their heads out the apex of the pyramid like the wings of a white phoenix. Their ritual initiated a chain reaction; the pyramid became a lightning rod for the planet.

"We will not die a second time," Miguel said.

A slow tremor began in the walls and floor of the chamber. They felt the vibration as stone scraped against stone, allowing the small door high up in the shaft to open. A thin ray of pale light entered the chamber and shone on the crystal. A prism of rainbow colors erupted and were reflected in the mirror. A spectrum of crystal starlight shone on Alexandria's face. She was transformed into a priestess. She raised her arms and spoke in a loud voice.

"I live in the eye of the lady of flame. I am light reflected by Hathor's mirror. The words of goddesses are bright and shining in my mouth. I create myself. I am the gods' secret. I have seen the great fire of perhaps, the beacon of possibility. I wake in the liquid light of a vision. Now Isis stands up and combs back her hair."

The three initiates stood in awed silence for several minutes. A shimmering rainbow of light bathed the chamber in delicate iridescence. They collected their belongings in silence and crawled back along the horizontal passage.

When they arrived at the bottom of the Grand Gallery, they waited in silence. After several minutes Miguel looked at them.

"Our work here is complete."

They climbed down the lower portion of the Grand Gallery and returned to the junction of Mamoun's entry and the ascending passage. At the eleventh hour of night, Miguel read the speech chosen for that moment with passionate intensity.

"It is one hour before dawn. In the beginning, the end is foretold, but we are not privy to it. We struggle on, strive to reach some end, the purpose of which escapes us, yet whose purpose is simply that we strive for the end. It is desire that propels us. Process alone has significance. You are one when the question is its own answer, when the answer is the quest."

Miguel smiled, his face was radiant. They made their way back toward the entrance and waited. At six a.m. they heard the sound of Mohammed's keys unlocking the gate.

Alex, Miguel and Erik emerged at morning twilight, coming forth into day in the tradition of millennia. A brilliant star hovered on the eastern horizon, rising in a moment of dazzling transcendence before the sun.

"You look like Moses descending from Mount Sinai," Mohammed whispered, his eyes wide.

They joined hands and ended their ritual in unison. Their voices rang like trumpets as Re-Khepher ascended in the east to bless the ancient land.

"Stars fade like memory the instant before dawn. Low in the east, the sun appears as an opening eye. That which can be named must exist. That which is named can be written. That which is written shall be remembered. That which is remembered lives. In the land of Egypt Osiris breathes. The sun rises and mists disperse. As I am, I was, and I shall be a thing of matter and heaven."

23
Eye of Horus

Alex heard water running in the shower. She rubbed her eyes and looked at her watch, three o'clock. She decided to phone don Miguel. "I'm starving."

Miguel's laugh echoed in the receiver. "Shall we have an early dinner? There is much to discuss."

Alex and Erik met Miguel and Mohammed by the swimming pool. They circled around an umbrella table in the shade of tall palms, gaining relief from the intense heat. Sun light sparkled on the surface of the water. Mohammed opened a paper sack brimming with fried falafel cakes wrapped in warm Egyptian bread.

"That smells delicious," Alex said.

Miguel and Mohammed drank iced tea, and Alex and Erik ordered beer. Alex bit into one of the sandwiches. Savory flavor filled her mouth, but her pleasure was short-lived.

"We had problems during the night," Mohammed said, his face strained from effort to suppress his emotions. "One of my men is dead."

"What happened?" Erik asked, his eyes widening.

"There was a struggle at the entrance to the pyramid. Someone wanted to join your slumber party," Mohammed said.

"We apprehended the killer, but I do not believe he acted alone."

"I am so sorry," Alex said.

Mohammed looked at her. "Thank you on behalf of those who serve in silence and in secret, giving their lives for the ancient ones."

Their eyes remained locked for several moments.

"Our next move is now more urgent," Miguel said.

"You realize you could be killed," Mohammed said.

"The priceless knowledge buried in those chambers belongs to the world, not special interests," Erik said.

"I believe we will be protected," Miguel said.

"We still need the key to unlock the door," Alex said.

"If the sound of a lion's roar closed the Hall of Records, what sound opens the way?" Erik asked.

Alex shrugged her shoulders. "I've been thinking."

"Uh oh," Erik said.

Don Miguel's black eyes sparkled like beads of jet.

"Cats are nocturnal," she said. "Why choose a lion as a solar symbol? In Astrology the sun rules Leo, but that seems too simple."

"Lions roar at sunset to rouse themselves for the nightly hunt," Mohammed said.

"Like football players before a game," Alex said.

Erik frowned at her over the top of his sunglasses.

"Look at this diagram of the zodiac of Dendara," Miguel said, placing a book on the table. "The figure representing Thoth is placed between Virgo and Libra, the autumn equinox. You saw the ceremony which sealed the Hall of Records at dawn on the spring equinox, the beginning of a cycle of darkness. Could the opening be signified by the autumn equinox?"

"Good question," Alex said. "If so, we're a couple months early."

"Perhaps we're missing the obvious," Erik said. "You said the Sphinx was a lioness, like Sekhmet. If this temple was dedicated to Isis and master-minded by Thoth, there's also a lunar connection."

"Correct. Thoth was a lunar deity," Mohammed said. "The sun was the right eye of Ra, and the moon was the left eye of Horus. Thoth was responsible for replacing the eye of Horus after he lost it to Set in their famous battle."

"And, the full moon rises in the east tomorrow night, directly opposite the setting sun," Erik said.

"So the Sphinx will gaze at the full moon after the sun sets behind the statue," don Miguel said. "Sheila also told you the moon will oppose Sirius as she waxes toward fullness. I sense a powerful significance about the lioness being aligned between Sirius, the sun and the moon."

"Not sun set, but moon rise," Alex said, smiling.

"The ancient Egyptians believed our sun revolved around the star Sirius," Mohammed said. "Sirius, and later Isis, was called the mother of the universe.

"Sometimes she wore a crown showing the phases of the moon. More often she was depicted as a cow with a large star between her horns," Mohammed said.

"A cow?" Alex asked, laughing out loud.

The men looked at her.

"That explains my vision in the pyramid. What is the sound of a sacred cow?" she asked.

Erik and Miguel smiled in recognition and together replied, "Moo."

"Mu, legendary motherland in the Pacific," Miguel said.

"The Egyptian vowel sounds were sacred and unwritten," Mohammed said. "Hieroglyphs were consonants, homophones and symbols."

"Eureka," Miguel said. "How exquisitely simple."

"And how exquisitely Egyptian," Erik said. He crossed his arms over his chest, pretending to pout. "But now I can't say 'open sesame.'"

Alex glared at him.

"You may be right, but this enterprise is madness," Mohammed said.

"Lunacy, to be precise," Erik said.

"Sirius business indeed," Alex said, biting into a falafel sandwich.

* * * * * * *

A brisk breeze blew across the Giza necropolis as they approached the Sphinx. The night air was chilly, and Alex was glad for the protection of a hooded sweat shirt. Her only jewelry was a necklace; a clear quartz crystal wrapped in silver wire was tucked beneath her shirt.

The leonine enigma crouched in the bedrock, guarding her secrets with the tenacity of a lioness protecting newborn cubs. Alexandria pondered her inscrutable features as the silent watcher gazed east. The stone sentinel had waited for millennia.

"Sciere. Velle. Audere. Tacere," Miguel said to the statue. "You are the embodiment of the four powers of the Sphinx."

"Latin," Erik said. "What do the words mean?"

"To know, to will, to dare, and to be silent."

"You echoed my sentiment," Alex said. "Thousands witnessed the sealing of this holy place. Tonight, only three of us return."

"Three who come in the name of many to honor our vow," Miguel said. "We will open the portal of memory, walk through the gates of yesterday and approach the pillars of tomorrow."

Alex didn't trust herself to speak. She nodded, giving silent thanks to those who watched this night.

Night is the province of the feline. As the silver orb rose in the eastern sky, pale moon light stole across the body of the Sphinx like a predatory creature of the night, transforming the solar symbol into a great nocturnal cat.

Starlight could not compete with the brilliance of the lunar disk. Sekmet, the powerful, protector of the High Priestess's scroll, looked into the argent Eye of Horus.

"In ancient times, silver light would have been reflected from the orb crowning her head And the uraeus cobra on her brow," Alex said.

"That would have been an awesome spectacle," Miguel said.

"At the time of the equinoxes, Sekhmet was aligned with sunrise and moonrise," Erik said.

Alexandria removed her hat and shook her hair loose. Her fiery mane was rendered monochrome in the ghostly moon light. The desert looked like a lunar landscape. Alex turned and followed the direction of the Sphinx's eastern gaze, imagining the lioness smiled as the moon touched the cusp of Aquarius. The promise of a new epoch, when both eyes of Horus might look upon a world of balanced polarities.

"Is it time?" she asked.

Miguel nodded. "Tonight we call upon the lioness, the cobra and the jackal. May their powers strengthen and assist us. We invoke the intercession of Thoth, Ra and Isis as we endeavor to fulfill our promise."

They walked around to the south side of the Sphinx and approached her right shoulder. A tarp covered the point of forced entry they had noticed earlier. They touched the place on the stone where Mohammed instructed them. A faint quiver seemed to move through the great statue. A limestone slab scraped across the bedrock, revealing a nearly square aperture three feet on each side. Musty air escaped from the opening.

"This seems too easy," Erik said.

"Remain focused and alert," Miguel said.

Alexandria's heart raced, and she felt dizzy.

"We're not inside yet. I can't think about what might be down there."

"I've heard stories of alligators, snakes and demons," Erik said.

Erik and Miguel shone flashlights into opaque blackness. They climbed into the opening masked by the fire box, pausing to allow their eyes time to adjust to the darkness.

They crawled through a horizontal passage, five feet beneath the bedrock, for fifty feet. They emerged in the underground chamber between the paws, detected by John Anthony West's seismic tests. They stood, and Erik shone his halogen lantern around the cavity. The smooth walls of the rectangular room were carved from solid limestone bedrock, similar to the Sphinx enclosure.

"Mohammed said they recently cleared the rubble from the passageway into this room, but they haven't been able to move beyond this point," Erik said.

"It's difficult to tell the dimensions of this room in the dark," Alex said.

"Roughly twelve by fifteen meters, according to Mohammed's source," Erik said.

"Scan slowly over the eastern wall," Miguel said.

The light revealed the suggested outline of a door, barely discernible on the eastern wall. They moved to get a closer look, and Erik shone the lantern on the edges of the outline. The door was constructed of the same limestone and devoid of ornamentation or carving.

"This is where we test your theory, Alex."

"Let us begin with the speeches we chose from Normandi Ellis's book," Miguel said.

Raising their voices in the chamber as they might have thirteen thousand years ago, the three initiates called out in unison.

"I am the servant of Ra, eldest son of morning, washing the eyes of gods and bathing in tears. I am the oar of his boat, a strong sycamore hewn for the rowing. I am a friend of water and fire. In this boat I cross the Lake of Flame, ferrying ancient souls."

Alex raised her arms toward heaven in the dank space as Miguel had shown her.

"As if I'd slept a thousand years underwater I wake into a new season. I am the blue lotus rising. I am the cup of dreams and memory opening -- I, the thousand petaled flower. At dawn the sun rises naked and new as a babe; I open myself and am entered by light. This is the joy, the slow awakening into fire as one by one the petals open, as the fingers that held tight the secret unfurl. I let go of the past and release the fragrance of flowers."

Then Erik spoke.

"This boat was hewn of cypress wood seven arms in length, green as crystal tourmaline, strong as the voice of Ra. The world has spread itself before me, washed with natron and ambergris. I sail through stars silver as fishes. I am a messenger of Ra. What grace I've seen no man can know; green words fly from the mouths of gods; ground and baked, red words rise like bread -- a perfect food for dead men. Yellow stone in the sea, golden light among stars, I am a messenger of Ra whispering the secret of ages."

Alex was grateful the darkness masked her uncertainty. What if their chant didn't work? She breathed, gathered her power and called upon Thoth and Isis.

They faced west where Sirius, mother of the universe and benefactor of Egypt, occupied the sky. Invoking her power and blessing, they intoned the sound 'Mu' three times in a long powerful note, holding the vowel at a low pitch. Alex felt the vibration of the sound reverberating inside her skull.

They turned toward the eastern door, where the full moon continued her ascent, and chanted three more times. The stone door vibrated in resonance with their chant like a hollow obelisk. A crack appeared, and the door opened inward, scraping against the floor. Limestone dust fell around the opening. A blast of cool damp air washed across their faces.

"We have passed the first test," Miguel said.

"Thank God," Alex whispered. Her knees shook from the intense effort of the chant.

"Good work, Watson," Erik said. "What's inside, Miguel?"

Miguel shone his light into the dark opening. "There appears to be a narrow descending passage continuing into the bedrock."

"I'll go first," Erik said. "Alex, you follow me."

They entered on hands and knees and progressed on smooth moist stone into the cramped space, sloping downward at an angle. Their lanterns cast dim streaks of light on the stone blocks in the musty passage. They moved at a slow pace on the slippery stones deep into the bedrock beneath the water table. Moisture seeped onto the rocks from an underground water source.

"Could anything live in here?" Alex asked.

"We don't want to know," Erik said.

Alex willed her mind to be still. After what seemed an interminable length of time, they emerged into a larger space. Darting flashlight beams displayed a narrow stone bridge, spanning an underground channel of water.

"I imagine we are under the remains of the Sphinx temple," Miguel said. "We have progressed another twenty meters."

"This was probably at ground level at one time," Erik said. "Looks like the remains of a canal, maybe even a boat dock." He shone his light on the ceiling.

"That area appears to be recent excavation from above."

"I hear noises in the water," Alex said, cringing.

"Snakes, rats or crocodiles," Erik said. "Nothing to worry about."

Don Miguel struck a match and ignited a preparation of copal incense. The flash of light disclosed an ample space carved into the limestone bedrock.

"There is little margin for error on this bridge," Miguel said. "Remember, we were part of the plan to protect this sanctuary; we must prove worthy to pass the guardians."

Erik went first as they crawled on hands and knees across the slippery stone expanse. Tensing her muscles, Alex concentrated on each movement as they advanced for twenty feet.

"Damn," Erik shouted. "The bridge ends." His words were followed by a loud splash. Alex screamed.

Don Miguel stood on the narrow channel, shining his lantern on the water. He began a sing song chant in Mayan. Erik's head poked above the surface; he clutched the bridge. Alex grabbed his arm and helped him onto the stone walkway.

"I lost the flashlight during a disagreement with a crocodile," he said.

"That's not funny," Alex said.

Miguel's lantern exposed a distance of more than twelve feet without a bridge.

"We could swim; I'm already wet," Erik said.

"The second test," Miguel said.

"I think we should chant again," Alex said.

"We have nothing to lose but collapsing the rest of the bridge," Erik said.

Alex centered herself and balanced on the narrow stone causeway. They intoned the notes as they had before.

When the stone bridge vibrated beneath her feet, she faltered. As they finished, a loud scraping sound wrenched across the ceiling above their heads. Alex feared the stone bricks would collapse.

Miguel shone his light in the direction of the sound. They watched as an enormous block of limestone descended into the open space, completing the bridge.

"The second challenge has been met," Miguel said.

They continued at a slower pace. Within twenty feet, they came to the other side of the water in an area where they could stand. Miguel shone his lantern in front of them. The beam of light revealed the startling sight of a circular alcove with three doorways. Two huge stone serpents, carved like menacing cobras with hoods spread, reared between the doors. The black diorite statues appeared to be twelve feet tall.

"Holy cow," Erik said.

Alex was startled from her state of shock.

"What a funny thing to say. I hope Sirius is amused."

When they stepped off the bridge, the circular space was illuminated. Lamps of unknown technology revealed two granite lionesses, crouching back-to-back on large blocks, in the center of the rounded alcove.

One looked east toward the doors, the other gazed west, on the alert. The lionesses were crowned with reflective orbs; serpents emerged from the top of their foreheads.

Vivid blue eyes probed the three intruders.

"Just like my vision," Alex whispered. "They must be perfect scale models of the Sphinx in her original form."

"Why two?" Erik asked.

"To protect the past, and to wait for the future," Miguel said.

"Something about these lions reminds me of the cherubim on the arc of the covenant," Erik said. "A potent and often lethal energy field was connected with those guardians."

"The third challenge," Miguel said.

"The serpents look Mayan," Erik said.

"Perhaps the Mayan ones look Atlantean," Alex said.

A design of three triangles fashioned like Alexandria's ring was emblazoned above the middle door. The center triangle was white, the left blue and the right red. The tops of the door frames were carved with designs like writing.

"Door number one, door number two, or door number three?" Erik asked.

"Three doorways and three of us," Alex said.

"We probably get one guess," Erik said.

"I believe all three pieces of the code must be present to pass the guardians," Miguel said.

"As Apophsis said, 'Adversary or redemption;' to survive we must embrace them. We should walk through the doorways together," Alex said.

"Then the center door is yours, Miguel," Erik said. "Do we choose the same or opposite polarity, Alex?"

She stared at the design.

"I'll take blue for water; you take red for fire."

"Agreed. Take a picture first."

Removing her camera, Alex photographed the amazing sight. When the camera flashed, the black serpents opened their eyes, revealing cabochon rubies and blue sapphires, matching the triangles above the doors.

The jeweled eyes of the serpents scanned the area like electronic motion sensors. The snakes opened their mouths, emitting energy fields like red fangs of laser light.

"Shit," Erik said.

"Those who were left as guards," Alex whispered.

"May not be passed until their regeneration in the mount, or until the fifth root race begins," Miguel finished the quote from the Cayce readings.

"These machines are scanning our DNA," Alex said. "They're like the serpents who spit fire from the Book of the Dead."

"A perfect blend of Atlantean technology and Egyptian mysticism, programmed thirteen thousand years ago," Erik said, shaking his head.

"There is no room for fear or hesitation," Miguel said. "Our initiation in the Great Pyramid prepared us to meet this challenge."

"The ultimate moment of truth," Erik said.

"It is time for the final prayer," Miguel said. He stood proud and erect, raising his arms in a gesture of invocation. The voice of the shaman rang in the hollow hall.

"The ibis and the ink pot -- these are blessed. For as the ibis pecks along the bank for a bit of food, so the scribe searches among his thoughts for some truth to tell. All the work is his to speak, its secrets writ down in his heart from the beginning of time, the gods' words rising upward through the dark belly, seeking light at the edge of his throat. We are made of god stuff, the explosion of stars, particles of light molded in the presence of gods. The gods are with us. Their secrets writ only in the scrolls of men's hearts, the law of creation, death and change inscribed in the blood and seed of man's love. In the beginning and at the end, the book is opened and we see what in life we are asked to remember. Hear then my words, the ringing of my speech, as the heart and the scroll of this life fall open."

Miguel led them as they chanted the seven notes of the musical scale, visualizing a rainbow of light moving upward through their spiritual centers.

Alex feared her legs would not move her body forward. Summoning every reserve of strength and courage, she willed herself to approach the entrance.

Scarlet arrows of light flashed around them as they advanced toward the doors. A high-pitched whine stabbed her ears.

They passed through the doors unharmed and entered another chamber. When they crossed the threshold, the next room became illuminated by the same light source. On the opposite wall were mirrored panels painted with life-sized murals of figures dressed in costumes from another time. Their own reflections were superimposed on the glass paintings, dressed in ancient clothing.

"Dear, God," Alex said.

"We see ourselves as we were the day the chambers were sealed," Miguel said in a hushed voice.

Alex approached the glass and touched her own reflection. "I have seen this face in a mirror before."

"I wonder if these designs above the doorways are names and dates?" Erik said. "This writing is unlike anything I've seen; block capital letters, Celtic runes and computer code homogenized."

"I'll nix the flash," Alex said and took a few photos. "Shall we travel through the looking glass, gentlemen?"

They opened the doorway of their own likeness and entered a catacomb of alcoves and chambers inlaid with alabaster, marble and stones.

Crystal light fixtures, resting in carved stone sconces, blinked on as they passed, powered by the legacy of an unknown technology.

"This place is in pristine condition, hermetically sealed," Erik said.

Miguel laughed. "The legend of these chambers is the origin of that expression. Thoth became the Greek Hermes."

They walked through a time capsule organized like a museum or library of priceless treasures arranged in attractive displays.

"The floor plan seems similar to the Sphinx temple," Miguel said.

A rush of familiarity washed over Alexandria. "I know where everything will be," she said.

"I believe your former incarnation was Mistress of Records, one who superintended the gathering and organizing of these contents in conjunction with Thoth," Miguel said.

Alex blushed and smiled. "And you shepherded the records in the Yucatan."

Paintings, sculptures and pottery adorned a room like an art gallery. Musical instruments, resembling lyres, harps, flutes and violas filled another hall.

Alex examined a display of jewelry, gem stones and crystals, delicately arranged on silk and linen cloths. She reached for a necklace inset with stones and beads of lapis, carnelian, turquoise and onyx. "This is exquisite," she said, admiring the delicate artistry.

Clothing, cooking utensils, childrens toys and woven blankets were spread across chairs and tables as if left yesterday. Erik picked up a toy that resembled a miniature airplane.

Miguel removed the stopper from an alabaster vial. He closed his eyes and inhaled the aroma. "Rose oil," he said.

Alex resumed the tour. "This seems to be the technology and transportation wing." Models of aircraft like dirigibles and water craft were displayed next to shelves of exotic looking equipment and machines.

"This place could keep archeologists busy for another thirteen thousand years," Erik said. "Nothing in my life prepared me for this."

"Something in a past life did," Alex smiled.

He squeezed her hand.

The history of humanity on earth was depicted in paintings, carvings and maps of the earth as the land masses shifted and evolved through earthquakes and volcanic upheavals. The progressive destruction of Atlantis was shown through a series of maps. Aerial views depicted the first continent, then a group of islands and the final large island Alex knew as Poseidia.

"From the looks of this, humanoids have been on this plant for a very long time," Erik said.

While Erik poured over ancient maps, Alex discovered a room like an astronomical observatory. Bright stars were painted on a domed indigo ceiling.

The floor was a circular map of the earth with monuments and locations reflecting a global pattern of astronomical monuments in relation to the stars above. Circular walls were covered with paintings, conveying the antiquity and the time lines. The cardinal directions were represented. A picture of the earth's globe and axis pointed to a circle of stars.

Alex nearly screamed. "Erik, come here."

The two men rushed to join her.

"A Cosmic Mirror," Erik whistled through his teeth.

Miguel stared at a circular representation of stars and constellations. "What does this represent?"

Erik moved to get a closer look. "Brilliant."

Alex and Miguel stared at him. "This circle denotes one complete rotation of a precession of the equinoxes. Those are the various stars the imaginary pole points to as it wobbles through the twenty-six thousand year circle. Here's Polaris in Ursa Minor and the constellation Cepheus."

"This one's larger than the others," Alex said.

Erik studied the picture. "Vega, the pole star thirteen thousand years ago. These astronomical references provide exact dating."

"So Vega was the pole star when this was painted, just like my dream," she said, eyes widening.

"Look at this," Erik said. "Paintings of constellations describing the night sky at that time. The written characters beneath them must be Atlantean and Egyptian."

"A Rosetta stone of stars," she said.

"As you said, Alex, Astronomy is the key to the puzzle," Miguel said.

"Sirius has a prominent role," Erik said, pointing to a large star in the center of another painting.

Alex photographed without flash as they explored the chambers.

A beautiful carved and painted relief of the city of Poseidia, the Atlantean temple and the great crystal, the Tuaoi stone was placed center stage in one of the rooms.

"This looks like my dream too," Alex said.

They approached an unusual display behind the relief panel. Thirteen green crystal cylinders were suspended in cases that looked like clear plastic.

"The emerald tablets of Thoth," Miguel said. "I always assumed they were legendary. Imagine what knowledge of sacred science is contained in these crystals."

"The technology that destroyed Atlantis. My grandfather must have had a hand in this," Alex smiled.

"This is what Selig wants. Knowledge of free energy that would destroy the current balance of power, or place that power in his hands," Erik said.

"A time bomb in a time capsule," Miguel said.

Alexandria moved on, then she came to a sudden stop, staring straight ahead.

"What is it?" Erik asked.

"The burial chambers."

They walked down a generous hallway that branched into seven smaller halls. Alexandria approached a door. A seven pointed star set with gemstones glittered above the arched opening. Erik and Miguel followed her into the sepulcher.

"Sleeping beauty," Erik said softly.

Alex stared at the painted likeness of the beautiful woman lying in state. She wore a crown with a seven-pointed star, inlaid with seven gemstones in the colors of the spectrum.

"Rainbow star," she said.

"Like the goddess Seshat," Miguel said.

Treasured artifacts were arranged with loving care. A depiction of the seven-rayed healing temple was painted on one wall. Alexandria gently touched the sarcophagus, weeping tears of joy and relief. "We have returned at last."

"Alex, look at this," Erik said.

Shaken, she walked toward where he pointed. Placed among other articles on a gilded table was the small star clock from her dream. The star chart from her dream hung on the wall.

"It's really here." She held the clock in her hands, feeling deep gratitude, stirring evidence that consciousness transcended lifetimes.

Miguel placed his arm around her shoulder.

"The legend promised we may each remove one artifact,"

Her expression was pained; she shook her head, fighting tears. "The star clock is too obvious."

She chose a pure white crystal orb, and tenderly placed the sphere in her pocket. "Perhaps this is a stone of light with a story to tell," she said.

Erik chose a beautifully cast gold coin, inscribed with the same mysterious characters.

Miguel selected a translucent alabaster urn, small enough to fit in his palm.

"For incense. We have accomplished what we came to do. The angels of heaven must guide the rest of the unfoldment."

Their reverie was interrupted by the piercing whine of the black serpents and a terrifying scream of agony. They ran back to the antechamber, toward the sound.

Alex gaped at the lifeless form of Selig, the raven. His crumpled body lay on the floor of the alcove, hands clutching his ears. Blood oozed from his eyes and nose. The acrid stench of charred flesh filled the room.

"He followed us," she said, feeling nauseous.

"We need to get out of here," Erik said.

They crawled back across the long stone bridge. Out of breath, they struggled up the slippery surface of the passage to the cavity beneath the paws of the Sphinx. Three dead bodies littered the room.

"Selig's work," Erik said.

"More valiant lives have been sacrificed," Alex said.

"We will honor their memory through what we accomplished tonight and our continuing quest for truth," Miguel said.

They negotiated the horizontal route back to the shoulder. Mohammed's face appeared in the opening. "Hurry. We don't have much time. They came for me as soon as they discovered he followed you."

They ran across the sand toward Mohammed's van. Alex barely had time to jump into seat before the driver sped off in the direction of Cairo airport.

"I collected your belongings from the hotel. Your new tickets are at the airport," Mohammed said. His expression was grim. "I have been busy for the past hour."

"Thank you, my friend," Erik said. "We recognize the true price of your support."

Miguel removed the alabaster urn from his pocket. "Protect this treasure, and use it as you see fit."

Mohammed accepted the small vase with trembling hands. "Then the legends are true."

"Beyond anything you can imagine," Erik said, handing him the gold coin. Mohammed turned the coin, examining the inscriptions.

Alex removed the film from her camera. "I don't know if these will develop. If any turn out, please send us copies."

Mohammed nodded and looked at each of them. "I'm sorry I doubted you."

Alexandria removed her silver necklace, pried the silver wire loose from around the quartz crystal and inserted the white orb from the Hall of Records in its place. Twisting the silver wire around the priceless treasure, she placed the chain outside her shirt.

"Sherlock Holmes claimed the safest place to hide something was in plain sight."

"Elementary," Erik said.

Alexandria's heart pounded as she stared at the full moon, now high in the sky. She wrapped her fingers around the crystal ball, wondering what secrets the tiny orb contained.

24

Queen of Sheba

Mohammed herded them through the Cairo airport. He ushered the three travelers to the front of the line for the two a.m. flight to New York. The airline official stamped their tickets and passports, returning them as if they were infected with plague.

Alex cried when Mohammed hugged her. "Thank you for everything," she said. "I hope we can return under better circumstances."

He looked deep into her eyes. "My thanks to you, priestess of Seshat."

With fierce hugs, Erik and Miguel bade silent farewells to their Arab comrade. They boarded the plane and claimed their seats in the first row of coach behind the bulkhead. The night flight was only half full. After take off, Alex stretched across empty seats in the middle section, staring at the ceiling of the plane. Erik plugged his computer into the phone and modem port.

"I'm launching a few missiles on the internet."

Alex listened to his fingers click on the keyboard, struggling to get comfortable. When she finally relaxed and fell asleep, troubled dreams filled her mind with images of robed initiates, deception and betrayal.

*   *   *   *   *   *   *

When Alex woke, they were two hours from Kennedy; she called Sheila from the plane and left a message on her voice mail.

"Phone Aldora, take the train and meet us at the Warwick hotel this afternoon."

She disconnected the phone, replaced her credit card and returned to her seat.

"A few time bombs have detonated on the net," Erik said, smiling. "Things are in an uproar."

"Atlantean technology reincarnated," Miguel said.

Alex smiled.

The plane landed in New York at six a.m. They moved through customs like robots, then took a cab into the city and checked into the charming hotel on Central Park. Alex collapsed on the bed and fell into a deep sleep.

They met Sheila and Aldora in the lobby at five o'clock.

"I made reservations at my favorite Ethiopian restaurant," Aldora said.

"Fabulous," Alex said, salivating.

After a manic cross town trek with a seasoned New York cabby at the helm, the motley group descended on the Queen of Sheba restaurant. A colorful mural, depicting the legend of Solomon and the Queen of Sheba covered an entire wall. The arc of the covenant was prominent in the painted scene. Alex pointed to the cherubim.

"Dwellers on the threshold," she said.

Erik fought a smile.

They sat around a cozy table, covered with a bright colored woven cloth and warmed by candlelight. A smiling African woman brought a circular woven basket brimming with Ethiopian delights arranged on warm bread.

Alex tore off a piece of the bread and scooped a serving of spicy salad. Her eyes rolled backward.

"This is heaven."

Aldora cackled. "I love to watch you eat, child. Did you hear that, Mandisa?" she called across the room to the owner. The round woman beamed.

"Have you seen the New York Times?" Sheila asked, shoving a copy at Alex.

She leafed through the pages. Buried at the back of the first section was an article Sheila had marked titled, "Bodies found beneath Sphinx: Mummy's Curse or Foul Play?" Alex read the headline aloud.

"The games's afoot, Watson," Aldora chuckled.

Erik howled. "I checked the net before we left the hotel. The web's as busy as a convention of spiders. The honchos in the Egyptian antiquities department are publicly denying everything, hurling hyperbole at the international media. Privately, they're threatening to charge us with murder unless we tell them how we got in there."

The three travelers shared their experiences over dinner. When Alex told them about discovering Seshat's tomb, she grasped the necklace, holding the crystal aloft. "There were dozens of these in different sizes and degrees of clarity."

"This came from the Hall of Records?" Aldora whispered. "May I touch it?"

Alex smiled, removed the necklace and placed it around Aldora's neck.

"I talked to Emma. There's an offer pending on Gran's house." She paused for dramatic affect, waiting until they all looked at her. "Mom's engaged to Arthur Livingston from the bank."

"You're kidding," Sheila said, eyes bulging.

"Thank God Almighty, free at last," Aldora laughed.

Miguel and Erik roared.

"What are you three planning for an encore?" Sheila asked.

"We've done what we can for now in Egypt," Miguel said.

"According to a friend of mine, divers identified anomlous findings in the gulf stream off Bimini," Aldora said. "Anomalous; I love that word."

"What do you think?" Alex smiled. "Shall we return to Atlantis?"

Awakening Osiris, Normandi Ellis

Order Information

Additional copies of *Messengers* may be obtained
from your local book store or by contacting:

Queen of Cups, Inc.
707 Thompson Drive
Richardson, TX 75080-5025

email:silver@airmail.net

As a result of a near death experience in Mexico in 1966, Julie Gillentine pursued her life long interest in angels, dreams and other dimensions. She has emersed herself in the symbols, myths and spiritual teachings of many traditions for thirty years while serving as an executive in two major corporations. Julie lives in Dallas, Texas with her husband and their animals. Their children, step-children and grandchildren are spread across the United States. This is her first novel.